The TROUBLE with DESTINY

ALSO BY LAUREN MORRILL

Meant to Be

Being Sloane Jacobs

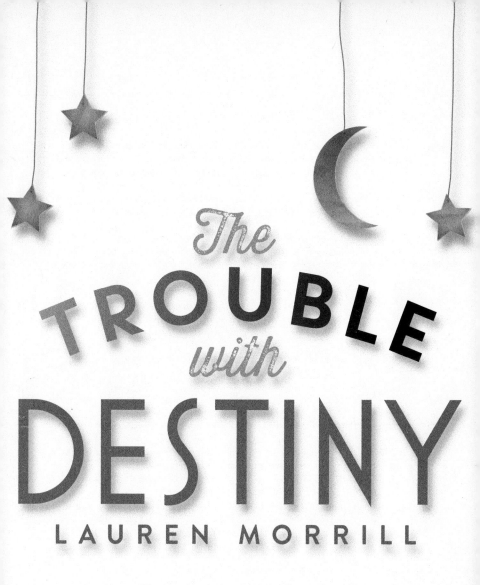

The TROUBLE with DESTINY

LAUREN MORRILL

DELACORTE PRESS

Text copyright © 2015 by Paper Lantern Lit, LLC
Jacket art copyright © 2015 by Erin Fitzsimmons

All rights reserved. Published in the United States by Delacorte Press,
an imprint of Random House Children's Books, a division of Penguin Random
House LLC, New York.

Delacorte Press is a registered trademark and the colophon is a
trademark of Penguin Random House LLC.

randomhouseteens.com

Educators and librarians, for a variety of teaching tools,
visit us at RHTeachersLibrarians.com

Library of Congress Cataloging-in-Publication Data
Morrill, Lauren.
The trouble with destiny / Lauren Morrill. — First edition.
pages cm.
Summary: A high school drum major must save her school band and navigate
romantic disasters when their cruise ship gets stranded at sea.
ISBN 978-0-553-49797-7 (hc) — ISBN 978-0-553-49798-4 (glb) —
ISBN 978-0-553-49799-1 (ebook)
[1. Drum majorettes—Fiction. 2. Marching bands—Fiction.
3. Cruise ships—Fiction. 4. Love—Fiction.] I. Title.
PZ7.M82718Tr 2015
[Fic]—dc23
2014025020

The text of this book is set in 11.25-point Electra.
Jacket design by Erin Fitzsimmons
Interior design by Heather Kelly

Printed in the United States of America
10 9 8 7 6 5 4 3 2 1
First Edition

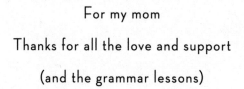

For my mom

Thanks for all the love and support

(and the grammar lessons)

CHAPTER 1

Destiny, it turns out, is not at all what I expected.

For starters, it has three pools, a bowling alley, and more buffets than I have fingers and toes. Its passengers are dragging rolling suitcases and hoisting cheap woven beach bags stuffed with shorts and tank tops and flip-flops and bathing suits in a rainbow of colors, and some of them already seem to be sunburned. And there are giant potted palm trees dotting the various levels and decks. *Palm trees.* Something about palm trees floating across the ocean blows my mind.

When I was eight, the same year my parents got divorced, my dad dragged me on a cruise of the great rivers of Europe. It was a trip my mom never would have agreed to. Given a choice, she preferred to drive up to the lake and spend a week in the sand reading a water-spotted paperback. She's always hated stuffy hotels and restaurants with unpronounceable menu items. And after that cruise, I was inclined to agree with her. All

I remember was wearing a really stiff, way-too-frilly dress in a shade of pale pink I *never* would have chosen to dinner on the first night, where I promptly used the wrong fork to eat what turned out to be a very bad oyster, and spent the rest of the trip alternately sleeping or barfing in our luxury cabin.

After only five minutes in the boarding terminal for the Sail Away Cruise Line, I can tell this trip is going to be different. I quickly scoop my long, slightly tangled dark hair into a sensible bun as I look around at the soaring glass ceiling of the station, with its glossy white steel girders and shiny white linoleum tile. I breathe in the salty smell of pretzels and hot dogs and fries floating in a hot grease bath. To my left, a sugared-up toddler with a fistful of Cheetos turns over an entire forty-four-ounce soda right into the lap of his mother, who seems too exhausted and bogged down by luggage to notice. Off to my right, an elderly couple in matching black leather fanny packs paws through a rack of souvenir T-shirts. It feels like I'm about to board a cruise ship from the food court of the Town Center Mall.

Dad would absolutely hate it, so obviously I love it.

"Attention, student participants of the Ship of Dreams performing arts competition," the terminal's intercom system squawks. "Please board the *Destiny* through gate D-one. Thank you."

My heart does a funny little flutter, like a fish just pulled from the ocean. This is it: my final chance to turn things around. *Our* final chance.

Of course, I'm the only one who knows that.

I spin on my heel to face my classmates, who have just dragged themselves off a bus after an all-night ride from our high school parking lot in Holland, Tennessee. Andrew and Ryan are still bleary-eyed and yawning from the nine-hour drive, clearly wishing they could carry the pillows tucked under their arms into a quiet corner and take a nap. Nicole is starting to look twitchy, possibly on the verge of a full-on panic. She's working on getting her overnight bus hair into a ponytail but can't stop smoothing her hand over the bumps, her toe tapping furiously to whatever is pumping through her earbuds (hopefully the soothing sounds of the ocean or some meditative chanting). But other than that, most of them seem excited to finally be here, rejuvenated by all the noise and bustle of the cruise line's giant, if cheesy, terminal.

"All right, listen up," I say, affecting the stern drill-sergeant voice I use on the field during marching practice. But with all the commotion, including the other groups of high school students who are also chattering and laughing and shouting to one another, no one pays any attention.

I stick my thumb and forefinger between my lips and give the high-pitched country whistle my mom taught me when I was five. Whenever we'd get separated at the park or in the grocery store, she'd whistle and I'd whistle back, a little family homing beacon that allowed us to find each other, never mind that Dad got me a phone in the fourth grade for this exact purpose. Immediately, all sixty pairs of eyes are on me. I clear my throat and give a little nod. *Game time.*

"Okay, guys, passports and tickets out, like we talked about. Section leaders, gather your crew and line up at gate D-one." I turn and wave like a crossing guard, my arm pivoting in the direction of the gate at the farthest end of the terminal. Already, crowds of other competitors are flowing in that direction. A perky-looking employee of the Sail Away Cruise Line is standing at the front of the gate, her jaunty white sailor hat falling off the back of her head as she checks tickets and passports. "And don't forget to double-check your schedules."

Immediately, the whole group begins moving en masse in the direction I've indicated, and I give in to a quick surge of optimism. After band camp and a semester's worth of practices and halftime shows, the group is more than used to following my directions—but that's when I'm on the football field back home, under bright lights, with white gloves and a very large, very fuzzy hat. That they're paying attention now, in the middle of this crowded terminal, gives me hope that maybe tonight I can actually get some sleep instead of lying awake in bed like I have recently, worrying about what's going to happen after this week.

Molly O'Dwyer leads the charge with her clarinet section, counting them off as they line up behind a group of twenty or so students from another school who are all wearing matching red T-shirts with tragedy masks screen-printed on the back. They're passing the time by playing some kind of improv game that involves them making rubbery faces and exaggerated hand gestures. *Great.* The Mechanicals. Despite all my prayers that they'd be stricken with some kind of temporary tropical disease that would make them unable to come on the cruise, it looks like they made it. And with energy to spare.

The Mechanicals are a group of drama kids from Centreville, our rival high school. They compete in improv competitions and stage one-act plays, but they'll basically participate in anything that will draw attention. They're forever staging flash mobs at the mall that sits right on the town line.

"Ugh, drama nerds," a voice says behind me.

I swivel around. Huck flicks me on the nose and I flinch. "Hector Martinez, how many times have I told you to stop flicking me on the nose!"

"Eight thousand seven hundred and forty?" He grins, stuffing his hands guiltily into his plaid bermuda shorts. His black hair is tufting out from beneath a black-banded straw fedora, and a pair of neon-orange sunglasses hangs around his neck on a bright blue neoprene band. Come to think of it, he looks a lot like a hipster version of the many Hawaiian-shirted, fanny-packed, gray-haired retirees boarding a few gates over. One glance in that direction tells me that someone at the cruise company has scheduled not only a couple of hundred high school students for this voyage, but also some kind of grand-parents' tour group. "And if you call me Hector one more time, I'm calling you Grandma, because she's the only one who can get away with that."

Just as I'm about to tell him to make that eight thousand seven hundred and forty-one, the entire group of improv kids lets out a moan that's a cross between those of a dying cow and a wailing widow.

I shudder. "Have they no shame?"

"Someone replaced their shame gauge with an overdose of confidence and a full tank of ego," Huck replies with an eye roll.

One of the drama girls spins around and shoots us a dirty look before turning back to her friends. I don't know what her problem is; we're not the ones passing the time pretending to be wailing farm animals.

"Whatever," I mutter to Huck. "We can take them, no

problem. What are they going to do, mime us out of the competition?" I keep my voice light, hoping that if I fake confidence, I'll make confidence, like my mom always tells me to.

A warm blast of air cuts through the arctic air conditioning as the glass doors of the terminal slide open with a quiet *whoosh*.

Russ Jennings ambles in, a blue Holland High School football team duffel slung over his broad shoulder. His blond hair is sticking up in a persistent cowlick on the back of his head, and faint red marks streak his face, probably from sleeping propped up on his arm. He blinks hard a few times while he scans the crowd, and when he spots our herd, he drops his sunglasses down on his face, yawns like a lion, and joins the back of the line.

"Could you keep an eye on *that*, please?" I say to Huck as Russ settles into some kind of sleeping-standing-up situation while he waits to board. He's nearly a head taller than everyone else, and I can't help but hum the tune to "One of These Things Is Not Like the Other" in my head. Russ definitely does *not* belong among the adorkable riffraff otherwise known as the Holland High marching band. And if it were up to me, I would have left him back in the school parking lot, sleeping in his Jeep.

I can't *believe* Principal DeLozier thought sending him with us to serve as band errand-boy was an appropriate punishment for throwing a football into Hillary's tuba during practice. What happened to the old standbys, like detention or, I don't know, paddling? When I complained to my mother, an elementary school teacher, about this pseudo-punishment, she launched into a twenty-minute ed-psych lecture on alternative

6

discipline and blah blah blah. I love her passion, but I had to stop listening. Having Russ come along is more like punishment for *us*. That the captain of the football team, the team that sucks up all our funding and treats us like lepers, gets to crash *our* spring break is a sign that there is *seriously* no justice in the world. What, if I skip fourth-period calculus, will I get a new car?

Huck nods at me, his face faux-serious. "I hope you know that if anyone else asked me to tail the captain of a team who thinks nominating me for homecoming king is some kind of *joke*, I'd reply with some very offensive hand gestures and a whole lotta *no*."

I roll my eyes. "First of all, that was Greg Milbanks, not Russ. And second, the joke was on them, because you rocked that powder-blue tux *and* the crown."

"Won't Demi have him pretty well distracted?"

I sigh. "They broke up, remember? Besides, I don't want Demi anywhere near us this weekend. She and the Athenas are our *real* competition. We have no choice here. I am not letting Russ or anyone else mess up our chances, okay? So please?"

Huck shrugs. "You got it, El Capitán." He gives me an exaggerated salute, then turns and pushes through the crowd to join the oboes in the line with the rest of the woodwinds.

"Oh, and Huck?" I call to him. He pivots gracefully to face me again. "Remember. *Best behavior*."

He raises one eyebrow, the opposite corner of his mouth turning up in half of a devious *who, me?* grin that doesn't inspire any confidence at all. "Always!" he shouts, then blows me a kiss and continues on to join the rest of the oboes and bassoons.

At the edge of the crowd, six porters in starched white shorts and polo shirts are struggling with carts overloaded with towers of black instrument cases. I hurry toward them, reaching into my messenger bag and extracting a manila envelope containing the instrument inventory I created last week.

"Hiya, fellas," I say, pressing a list and a crisp twenty-dollar bill into each of their hands. "I would *super* appreciate it if you'd triple-check that everything on this list is here when you get on board." I make a show of fumbling with another wad of twenties as I stuff everything back into my bag, all while saying a silent thank-you to my father. Our preboarding packet from the cruise company detailed the ins and outs of tipping (the one thing *not* included in this all-inclusive week, during which our shipboard ID cards will function as debit cards), but I need no instruction when it comes to pressing bills into someone's hand. Even though I see my dad only a few times a year, he frequently sends cash to make up for the fact that he joined a law firm on the other side of the country. Occasionally, it really pays to have a guilt-ridden absentee parent, especially one who believes that bribery and flattery will pretty much get you everywhere.

All six porters nod, and the luggage carts, which were previously moving in a slow and slightly circuitous path, suddenly pick up speed and move in a straight line toward the cargo loading area. I mentally place a big red check mark next to "instruments on board" on the giant to-do list that lives in my brain.

"Liza, I don't think I can do this."

The quaver in the breathy, high-pitched voice is unmistakable. I whirl around to face the tiny person that goes with the tiny voice. Never in my life have I met a human being more aptly named than our first-chair flute player, Nicole Mauser. To say that Nicole is slight would be like saying the Incredible Hulk is large. At five foot nothing, she looks like a stiff breeze could snap her in half. She has a narrow face and small features that appear to be continuously twitching. Nicole is also the best flute player in the Southeast, and if she can manage to convince herself that she won't be murdered on the subway, she'll be off to Juilliard in the fall.

While most of my classmates are dying to get on board for sun, fun, and all-you-can-eat buffets (oh, and to compete against nine other groups for a $25,000 prize in a high school performing arts competition), Nicole sees the trip as one giant opportunity for premature death. When I find out who showed her *Titanic*, I swear, I will make that person's life very, *very* unpleasant.

I grab Nicole by the shoulders, rubbing them like my mom used to do when she was trying to get me to go to bed at night. "Nicole, it's going to be fine. We talked about this. The ship is perfectly safe."

Her eyes grow wide, the wrinkle in her forehead deepening so much that you could use it to hold a pencil. "But—"

"But nothing," I say, keeping my voice cheerful but firm. "Why don't you get in line and practice those relaxation breathing techniques I gave you. Deep, cleansing breaths, remember?"

Nicole nods, her eyes still as wide as silver dollars, and takes a practice breath so deep her nostrils collapse. But her quivering slows, and something that might be in the neighborhood of calm comes over her.

"Oh my God, what would I do without you?" she asks, between yoga breaths.

"Pass out from hyperventilation?" I say, and she actually cracks a smile. "See? You're golden. It's going to be fine."

Once again I reach into my bag, this time for the blue file folder I prepared a week ago. It's nestled between a red one, which contains copies of every band member's insurance cards, health forms, and emergency contact information, and a green one, which holds room assignments and a flash drive of all our sheet music. I raided my mom's classroom supplies to ensure that I've left nothing—not a single thing—to chance. I double-check the schedule provided by the cruise line alongside the schedule I prepared for every member of the band, then unclip my ticket and passport from the back cover.

It's all going to be fine, I tell myself. *Everything is going according to plan.*

I hang on tight to that plan (win the $25,000 prize money) and try to push aside thoughts of what will happen if the plan goes awry (too horrible to imagine).

"Uh, Liza?"

A light tap on my shoulder sends a shiver up my back.

"Huck, I thought I told you—" I start to say. But as I turn I see that it's not Huck at all.

The guy behind me is tall and lanky, a few inches taller than my own five-foot-ten frame, and is wearing a vintage T-shirt and scuffed-up jeans. His hair is short, like he shaved his head a month ago and it's only now starting to grow back. What's there is a sandy, almost strawberry-blond that contrasts with stormy gray eyes and a slightly overgrown five o'clock shadow.

He looks infuriatingly familiar.

While I'm looking him over, trying to figure out where I know him from, the corner of his mouth turns up, his nose wrinkles slightly, and in a flash I'm twelve years old and standing on the warped wooden stage of Centreville Community College dressed as a bird, while the boy in front of me skips around onstage and sings the opening number of the *Stuart Little* musical, wearing mouse ears and whiskers. His hair was much longer then, falling down over his ears and eyes and requiring a near-constant head shake to maintain his vision, but no doubt, it's the same kid from Rising Stars Theater Camp.

I feel my heart pick up speed from moderato to allegro. It *can't* be him. Can it?

"Lenny?" I squeal.

CHAPTER 2

"Liza!" The guy who I now realize I have definitely correctly identified as Lenny throws his arms around me in a hug, and though the big fancy camera around his neck smashes painfully into my chest, I can't help noticing that my twelve-year-old friend has grown into a lean, well-muscled seventeen-year-old. His T-shirt is well worn and super soft, and he smells woodsy, almost like a campfire. When he pulls away, I see that the freckles that used to dance across his nose have faded, and some primo orthodontia must have straightened his incisors, which used to look like they were trying to stage an escape from his mouth.

"What are you doing here?" I ask, suddenly all too aware that my denim cutoffs and blue Holland High Style Marchers T-shirt must be awfully rumpled from the red-eye bus ride from Tennessee to Florida. I reach up to my messy bun and hope there aren't too many bumps or flyaways. "Are you competing? Is your school here?"

I'm talking way too fast. *Zip it, Liza.*

But Lenny just shakes his head and laughs. "Nah, I don't really perform anymore. I'm more into behind-the-scenes stuff these days." He lifts his camera from around his neck. "I'm actually just tagging along with my dad this week. My mom's on a business trip, and he thought we could use some father-son bonding time." He rolls his eyes, jerking his thumb over his shoulder at an older, taller, skinnier, and *way* less hot version of Lenny. The man currently wearing his everyday uniform of khaki pants and a black polo with the Holland High School crest embroidered on the chest.

I can see only the top of his head, since his face is buried in his phone, but it doesn't matter. I'd know him anywhere. I've only been staring up at him from my seat in the first row of flutes for the past three years.

"Your dad is Mr. Curtis?" I practically shriek, pointing at our band director. My jaw drops so low I worry Lenny can count my fillings. I force my mouth closed. *"Seriously?"*

Lenny nods the nod of someone who's more than a little embarrassed to have to claim a teacher for a parent, a feeling I know all too well since my mom teaches third grade and has more than her fair share of those awful apple- and pencil-themed teacher coffee mugs.

"I normally live with my mom in Brentwood," he explains, a fact I remember from our summer at performing arts camp. We'd bonded over our divorced parents, swapping stories about split holidays and tales of awkward parental dating disasters. I didn't go back the following year because Dad insisted I spend those weeks in Hawaii with him and Shannon, the boring red-headed CPA he was dating at the time, and so I lost track of

Lenny. And looking at him now, with his Ray-Bans perched on top of his head and his eyes that seemed to have lightened with his smile, I'm sorry that I didn't give that camp another try. "This is so crazy. I had no idea you were the conductor in my dad's band."

"Drum major," I reply, out of habit. The distinction is important, at least to me. The drum major doesn't just wave her arms to the music. She's a drill sergeant. She's a leader. She's the go-to girl for every single member of the band. She's responsible for everything from marching to music to instrument maintenance to the personal and mental health of everyone on the field. She's the person everyone else relies on.

"Oh, right," Lenny says, though I suspect he doesn't quite get the difference. "Anyway, my dad sent me over here to lend you a hand."

"With what?" I ask, and Lenny laughs again, pointing to my luggage: two brand-new, high-tech rolling suitcases my dad got for me, my duffel bag, and a cardboard box. I've had to pack my own stuff (suitcase #1); contingency supplies like first aid, extra sunscreen, sewing kits, and seasick patches (suitcase #2); my flute, instrument maintenance supplies and extra mutes, cleaning cloths, reeds, tuning forks, and slide grease (duffel bag); and two extra copies of every piece of sheet music for every instrument for shipboard performance (cardboard box).

"Looks like you're planning to move in," he says, eyes sparkling.

I meant to toss most of it on one of the luggage carts, but with Nicole's near meltdown and Huck and the Mechanicals, I forgot. "They're not all mine," I say quickly. "I mean, they *are*.

I mean, they're the band's. Which I'm in charge of, so I'm in charge of those by proxy, I guess."

I have to bite the tip of my tongue to keep myself from further babbling. In just ten minutes, I've gone from leadership to loserdom.

Lenny bends down, and in one swift, effortless movement he has the duffel bag over his left arm, the box cradled in his right, and is pulling one of the suitcases behind him.

"Ready?" He smiles at me, and it's all I can do to keep my knees from turning to the type of Jell-O they probably serve for dessert on this boat.

I hand my passport to the girl in the sailor hat, who scans it and mutters something about my destiny through a clenched-teeth smile. I drag my suitcase up the covered gangplank as Lenny walks next to me, the rest of my luggage hanging all over him, his camera bouncing on his chest, which I can see is taut and muscled through the tissue-thin fabric of his faded red V-neck, which—*Oh my God, stop it, Liza.*

As I step through the rounded opening at the end of the gangplank and onto the ship—which, with its beige carpeting, narrow hallways, and fluorescent lighting, looks like I'm stepping onto a floating Holiday Inn—I'm struck by another memory from our shared childhood.

It's the last night of theater camp, and we're performing the musical for our parents—or in Lenny's and my case, for our single mothers—who have come to collect us at the end of the two weeks. I'm standing just off stage left, waiting for my entrance. Lenny comes bounding into the wings, having just finished one of his big solo numbers. His crooked smile widens as soon as he sees me, and when he's out of the spotlight he grabs my arm and pulls me into the deep folds of the heavy red velvet curtain just offstage. The dust and must from the curtain nearly sends me into a sneezing fit. Then Lenny leans in and plants my very first kiss right on my lips, lightly smearing the bright red stage lipstick onto my chin.

It was thoroughly closed-mouth but still soft and sweet, and the memory turns my knees back to Jell-O and sends me stumbling down the hall, my rolling suitcase tipping off its wheels and crashing into the back of my legs, then the wall.

"You all right?" Lenny asks as I struggle to right my suitcase. It's so overstuffed with every possible contingency for the week that it keeps flopping over from one side to the other.

I quickly look away and place my hand on the smooth white wallpaper with a jaunty nautical pattern of blue anchors and steady myself before continuing. At least my stumble hid the fact that I'd been staring at him so hard I wouldn't be surprised if there were two laser-beam-burned holes in the back of his shirt. "Yup, just fine," I say, though the words come out sort of breathy. *Down, girl.*

We wind our way down a staircase and turn onto . . . another narrow beige hallway. I glance at my key card, nestled into a little blue cardboard folder with the number 298 written in ballpoint pen. The brass plaque on the wall next to my head tells me that my room should be just down this hall, so I charge on, glancing over my shoulder to make sure Lenny is behind me. He catches my eye and grins, and all speech leaves me. My friend from when I was twelve is a supreme hottie.

And we're on a boat. Together. For a week.

I stop in front of a white door with a brass plaque on it

bearing the numbers 298. I stick my key card into the lock and jerk it out, but the indicator light blinks red. I try again, only this time I miss the slot and smash the card directly into the wooden door, leaving a tiny scuff in the white paint. I gasp and lick my finger, scrubbing at the spot to try to remove it before the band gets charged for damaging the ship after just four minutes aboard. My face is burning so badly by this point, I'm worried flames might start shooting from my ears. Lenny leans against the wall, his arms weighted down with luggage. I give myself the three seconds it takes to reach down and pick up the card that clattered to the floor to give myself a pep talk. *He's just a guy. You know him. Chill out.*

I place the card into the reader and yank it out. The third time's the charm—I hear a mechanical click and the light turns green. I turn the silver knob and push open the door.

The room is tiny. I expected small, but the Sail Away Cruise Line must have used some kind of special lens or photo trick when they photographed the rooms for the website, because I was not expecting *this*. I have to step in all the way to the back wall in order to get Lenny and the rest of my stuff in and still have room to close the door. I'm pretty sure this entire cabin is the size of the bathroom on my last cruise, but on that trip I felt like some dirty-fingered little kid who wasn't supposed to touch anything. I'll take a tiny cabin on a boat with my best friends over a stuffy vacation any day.

Most of the room is taken up by two twin beds, side by side against the outer wall, both topped with identical nautical-themed bedspreads in shades of blue and green. The bed on the right already has Hillary's vintage duffel covered in patches of classic rock bands on it, so I heave my suitcase onto the bed on the left. Lenny puts the box down next to it and stacks my other suitcase and my duffel bag on top of it. Then he takes a seat on Hillary's empty bed.

Suddenly, I can't remember what I'm supposed to do with my hands or even what hands are for. I've never been alone with a boy in my room (unless you count Huck, but Huck has known he's gay for as long as I've known him, so I don't). It feels too awkward to keep standing, but the thought of sitting on a bed next to Lenny has my heart racing at a rate composers would call presto. Instead, I drop onto my bed, wedging myself between my suitcase and my tower of other luggage, which sways like it's about to topple onto my head.

I place my hands on my knees, which brush up against Lenny's knees in the narrow space between the two beds. The feeling sends me jumping to my feet again.

"Oh my gosh, this room is so small! Can you believe it? It's itty-bitty! Like, smaller than the dorm rooms at band camp! I mean, those aren't as nice, of course, because we have to bring sleeping bags and the carpet is *gross* from all the years of college students spilling soda or beer or whatever and those have cinder block walls that always have leftover pieces of sticky tack on them, so this is definitely nicer, but still, this is small. I've never seen anything like this." I hear myself rambling on about the aesthetic qualities of the rooms at Cherokee State College, which hosts us for band camp each summer, as if it's the most exciting thing on the planet. I really need to get this nervous babbling under control. It's not a cute nervous tic.

Lenny just reaches out and runs a thumb along the monogram on my duffel. HHS STYLE MARCHERS, it says, and below that, DRUM MAJOR. Mom hand-embroidered it for me to celebrate when Mr. Curtis announced last spring that I got the job. I'd been up against three rising seniors, all boys, two trumpets and a percussionist. Beating them as a girl had felt pretty great, but beating them as a rising junior had been pretty well unheard of. Turns out the weeks I'd spent in my bedroom directing along to YouTube videos of marching bands had paid off. "Bummer about the band, huh?"

I stop in my tracks, thoughts of my tiny shower and the boy on the bed suddenly gone. I whirl around to face him. "You know about that?"

"Yeah, my dad told me," he says, rolling his eyes. "Of course admin thinks the answer to a budget deficit is to cut the arts. God forbid they take some money from sports."

Blood starts pounding in my ears like a bass drum. "It's not going to happen," I say quickly.

"What?"

"It's not going to happen," I say again, clearing my throat. This time my voice is loud and clear. "I won't *let* that happen. Those cuts only matter if we can't raise the money to keep us going, which we will totally do. Losing the band is *not an option.*"

They're words I've repeated to myself over and over again since I first overheard the conversation between Mr. Curtis and Mrs. Buckner, the art teacher, back in October. I knew cuts were coming, but I figured they'd cancel construction on the new football team weight room or skip repaving the student parking lot. Not cut the buses they use to transport us to away games and sell off all the school-owned instruments. Without the buses we could at least figure something out, but without the sousaphones, the baritones, or the drums, there's no band left. I'd never betray my woodwind sisterhood, but let's be honest, flutes do not a marching band make.

I spent weeks trying to brainstorm ways to raise enough cash to keep us going. Then, an email from a newsletter I subscribe to gave me the perfect solution:

A spring break cruise for high school performing arts groups. A week of showcases concluding with a shipboard competition. A $25,000 grand prize. It would be more than enough to fund instrument maintenance and pay for the buses that take us to away games. All I had to do was write an essay on why we wanted to compete (Uh, hello? The future of the band?) and send in a video of a performance (luckily our performance at our town's annual fall festival this year was flawless), and we were in. And now only one week and nine other groups stand between us and the money we need to exist next year.

That money will be our savior, and my legacy.

A wrinkle of concern appears in the space between Lenny's blond eyebrows. I realize I sound like one of those high-strung mothers on the Lifetime movies my mom loves to put on while she cleans the house. In those, a crazed mom invariably attempts to knock off the competition to get her child to the top. This is *not* the impression I was hoping to give off.

I take a breath, rubbing my sweaty hands on my shorts. "I have a plan," I say slowly. "But it's important that everyone stay calm. That means they can't know that we're in danger of losing the band."

"They don't know?" Lenny asks.

"They *can't* know," I say, especially not now, this close to the competition. I've managed to keep the secret to myself for months, not even breathing a word to Huck. I didn't want the panic and pandemonium I knew would come if they knew how close we are to losing one another. I needed them to focus. It hasn't been easy, especially as everyone started making plans for roommates and band camp this summer and suggesting new songs to add to our game-day repertoire. I almost slipped once, after homecoming, when Huck asked me if I was going to try out for drum major again next year, but I held it in. I've come this far. I'm not going to let the secret out now.

"Understood," Lenny says, nodding slowly. He stands up and adjusts his camera strap around his neck, then reaches up and turns an invisible lock at his lips, flicking the imaginary key over his shoulder. "They won't hear it from me."

"Thank you," I say, and smile at him. I can't help but notice that despite the fact that he's become a tall, hot photographer, I can still see the grinning, freckled Stuart Little in there. It makes my heart flutter like a tremolo.

"Not a problem at all," Lenny says. "I should probably get going. You know, make sure my dad didn't lose *my* suitcase."

"Oh, sure," I reply. I flatten myself against the wall as he edges past me toward the door.

He has to duck just a bit to get through it. Then he stops and turns, his old friendly smile back. "I'll see you, okay, Birdie?" The reference to his summer nickname for me, after Margolo, the character I played opposite him in *Stuart Little*, makes me want to do a happy dance right then and there, but I manage to contain myself.

"Yup, see you!" I try to sound light and playful, but instead I sound like I've swallowed a piccolo. Lenny just gives a quick wave and pulls the door shut behind him.

Crap.

Now that I'm alone, all the tension of his presence, all my worries about the loss of the band, and all the pressure of the competition rush out of me in a *whoosh*. I fall back onto the empty bed, my hand running over the warm spot where he was sitting.

A red light catches my eye from the narrow bedside table between the two beds: an iPod dock reading 11:00. The team leaders meeting has just started. And I'm going to be late.

Double crap.

As I leap to my feet, I can feel *Destiny*, all fifty thousand tons of her, rumble to life beneath me. I glance through the tiny porthole and see the terminal sliding away. We've left port. With each passing second we get farther away from land—and closer to a win.

CHAPTER 3

I take the stairs three at a time and bolt down the hall toward the Sunset Pavilion, a smallish theater with bright orange walls and no windows. There are ten groups participating in the shipboard competition, and a quick scan of the two dozen or so people in the auditorium shows that I'm the last of the group leaders to show up.

I spot Mr. Curtis in a seat in the back corner of the theater, and I set off to join him while I attempt to catch my breath. On my way up the stairs, I pass Mrs. Haddaway, the advisor for Holland High's all-girl show choir, the Athenas. I almost don't recognize her with her hair tucked up in an orange Tennessee Volunteers baseball cap, the bill pulled down low as she hunches over some pink-and-green knitting project. Two rows up are Demi Tremont and her best friend, Missy O'Brien, the captain and cocaptain of the Athenas. In their identically worn-in denim miniskirts and candy-colored tissue tanks, they look like Tweedle Mean and Tweedle Meaner. When Demi spots me coming up the stairs, she sneers at my rumpled clothes and messy bun, then turns to Missy.

"Thank *God* my mom got us upgraded," she says in an exaggerated stage whisper. "She's dating this totally hot travel agent, which means VIP *everything*. I can't imagine being squeezed down in the ass end of the ship, practically bunking with the freaking *crew*."

I've spent most of high school ignoring my ex–best friend, but her comment makes my blood boil. After I found out about the cruise competition, we fund-raised for months to earn the money for the tickets, selling candy bars, wrapping paper, magazine subscriptions, anything that would bring in the cash to cover our rooms. I practically turned my band into a living production of *Death of a Salesman* just to get here. On the other hand, the Athenas hosted exactly *one* bikini car wash and are staying in deluxe suites. *Unfair.*

Demi and I were born on the same day, in the same hospital, one hour apart in rooms right next to each other (she came first, which would turn out to be a theme between us). This basically ensured that we'd be either best friends or mortal enemies, and for the first twelve years of our lives, we were the former. While our moms drank coffee and shared neighborhood gossip, we babbled and played and eventually became best friends. We were in the same preschool class, the same ballet class, played on the same soccer team, and sat next to each other in the same Sunday school class. And when we weren't shuttling around to various activities together, we were in each other's bedrooms playing endless hours of pretend.

There's only one thing to know about Demi: Demi is a winner. Demi wins. From the time we were little, she was always the best soccer player, the prima ballerina, and the first to raise her hand to name the writers of the Gospels. When we played school, Demi was the teacher. When we played hospital, Demi got to perform lifesaving surgery. In the confines of her cotton-candy-pink bedroom, Demi racked up an Oscar, a Grammy, the *American Idol* title, and a Super Bowl ring. And honestly, I never minded much. I liked opening the envelope, and covering myself in ketchup to play a surgical victim was fun (though we got in mega trouble for the mess we made on that one). I've just never been that competitive. It wasn't until I tried out for drum major that I'd ever really competed for anything, and I like it just fine that way.

Then sixth grade rolled around and middle school happened, and Demi discovered a whole new world ready for the taking. Now she didn't just have to pretend to win; she could simply *win*. And so Demi set out to always wear the cutest outfits, have the most friends, sit at the best table in the cafeteria (and in the best seat, of course, right in the middle of the action), and go out with the most sought-after boy at Holland Middle School.

And me? When it wasn't just the two of us playing pretend anymore, it wasn't as fun. Not for me, at least. I just got tired, first of trying to keep up, then of always playing second fiddle. Every day with Demi was like running a marathon. But no matter how fast I ran, I was always guaranteed to come in second. So on the first day of seventh grade, when we had agreed to sign up for auditions for the fall musical, I walked over to a different table and signed up for the one activity I knew Demi would never, ever deign to do. There would be no competition, and I definitely wouldn't earn any points in the race to be cool.

Demi won the lead in *My Fair Lady*, and I became a flautist in the middle school band. Without shared activities, our carpools disappeared, and with Demi in rehearsals, so did our sleepovers and movie dates. I started eating lunch across the cafeteria with my new band friends, which turned out to be way more fun than watching Demi flirt and everyone else fawn over her. And with all my newfound free time I gained from not applauding for Demi every day, I even became a kickass flute player. I didn't realize we'd broken up until long after it had happened, leaving me to wonder if Demi and I were ever real friends, or if I was just her tagalong. Regardless, Demi and I never competed against each other again.

Until now.

I open my mouth for some kind of smart retort, but Demi has already turned back to Missy. The pair of them start pointing at our competitors and whispering behind cupped hands, throwing narrow-eyed glances around the auditorium. I make my way to the back corner and take my seat next to the ever-quiet Mr. Curtis, who once again has his nose buried behind his phone. We don't get cell service out here, but the website boasted about the ship's superior Wi-Fi capability.

"Hi, Mr. Curtis," I say as I plop down in the chair in the row in front of him.

"Hey there, Liza," he says, a relaxed smile on his face that I would attribute to the cruise, except Mr. Curtis always seems to run on half speed. He's the calmest, most Zen teacher I've ever had, which is probably why I feel like I have to be doubly motivated to get anything done with the band. Without me taking the lead, I'm pretty sure half the woodwinds would still be in the parking lot of the cruise terminal, and at least one student would have been left back at the school.

I think about Lenny and his laid-back smile. I guess he does get *something* from his dad, though I have to push the thought away quickly. I don't want that like-father-like-son image to come creeping into my head later. *Ick.*

I start to apologize for being almost late, but Mr. Curtis is already back on his phone, where I notice he's playing some kind of game that involves tapping on pictures of flaming candy bars. Which is just as well, because a crew member clad in the ship's uniform of crisp white shorts, matching polo, and white socks and sneakers is starting to pass around a stack of stapled papers. When he gets to the back row, he hands two to me, and I pass one over to Mr. Curtis. I leaf through the packet, recognizing most of the information as stuff I already pulled off the web, mostly maps, schedules, rules, and programs. There's also a list of all the other competitors. I take a moment to scan down it to see that the only groups I know are the Athenas and the Mechanicals. There's an orchestra listed, and some kind of dance troupe, plus two other bands. The other three I can't determine from their names alone.

The crew guy, who introduces himself as First Mate Kevin without a single note of irony, runs through the performance schedules, locations, and rules of the competition. He reminds us all to double-check that the judges have the most up-to-date programs for each of us, a task I took care of via email last week. We've been working on our program since January, so there was no reason to wait to submit our music. He also reminds us to arrive at the auditorium by 6:30 sharp for tonight's showcase, and I make a mental note to get there at least fifteen minutes early. Definitely on time in Mr. Curtis's book.

First Mate Kevin finishes right as the auditorium door swings open and the rest of the student performers start to stream in to join their team leaders. The remaining Athenas, all dressed like they shopped on the same really expensive website, all wearing variations on the short skirt and brightly colored tank top, stream in. A few have accessorized with matching candy-colored sunglasses or bright bauble necklaces, but they all have their hair flat-ironed shiny and cascading over their shoulders. They squeeze in past Demi and Missy and occupy the row of seats right in the center of the auditorium. Of course.

The Mechanicals file in behind them, still in their matching shirts, all stumbling in doing spot-on impersonations of zombies for reasons I can't possibly guess. It's like they don't even care about the competition; they just want to be the center of attention. Though only one town over from Holland, Centreville is a much more affluent community, so the Mechanicals probably aren't facing the same cuts we are. Which is good, because if they don't *need* the money, maybe they'll let their guard down enough for us to squash them.

As they plop down in seats, laughing and talking and high-fiving, I almost envy them. They look like they're having *fun*, which is what I'd be doing if we weren't in dire financial straits. While the rest of the crowd trickles in, I give myself a moment to imagine what it would be like to be on this trip without the black cloud of the cuts hanging over my head. I'd probably spend most of my time sitting in a lounge chair with Hillary on one side of me and Huck on the other, a stack of trashy magazines on my lap. I'd eat my weight in buffet food and belt out songs in the karaoke lounge and probably act just like the Mechanicals.

But this week isn't about fun. It's not about hanging out with my friends or scarfing belgian waffles while I read about which celebutante is dating which heartthrob. It's about making sure that next year, I get to keep the band and my friends. And that thought has panic washing over me, first as a trickle, then as a flood.

I squeeze the arms of my chair tightly, willing myself to breathe. Huck comes through the door, tailed by the other four oboe players, the rest of the woodwinds, and all the brass. The percussion section brings up the rear, as usual. They're a scrappy group of dudes who are always in motion, drumming on themselves, one another, or anything within reach. Huck trots up the steps and drops down in the seat beside me, and I immediately feel a little better. Huck may be drawn to trouble like a starlet to a scandal, but he's also my best friend.

"I can't believe I have to spend the week dealing with *that*," I say, gesturing down to the row of Athenas. "I know we're here to work, but I was at least hoping for a little break."

"A break from what?" The row of seats bounces and groans as Russ, Holland High's quarterback—and Demi's ex-boyfriend—drops his solid frame down in the empty seat next to mine. He reaches up and tucks his long, nearly chin-length blond hair behind his ears, where I notice a hole, the remnant of the time the starting line decided it would be cool to pierce one another's ears as some kind of warped demonstration of toughness and solidarity. Coach Morrison went ballistic and made all his players remove the earrings, but the mark remains.

When Russ catches me staring, he nods at me with a jock-like "'Sup?" At well over six feet tall, his knees thud into the seat in front of him, his arms more than taking up his armrest and starting in on my own. I nudge him hard with my elbow in an effort to confine him to his own space.

"You were saying about work?" Huck mutters under his breath. He leans back in his seat so as to disappear behind me, and thus out of Russ's view. Huck has never forgiven the HHS football team, Russ included, for the incident during the pre-game show sophomore year. We'd just finished the national anthem and were about to march into the tunnel formation, when the football team accidentally (on purpose) stormed the field early. Huck went flying ass over ankles into the end zone in front of a cheering crowd of Bulldog fans.

"Uh, Russ? Could you, um—" I search my brain for a task that will occupy him somewhere else, somewhere far away from me so I don't have to spend every second babysitting him. "Could you double-check that our instruments got loaded into the practice room?"

Russ leaps out of his seat with all the eagerness of a golden retriever sent after a tennis ball.

"Sure thing, Coach," he says, and flashes me a grin like he's starring in a Gatorade commercial.

"You don't have to call me Coach, Russ," I say for the ten thousandth time.

"Wait, so what are you, then?" His face gets quizzical, as if he's trying to solve a complex geometry problem.

"You mean existentially?" Huck chimes in, still slouched down in his chair. I slap him in the chest.

"I'm the drum major, Russ," I say, channeling my mom

when she's trying to get her third graders to settle down and work on subtraction. When the look of confusion doesn't fade, I clarify. "I'm like the leader."

Suddenly he's all smiles, deep dimples you could deposit Skittles in appearing on both cheeks. "You mean like the QB."

I sigh and give a resigned shrug. "Sure, I'm like the band's QB."

Huck swallows back a snort.

"I can respect that," Russ says, raising a hand for a high five. His hand whizzes toward mine with so much speed it actually produces a breeze. The impact sends my hand flying backward into my own face. Russ, who thinks this is all some kind of funny act, grins, then turns and bounds down the stairs two at a time.

All around me, my friends bust out in riotous laughter. Even Huck is doubled over, hiccuping.

"Traitor," I snap, shooting him a warning look, but he only laughs harder.

"C'mon, Liza," he says between desperate gasps for air. "That was funny."

I reach up and pop his fedora right off his head. He bends down to retrieve his hat from Clarice Cartwright's lap. Clarice is a freshman who plays clarinet. Seriously, Clarice, the clarinet player. I sometimes fantasize about handing her a saxophone and whispering, *"Hurry! There's still time!"*

"I do *not* envy you this week," Huck says, straightening up again.

"What do you mean?" I ask. But he doesn't have to answer, because I feel a sudden twinge, an unpleasant feeling of being watched. A familiar pair of sea-green eyes is glaring at me. Demi. She's giving me a look so sharp it could draw blood. As soon as she catches me staring, she pivots around and fixates on the door, where Russ's broad shoulders are disappearing out into the hall.

"Great," I mutter. "Just what I need. *More* drama." I heard Demi dumped Russ pretty spectacularly about a month ago, so I don't know what she has to be pissed about. Besides, if I could offload Russ, I would. Gladly. In fact, I plan to spend the week giving him enough mindless tasks to keep him completely out of my hair. I make a mental note to brainstorm a list tonight.

Up onstage, First Mate Kevin taps a mike and introduces himself to the new arrivals. This time his title draws a round of suppressed snickers from the crowd. First Mate Kevin either doesn't hear them or pretends not to, because he charges on.

"Welcome to Sail Away Cruise Line's Ship of Dreams high school performing arts competition!" He pumps his fist in the air, and this draws a round of cheers. The Mechanicals jump out of their seats and stomp their feet. *Off switch,* I think in their direction. Kevin grins, then waves at the crowd like he thinks he's a late-night television host trying to silence his audience so he can finish his monologue. "From the looks of all the talent in this room, I know we're going to have a fierce competition this week," he says while shielding his eyes and scanning us all, "but we're also going to have a *heck* of a lot of fun!"

Kevin pumps his arm again, but this time the reception isn't quite as hearty. Undeterred, Kevin launches into another summation of all the rules and regulations of the competition. Finally, he gets to the *just say no* portion of the presentation.

"And, kids," he says, his voice affecting a kind of sitcom-dad tone, "when we get to Nassau, there are going to be some unsavory characters hanging around. They might even offer you some *illicit substances.*" He hooks his fingers into air quotes, and I feel a shift in the audience that feels like a collective eye roll. "But I know you'll say no. After all, you'll be having so much fun aboard the ship that you won't need drugs to get high. You'll be high on life!"

The giggles start quietly but soon spark a roaring fire of raucous laughter. It seems First Mate Kevin is unaware that everyone is laughing *at* him and not *with* him, because he just stands there beaming like he's accepting an Emmy.

But I'm too distracted by the sight of Lenny to join in.

He's only just arriving, so instead of making his way up the aisle to sit with us, he leans back against the bright orange wall, arms crossed, one leg propped up against the wall behind him, one hand cradling his camera.

"High on life indeed," Huck whispers, his gaze following mine and every other girl's (and more than a few guys'). "Who's the hipster James Dean?"

"Mr. Curtis's son," I reply, trying to keep my voice from betraying the nervous energy racing through my veins. "I actually know him. . . ."

But before I can give any more details, First Mate Kevin adjourns the meeting and bounds off the stage. I know from experience that I have exactly four seconds before I lose control of the band completely. I leap to my feet and turn to face them, raising my arms for their attention like I would on the football field. All heads snap to me in unison.

"Guys! Don't forget. Lunch next, followed by a rehearsal at two-thirty. The practice room number is on your schedule. Do *not* be late."

Everyone nods, and I get a scattering of "Sure thing, Liza." But as soon as I drop my arms, they start moving for the door *fast.* They're probably hightailing it to either be first in the buffet line or to steal some extra time to explore the ship. I don't blame them. If I didn't feel so responsible for their well-being on the ship and for the band's *entire future,* I'd be pretty psyched to check out the three pools, six sundecks, bowling alley, and zip line. A *zip line,* for goodness' sake.

"Meet me in the room. We'll go to lunch today, okay?" Hillary calls from the bottom of the steps.

"Definitely," I reply. "Fifteen minutes?"

"Early is on time," she says, rolling her eyes, and we share a laugh.

When the stampede clears, I head down the aisle with Huck. On my way, I practically collide with Demi, who's making her way up the stairs. Her pouty, pink-glossed lips are pursed as she scans the auditorium.

"Looking for something?" I ask.

"Or someone?" Huck mutters, throwing a glance down toward the door, where Lenny is talking to his dad. Leave it to Demi to set her laserlike focus on the hottest guy on the boat. Just another trophy for her collection, I'm sure. But before Demi can reach him, Lenny disappears out the door.

Demi spins on her heel, her eyes going from my frayed cutoffs to my rumpled tank to my messy bun and down again. "Don't even try," she says, rolling her eyes. "It's too sad."

Missy appears, trotting up the aisle. "Did you find him?" she asks, but the question dies in her throat after a death glare from Demi. Missy's eyes go wide as she catches sight of me. Then her expression turns smug. "So what are you guys going to do for your showcase? Like, march back and forth across the stage?"

"It's concert band, Missy. We sit in chairs," I deadpan. Missy may be cute, with the voice of a pop tartlet, but she's not exactly the brightest spotlight on the stage.

"Did you bring your army jackets?" Demi asks, all syrupy and sneering.

"Still looking like a walking explosion at the sequin factory?" I retort. Say what you will about the band uniforms (and you could say a lot about our British army–inspired red jackets with epaulets and gold buttons, purchased thirty years ago and sporting an almost vintage fade), but they're nothing compared to the sock-hop skirts, spandex turtlenecks, and sequined vests the Athenas have been wearing since at least the midnineties.

"Well, *when* we win the twenty-five K, we're going to buy new designer dresses. In gold," Demi says, taking a step toward me, "to match our trophies."

I open my mouth to reply, but she holds up a tanned, manicured finger in my face. "Save it," she says, arching an eyebrow at me. "You know y'all don't stand a chance against us."

They pivot on their ballet flats and strut toward the door. Before they even make it out, both Missy and Demi have peeled off their tank tops to reveal brightly colored, barely-there bikini tops. Their VIP rooms may all come with private balconies, but I know Demi & Co. won't miss a chance to show off their stage-ready bods to the whole ship. Even when we were little, Demi loved prancing around the neighborhood pool in her hot-pink suit, while I preferred to curl up on a towel with my iPod and the one trashy magazine I'd allowed myself to bring.

"Don't worry, Liza," Huck says, placing his warm hand on the small of my back. "They're just trying to get in your head."

"I know," I reply, and I wish I could tell him it wasn't working, but the truth is, I'm nervous. I'm nervous we're not as good as I think we are and that the Athenas are better. I'm nervous that we won't get the money and about what will happen if we don't. Of course, he doesn't know that. "I just . . . I really want to win. I *need* to win."

Huck puts a hand on my shoulder and pivots me around to face him. "Is this about band camp again?" he says, suppressing a small sigh.

It's not just band camp. It's Senior Speeches, where the outgoing seniors get up and talk about the band and memories and how much everything meant to them. They remind us of all the traditions we're supposed to carry on, where they come from and what they mean. Senior Speeches are fun and hilarious, if not a mild threat to the underclassmen not to screw everything up in the coming year. Every year, the seniors who've just graduated drive up for the last day of band camp, which usually happens a week or two before they all leave for college. On the steps of the library at Cherokee State College, the tiny liberal arts campus in the woods that hosts camp every year, the outgoing drum major gives the final speech. Last summer, Sam Jacobs, a short, curly-haired clarinet player and certified genius who was off to Swarthmore in the fall, gave his entire speech while staring directly into my eyes.

"Liza Sanders, youngest drum major in the history of the Style Marchers, I leave my legacy in your hands. My legacy, and the legacy of all the drum majors before me! We kept this band marching. We kept the music going. We kept the crowd cheering. We kept the spirit of the Holland High Style Marchers alive. This legacy is yours to carry, and yours alone."

He was probably a little drunk when he said it (okay, a lot drunk; rumor had it that the seniors passed around two handles of Jack before they gave their speeches), but something about those words resonated with me.

They're more than my bandmates, they're my *friends*. The band has always been my home, a safe haven where I escaped Demi and the rat race of popularity happening in the cafeteria and in the halls. Every morning before first bell, between classes, and after school, the band room is where I can go and talk about who had the best Dr. Frank-N-Furter costume at last week's *Rocky Horror* sing-along, or debate who has the best female superheroes, Marvel or DC. Our weekends are spent at bonfires out at Hillary's family farm or singing along to the *Grease* sound track, the only songs on the ancient jukebox in Ben Tucker's parents' living room. And every year, Molly throws a Halloween party in her backyard, where you won't find a single person dressed as a slutty nurse, slutty mouse, or slutty *anything*, except for the year Huck decided to dress as just "slutty" (let's just say Nicole's red bandage dress was working very hard that night). I have three years of memories with these people, and I'm supposed to have one more.

So when I overheard Mr. Curtis talking about cutting the band, it felt like he was talking about cutting off my arm. And Sam's words sang through my brain like a chorus. *Keep the band marching, keep the music going . . . the spirit of the Holland High Style Marchers.* I can't imagine making it through senior year without the band.

I *won't* imagine it.

The rest of them are counting on me. And they don't even realize it.

"Liza? Earth to Liza?" Huck snaps his fingers in front of my face, and I have to blink a few times to get my focus back. "You know Sam had had like, six shots of Jack and a pot brownie that night, right? You have to let go of the legacy speech. It's going to drive you insane. The speeches are just overblown stand-up routines. Yours is going to be fine."

I nod, letting out a breath so Huck will see that I'm relaxing. But he's totally wrong. It's not the legacy *speech* I'm worried about.

It's our *actual* legacy.

CHAPTER 4

"I did not realize there were so many ways to prepare shrimp."
Huck rubs his belly with a muted groan.

"Well, maybe sampling them all wasn't the best idea." I've
avoided seafood since my oyster incident, preferring to stick
to a burger and fries for lunch. Since the ship set sail only
two hours ago, we're still working on picking up speed. This
means that while feasting on the largest buffet known to man
or beast, we're simultaneously working to develop our sea legs.
For some, a lethal combination.

"If you need one of these, let me know," Hillary says. She
lifts the sleeve on her I ONLY DATE BEATLES FANS T-shirt to reveal a three-inch square stuck to her arm just above her tattoo
of the opening notes to "A Day in the Life," which was her
eighteenth-birthday present to herself. "Seasickness patch. I
bought the family-sized box at Costco."

Hillary is a senior and off to Northwestern this fall to study journalism. She sort of adopted me as her little sister back when I was a freshman. Huck has always been my best friend, but Hillary has been there when I needed a girl on my side, like when I needed a roommate for band camp or that time I started my period during the first quarter of a playoff game and Hillary produced a tampon she'd wedged between the valves of her tuba. Her self-styled pixie cut makes her the Queen of the Home Haircut, and she can often be found before rehearsal giving out free trims in the tiny restroom in the corner of the band room. Thanks to Hillary, my bangs are always the perfect length.

"I read in the brochure that the first few hours are the worst," I reply, thankful that my stomach appears to be cooperating with the motion of the ship. At least one thing is going right for me. "Once we hit full speed on the open ocean, we'll barely feel the waves."

"Ugh, then full steam ahead," Hillary says, bumping my hip with hers.

The three of us make our way down a mirrored hallway toward our practice room, a space called the Copacabana Canteen. When we arrive, we find band members gathered outside the door. The clarinets are sitting in a circle playing some kind of hand-slapping game, while the trumpets kick around a Hacky Sack while trying to avoid beaning the head of Susan Bryan, a french horn player sitting against the wall nearby. Behind them, the drum line practices an impromptu step routine.

"Is the door locked or something?" I ask the waiting crowd.

"Or something," a skinny freshman saxophone player named Alex says, tossing her impossibly long red hair over her shoulder. She points to the door. I peek through the porthole window and see Demi leading the Athenas through a dance routine that involves knee bends and a shoulder shimmy.

Without a word, I burst through the door, sending it clanging into the wall behind it. The dancers halt midshimmy, and a tall brunette in the back row actually lets out a small shriek.

"Excuse me, rehearsal in progress," Demi snaps as if she's the dance teacher from *Fame*, a role she's been dying to play since we were kids.

"Yeah, it's supposed to be *our* rehearsal in progress," I reply. I reach into my bag and produce my blue folder. I flip it open to the page with the schedule First Mate Kevin handed out and shove it under Demi's nose. It clearly shows that the Copacabana Canteen belongs to the Holland High band. I cross my arms and tap my foot theatrically on the parquet floor. Not the best venue for a loud band rehearsal, but at least the cavernous room will be big enough for all of us and our instruments. It practically dwarfs the twenty Athenas and their rump shaking.

"Oh, sweetie, didn't anyone tell you?" A mocking pout spreads across Demi's red lips, and she cocks her head in faux sympathy. "There's been a change."

I glance around the room and notice a distinct lack of oversized instrument cases. All I see are mirrored café tables pushed up against the wall with black chairs stacked on top of them. One of the freshman Athenas has dragged a chair across the shiny tiled floor and is balancing on top of it while she tries to take down a disco ball that's hanging low over what I assume is a dance floor.

The band crowds into the open door behind me, jockeying for position to watch the showdown.

"What did you do with our instruments?" My blood is pounding in my ears. I'm already picturing them settling onto the ocean floor, a cloud of sand rising up while tropical fish swarm around them. She's not *that* evil, is she?

A stormy look crosses Demi's face. I follow her gaze and see that she's glaring at Russ, who's just wedged himself through the crowd.

"Hey, Coach," he says, then catches the combination stress-and-rage face I'm making. "I mean, uh, Liza. I was looking for y'all. I thought we had practice."

Staring at his innocent smile, I worry my brain might explode and ooze out of my ears. I take a deep breath, determined not to lose my cool in front of either the band *or* Demi and her posse of singing dancebots.

"We do, Russ," I say in a voice so icy and controlled that I hear Huck gasp. "Do you not remember me asking you to make sure our instruments got to our practice space? Which is here?" I gesture around the room, empty of instruments.

Russ grins. "Yeah, but Missy said that there was a mix-up, so I moved our stuff. She gave me a luggage cart and everything. C'mon, I'll show you." Russ turns back toward the door. I shoot Missy a death glare. She gives me a smile and a finger-wagging wave.

"Let's just go," Huck says. He loops his arm through mine and leads me through the door after Russ. The rest of the band falls in behind us. "Not worth it."

We make our way back down the mirrored hallway. "Huck, what am I going to do?" I whisper.

"About what?"

"What do you mean *what*? It was already going to be an uphill battle to beat the Athenas, but now they're using Russ as a saboteur!"

"Um, I doubt Russ is a saboteur. I think he's just dumb," Huck says. I glance at Russ's back, a gray Holland High Football T-shirt stretched over his broad shoulders. We follow him down two flights of stairs. "Besides, didn't Demi just dump him?"

Huck has a point. Still, better safe than sorry. "Please, that's probably all just a ruse. Or maybe he's trying to get her back by sabotaging us. Either way, he can't be trusted."

"Uh, *drama* much?" Huck rolls his eyes, but I ignore him. I don't trust Demi, so I can't trust Russ.

Russ leads us down a third flight of stairs, down another hallway, and around a corner to another doorway. A sign overhead reads PARADISE ALLEY BOWLING, and a handwritten note taped to the door reads *Sorry, Closed for Repairs*.

Russ throws me another grin, then shoves through the door into the darkened bowling alley. He flicks on a light, and I see all our instrument cases stacked in an impossible tower, crowding the small lobby area and reaching over into the seats at the end of the four lanes. Against the back wall, a ladder is set up surrounded by caution tape, an open duct exposed on the floor. The room is almost the same size as the studio upstairs. Unfortunately, most of the space is taken up by orange plastic seats bolted to the floor, racks of bowling balls, computer scoring units, and a *freaking bowling alley*. The rest of my fellow musicians crowd in behind me, leaving almost no room to turn around, much less rehearse.

"This won't work!" I hiss to Huck, my panic level reaching

code red. My iron grip on my cool is loosening with each passing second.

"Maybe if we unpack everything and move the cases out into the hall, there might be some space?" Russ runs his hand through his beach-blond hair. Everyone looks at me, their fearless leader, for instructions. I'm tempted to call it a day, but that means I give Demi another in a series of wins. This is *my* band, and *I* decide when we practice. Maybe not *where*, but *when*.

"All right, guys, here's what we're going to do," I announce loudly, and tell them to unload their instruments and stack their cases by the door. Then I direct all the section leaders to gather their players into groups so that we can do a standing rehearsal like we would out on the practice field during marching season.

Everyone gets to work. Russ has stacked the cases carefully to make them all fit in a complex jigsaw-puzzle formation, with the smallest instruments at the top. This means that our tiny woodwind girls are having to practically scale a mountain to grab their stuff, and then, in order to make space for others, move out into the lanes. Andrew, a lanky baritone player whose vision is partially obscured by a dark mop of curls, loses his footing on the greased-up floor. His baritone case hits the lane and careens toward the pins at the end just as he hits the floor with a thud. His girlfriend, Clarice, the clarinet player, yelps and rushes to his aid, but is blocked by Russ, who is standing over Andrew.

"Strike!" Russ laughs. He offers a hand to Andrew, who stares at it suspiciously before ignoring it and pushing himself gingerly to his feet. I don't blame Andrew. It wasn't long ago that the defensive line mistook him for a tackling dummy as he crossed the practice field to our rehearsal and sent him skidding butt-first across the wet grass. I had to help him sew up his jeans so his jack-o'-lantern boxers wouldn't be on display during his European history presentation the following period.

"This is a nightmare," I mutter to Huck, who is clutching his oboe case and trying to contain his laughter. Across the alley, Ben and another trumpet player named Nate, both of whom fancy themselves the jocks of the band, have started a game of catch with a hot-pink bowling ball.

"Put that back!" I call, but in all the commotion, they either don't hear me or pretend not to. I set off through the crowd, climbing over a bass drum and a tuba. Russ has already joined in, and has the pink bowling ball hoisted for a toss.

"Put that back!" I bark at full volume.

Russ jumps, and the ball drops out of his hand and lands on the floor with a crash. It rolls—slowly at first, then faster—straight toward the open duct in the floor.

"Oh God," I whisper. I watch its path, my rolling stomach picking up speed with the ball.

"Get it!" Russ shouts, and all three boys spring into action. The slick floor sends them all skidding headfirst after the ball just half a second too late. It drops through the duct in a flash of pink.

The entire room goes silent while we wait to hear it land. It feels like we wait for three eternities. Finally, there's a loud *crack*, a crash, a clang . . . and then a long, low hissing sound, like the air being slowly let out of a balloon.

"What's that?" Russ says, wrinkling his nose.

Before I can answer, a stream of white smoke begins pouring out of the duct. It rolls low over the floor, curling around our ankles, then begins to rise until we're fanning our faces just to see. There's a hot, damp smell that makes my eyes water and my heart pound.

"Oh my God!" Clarice the clarinet player shrieks. Images of lifeboats and a sinking ship flash before my eyes, making me break into a cold sweat. Nicole Mauser clutches her flute case and looks like she's seconds away from throwing up or passing out—or both. Russ uses his huge arms to try to fan the smoke away from the opening, but it's like sticking a teacup underneath a waterfall. The smoke is getting thicker, and it's rolling toward the back of the alley.

I have to do something before . . . I don't know what. We sink? We get in trouble? We get disqualified from the competition?

Suddenly death at sea seems less scary than what will happen if we lose the competition.

"Everybody get your stuff—*fast*. We were never here." My voice comes out as a yelp. "Our practice space was full, so we just stored our instruments in our cabins and enjoyed a free afternoon. Got it?"

I haven't seen a group of band kids move this fast since that time the homecoming game went into overtime and we nearly missed our postgame trip to Dairy Queen. Brass and silver disappear into the velvet guts of instrument cases. Stacks of sheet music are shoved into folders and bags, and for once, I'm not worried about folded corners or crumpled pages. Within minutes, the room is clear.

"You coming?" Huck calls from the doorway.

The air is still cloudy and scented with a bitter, chemical tang. I have a sudden image of smoke pouring out of the portholes, of the ship tipping, of slowly sinking into the ocean while we bob around it in tiny lifeboats. My stomach has climbed up my spine and blocks my windpipe.

"Yup," I reply.

Then Huck and I duck out of the bowling alley and race down the hall.

CHAPTER 5

Three hours have passed since the bowling ball incident, and I spent almost every second of them waiting for some kind of wailing alarm to signal us to report to our lifeboats, all the while fighting the urge to confess what we did. I barely managed to choke down my caesar salad at dinner.

But as we take the stage for the opening showcase, still afloat, still with no indications of trouble, I start to realize how ridiculous I've been. No way could a runaway bowling ball sink a *cruise ship*. No doubt the cleaning crew has long since discovered the damage and set about repairing it. No one needs to know the band was involved in any of it.

I look around at the Grand Auditorium, built to look like a miniature Lincoln Center, with the luxury boxes painted onto the walls as murals and small versions of the famous modern diamond chandeliers hanging from the ceiling. The Mechanicals just left the stage to riotous laughter and raucous applause after performing a selection of scenes from *Spamalot*. It takes several minutes to get the chairs, stands, and instruments set up afterward, and it doesn't help that Michael Narducci, the pit leader, drops the gong.

I swallow hard, wishing I weren't troubled by such a bad case of preperformance jitters, which make me feel as if there's a major grasshopper infestation in the bottom of my stomach. What I do *not* need right now is to barf all over Nicole Mauser, who is practically vibrating with nerves far worse than mine. When she catches me staring at her, I mime a deep breath. She sits up straighter in her chair and mouths a silent thank you.

The audience is made up mostly of our fellow competitors, who stuck around after their performances to scope out the competition. The rest of the crowd includes a collection of retirees who think a performing arts showcase is a lovely way to spend a Friday night at sea. Their gray and silver hair catches the light in the theater, and I wonder if any of them could be bribed to turn down their hearing aids. I'm not exactly feeling confident after today's "practice"—if you can even call it that—and from a glance at the band gathered around me in all black, they're not feeling great either. Everyone looks nervous or traumatized . . . or both.

The Athenas, next up on the program, are waiting in the wings. All of them are huddled in a group, whispering and snickering. Except Demi. She's standing off to the side, eyes closed while her mouth moves in what I recognize as her traditional preshow good luck ritual: reciting the Debbie Allen dance teacher speech from the TV series *Fame*. Demi's older sister got her the DVD set for her tenth birthday, and we watched the episodes so many times we practically wore out the discs. As I watch Demi now, I have to stop myself from reciting along with her, as I did so many times when we were kids. *You've got big dreams? You want fame? Well, fame costs. And right here is where you start paying . . . in sweat.*

I force my eyes away from Demi and take one final visual sweep of the band in front of me. Everyone is seated, their instruments poised on their laps, just waiting for my signal. It's time.

I raise my hands, and everyone lifts their instruments with my motion, their eyes on me for the count. I take a deep breath, letting myself wish one last time that we'd gotten that practice in. Or at least hadn't caused property damage such that my band is traumatized. But it's too late for that now. As my grandpa Sanders used to say, *Wish in one hand, spit in the other, and see which one fills up faster,* an expression that always makes Dad grimace in disgust.

And then we begin. We manage to all hit the downbeat at the same time, but my pride is short-lived. Huck and his oboe immediately skip a measure, a mistake he's made at nearly every performance this year, letting out a series of ill-timed, squawking trills. This sends Jared, the snare drum player, into a minor panic, since those trills are his cue. He sweeps his shaggy bangs out of his eyes, and with a *better late than never* shrug, he starts banging away. The trumpets seated in front of him jump in surprise.

Sweat starts moving from my neck to my waist. With one hand I flip forward in the sheet music, frantically scanning the measures. I have absolutely no idea where in the music they are.

Then—like a phoenix rising from the ashes—Nicole stands

for her flute solo. Her solo is beautifully performed, if seven measures early.

When she's done, she walks quickly and deliberately off-stage, where I see her bend over a trash can in the wings. Thankfully, the band is playing so loud that no one can hear her retching. I don't think any deep breathing is going to help her out of that one.

At this point, I just need to get them all to wrap it up, more or less at the same time. I hold my hands up to indicate a fermata, a moment where they all hold their respective notes until my signal. The few that are actually watching me hold, but it takes a good twelve counts before the rest of the band catches on. Like musical dominoes, they fall in line, one after the other. And when I've got all their eyes, I give them the final cutoff.

"Oh, thank God," I mutter as merciful silence takes over. I catch Huck's eye. He mouths, "I'm sorry."

I can't even respond. What would I say? *Thanks for missing your cue yet again and messing everybody up, Huck? I wish you'd do us all a favor and quit?* Even if it's true, I can't say that to my best friend. I feel dizzy and hot, and like maybe someone's shoved cotton balls in my ears. Everything is oddly muted, and I wonder if I'm having an aneurysm. Or a psychotic break. I can feel the eyes of the audience boring into my back like a sea of hot laser beams.

A tentative smattering of applause begins, and even though I'd prefer to drive blunt pencils into my eyeballs, I turn to face the audience. The applause picks up to something that borders on respectable when I, followed by the rest of the band, take a bow. I focus on the empty seats so I don't have to see anyone looking at me with pity or bewilderment. I wish again that I were back on the football field, where the crowd is farther away and I can hide behind my bulky red and black uniform and my drum major hat with the giant plume on top. Standing there in my black pants and black long-sleeved shirt, I feel entirely too exposed.

I practically bolt off the stage, eyes planted firmly on my feet, and nearly steamroll Demi. The rest of the Athenas are behind her, all clad in their sequined vests.

"Don't worry, I started a rumor that you guys are from the deaf school, so everyone understands." She grins, and I swear, her bright white smile actually twinkles. "You're welcome."

She nods to the Athenas, who nod back at her. Then, like a herd of Broadway cheerleaders, they bound onstage, their black circle skirts and ponytails tied tight with matching grosgrain ribbon bouncing in unison. Unconsciously, I let out a groan.

"Cheer up," Huck says. He cradles his oboe in one arm and throws the other around my shoulder. "They could choke."

"Or we could sink," I reply, scuffing the toe of my shoe against the floor. "Literally." After our horrible performance, I'm almost *hoping* we will.

"Dude, it was a bowling ball. Have you seen this boat?" Huck gestures out at the theater, which makes up about one-eightieth of the total square footage of the ship. "There's no way one little ball could break an entire ship."

"You're right," I reply, but my voice shakes just enough to betray my lingering nerves.

"And like I said." Huck nudges my shoulder with his, a playful smile on his face. "They could totally choke."

But they won't.

The Athenas have always been good, but under Demi's leadership, they've turned into a tiny, perky show-choir army. They're as talented as they are snotty—which is to say, extremely. They perform at every pep rally, at every holiday assembly, and without fail, they have our entire school of jaded teenagers cheering. My classmates barely tolerate the band, but they *love* the Athenas.

The Athenas take their positions onstage in two lines, heads bowed, arms crossed behind their backs. Demi gives an almost imperceptible nod, and then they're off, singing and dancing in such perfect time that I wonder if they were animated by Disney. All thoughts of our monster truck rally of a performance (*Crash! Clank! Eek!*) are gone as the crowd starts clapping in time with their medley of throwback boy-band classics from the late nineties. When they perform, their twenty bodies suddenly look like forty, or more. Their movement, their enthusiasm, their smiles, it's all bigger than life. They make use of the entire stage, spinning and jumping and moving down to the floor, legs kicking in the air. The electricity of their performance sizzles through the auditorium. I have to admit, Demi is amazing, but when they perfectly execute classic boy-band harmonies and the video-ready dance moves that go along with them, I know I've had enough.

"I can't watch," I say to Huck.

I turn and start to make my way into the blackness of the backstage area, stepping over bundles of sound cords and around sandbags, considering disappearing into the folds of the heavy velvet curtain, until I smash directly into Lenny and his camera, which is hanging around his neck. The lens smashes into my sternum, partially knocking the wind out of me. Onstage, another *NSYNC song is kicking up loud enough to mask my gasp.

"Whoa, easy, Birdie," he says, putting his hands on my shoulders. A small thrill runs through me, starting at the point where his strong hands rest on my shoulders. Then I remember that he must have seen what happened a moment ago onstage, when I basically led the band through a rousing performance of *What-the-Heck-Was-That?* And that thought makes me want to sink into the floor. "Are you okay?" he asks, as if to confirm my worst fear. He wasn't struck temporarily deaf or unconscious. He saw our performance.

"Not really," I mutter. I wave one hand at the stage and rub my forehead with the other. "We didn't get to practice today. And well, you saw the result."

"Hey, it wasn't that bad." Lenny gives me a slightly embarrassed smile that tells me he knows how big a lie he's telling. A *real whopper*, as Grandpa Sanders would say. "First-night jitters, right?"

"Times ten," I reply, my voice weak and resigned.

"Remember what Shandy used to say about jitters?"

I can't help but laugh at the mention of our drama camp counselor, a senior theater student at the community college famous for her massive mop of fiery red curls and genuine belief that she would be the next Meryl Streep. In unison, we both wave exaggerated jazz hands and say with Shandy's trademark lisp, "Shake 'em out!"

Onstage, the Athenas fling their hands in the air to hit the last chorus. As soon as the music kicks off, all the lights go with it, blinking out with an audible snap. The auditorium is plunged into darkness. But no one cares. Applause thunders through the room. I swear, the only light comes from the twenty Athena grins up on the stage.

The audience is still cheering when a backup generator kicks in. It grinds up to illuminate about half of the overhead lights . . . just enough to show the curls of white smoke creeping across the stage.

"Dang. The smoke machine's a nice touch," Lenny says, nodding at the stage.

But as the smoke begins to rise and creep out into the audience, the sour smell from the bowling alley tickles my nose.

My stomach twists like the guts of a french horn. Something isn't right.

And from the looks of disgust that cross the faces of the audience, it's clear they know this isn't part of the show. It's only then that the cheers turn to confused chatter, the heads out in the audience pivoting around for an explanation.

First Mate Kevin bounds out onto the stage wearing a Britney Spears–style headset attached to a walkie-talkie held in his hand. With no microphone, he has to resort to exaggerated hand gestures to quiet the crowd.

"Settle down, everyone. Please take your seats," he booms, trying to compensate for the nonworking mike. He waves his hand in front of his face to clear the smoke. Down in the audience, white programs fan frantically to keep the smell away. In the front row, an ancient, wrinkled lady with a silver pixie cut and thick Coke-bottle glasses erupts into a coughing fit. "It appears we're having a few mechanical difficulties at the moment. Please remain calm and we'll get it solved *tout de suite.*" He lets out a nervous giggle that, thanks to the acoustics of the theater, bounces around the room without the aid of a microphone.

There are some groans and grumbles. The smoke is starting to clear, but the stench of something burning remains. The Mechanicals give one another exaggerated high fives, thumbs-ups, and even a few dramatic bows. But the words hit me hard, as if that stupid pink bowling ball has now dropped straight through my chest.

Mechanical difficulties.

The vent. The steam.

A *bowling ball couldn't do this. A bowling ball couldn't do this. A bowling ball couldn't do this.*

My mind goes into overdrive trying to convince my body that everything is fine, but my body isn't listening. My hands start shaking, so I clench them into fists, my nails digging half-moons into my palms.

"I'm going to go find my dad," Lenny whispers. "See you in a minute, okay?"

I barely manage to nod. He hurries around the curtain and down the steps on the side of the stage, and Huck once again sidles up next to me.

"Everything will get cleared up shortly," First Mate Kevin continues, his finger to his earpiece as he receives an update. "In the meantime, we've shut down the engines and primary power until we can get it fixed. We'll have the generators for now. I encourage you all to take a stroll on the deck or relax in your rooms. We'll keep you posted on the progress."

"This is a nightmare," I whisper to Huck.

"Worse than what happened up there?" Huck cocks his

head toward the stage, where the Athenas are patting one another on the back in their postshow huddle, too high on adrenaline to worry about a little thing like an electrical failure. I watch their enthusiasm, their collective triumph, and all of a sudden I worry that I really might throw up. A shiver runs up my spine as I remember our final, cacophonous note.

Huck pulls my head to rest on his shoulder. "At least if we sink we won't have to play again," he says.

"You don't think . . . ?" I swallow hard. "I mean, what happened earlier . . . ?"

"No, Liza," he says firmly, gripping me by the shoulders. "This is *not* your fault. You heard that first mate guy. This is nothing to be worried about."

"Well, Kevin needs to work on his poker face, because one look at him tells me we're going *down*."

Huck gives me a slight shake. "Liza, the man's a glorified babysitter, not an electrician. So stop taking cues from a grown-up in a sailor suit and chill out."

But the longer we sit in semidarkness, the less I believe it. I try to block images of Bahamian jail cells and shark-infested waters, but it doesn't work. I suddenly feel like it's roasting in here, and not just because the power outage caused the air conditioning to click off. Pricks of sweat are starting to form on my forehead, under my arms, and down my back. I try to swallow, but my tongue feels like it's made of steel wool.

"What's going on over there?" Huck points toward the audience. Near the stage, First Mate Kevin, his mouth set in a straight line, is nodding at Mr. Curtis, who keeps flinging his arms around, as if to say *Look at this disaster*. Behind them both is a greasy-haired, pudgy man I don't recognize, and he looks even more unhappy than Kevin and Mr. Curtis. Lenny is nowhere to be seen.

Mr. Curtis turns and scans the stage, where he sees me. He waves me over with a hard flip of his hand.

"Do you need backup?" Huck whispers.

I shake my head. "I'm okay," I say, which is a total lie. I can't tell if it's my imagination, or if the ship is rocking more violently than before, but it's definitely harder to walk a straight line. Never have I felt more like I was walking the plank. *Please let me not be in trouble.*

"What's up, Mr. Curtis?" I say, trying for a smile and managing only a grimace.

Mr. Curtis doesn't even attempt a small grin. Instead, he turns to Kevin and the greasy-haired man. "Liza," he says, pointing to the walking garlic knot of a man. "This is Raoul Ferengetti. The cruise director."

I feel the floor swaying beneath me. The room spins. Mr. Ferengetti scowls.

Goodbye, band, I think fleetingly. *I'll write to you from prison. . . .*

CHAPTER 6

I am the kind of girl who always seems to be working ten times as hard as everyone else for about 0.06 percent of the credit. Even I, despite being terrible at math, know that those odds suck. I can seriously count on one hand the number of times in my life I have truly gotten off easy. There was the time in fourth grade when I called Ethan Kline a four-letter word, and when he tattled, my teacher said I was a nice girl and didn't believe him. And then there was the time sophomore year that I convinced my history teacher that my computer ate my midterm paper, when in reality, I fell asleep watching an eighties movie marathon on TV. I got an extension for the weekend. That's it, a list so short I can't help but commit it to memory.

But as Mr. Curtis continues talking, and I notice that Mr. Ferengetti appears to be frowning *in general* instead of specifically *at me*, it occurs to me that this moment might in fact be one I can add to my list.

"I will *not* have the students in my care put in danger," Mr. Curtis is saying now, his voice stern. I notice that his hands are clenched into fists so tight his knuckles have turned white. The collar of his HHS polo is sticking up on one side, and his hair looks like it has suffered through an accident at the gel factory. The only time I've seen him even close to this upset was when he caught the flute players twirling their instruments like batons on the last day of band camp. "I want to know *exactly* what's happening. Why are the engines in trouble? How could this happen? I demand a full report. And what's this I'm hearing about a storm coming? Are we adequately prepared for this?" All sense of Mr. Curtis's trademark calm is gone, and questions continue flying from his mouth. He waves his phone in Mr. Ferengetti's face, the weather app on the screen showing little cartoons of clouds and lightning bolts.

I am about to respond when I realize that he is talking to Mr. Ferengetti, not me.

"Of course, sir, of course," First Mate Kevin chimes in, while the cruise director simply nods, slowly twisting the end of his mustache, which is, if possible, even shinier than the hair on his head.

I lean against one of the oversized Roman columns that frame the stage. My initial relief—he's angry at the cruise line, not at me—turns just as quickly to dismay. If Mr. Curtis gets the investigation he demands, it might just turn up a hot-pink bowling ball and a certain band practicing in the closed bowling alley. Forget saving the band. I don't know how much it costs to repair a cruise ship, but I know we'd have to have a whole lot of bake sales to even come close. Like, a million of them.

Over the years, I've learned that the best way to avoid panic is to make a plan. Working through steps and organizing your problems keeps you from thinking about all the ways things could fall completely apart. It's how I got through my parents' divorce, it's how I got through drum major tryouts, it's how I got through the idea of losing the band, and it's how I'll get through this.

"Mr. Curtis, can I talk to you?" I say quietly, directing a smile at Kevin and the cruise director that's meant to say, *Well, what can ya do?*

Once we are safely out of earshot, I lean in and gesture for him to do the same. "Everyone's *really* freaked out about the malfunction," I begin, glossing over the fact that no one seems more frantic than he is. "We should probably focus on keeping everyone calm, and direct them back to their cabins to make sure they're safe. I was wondering if maybe you could help me with that." I smile, channeling Shandy's acting lessons. Because I may be freaking out right along with him, but I can't let him see it. I let the smile grow slightly before continuing. "Sometimes you just really need assurances from a grown-up, you know?"

Mr. Curtis seems to realize for the first time that *he's* the grown-up and that *he's* supposed to be the calm one. I see him mentally try to get ahold of his horses, and I pretend not to notice the gross sweat rings now forming under his arms.

"Yes, yes of course, that's a great idea, Liza," he mumbles. He nods so hard his head looks in danger of rocketing off his shoulders. "That's a great idea."

And then, without meeting my eye or uttering another word, Mr. Curtis makes a beeline for the nearby stairwell that leads down to our block of cabins. I'm not sure if he's going to throw up or cry or take a sedative (though I certainly hope it's the latter). Whatever it is, it's taking him away from questions about what happened and any conclusions about what his students may have done to cause it.

Mission accomplished. For now.

I buzz through the auditorium, grabbing all the band members I can find and telling them to spread the word: HHS band needs to get below deck. Once I no longer spot any of our stiff black concert dresses or black suits in the crowd, I head down toward our rooms.

The elevator doors slide open to reveal that the hallways of the Riviera Deck, also known as the lowest floor of the ship not occupied by the crew, have become a mini dance club. Someone's turned up their iPhone speaker to full blast, but the tinny tunes are drowned out by the voices of my bandmates singing along. Almost all of them are crammed into the narrow space, hands on hips, stepping to the right, executing the Time Warp from *Rocky Horror*. Despite having come extremely close to losing everything and possibly getting sent to some juvenile detention center on a remote island, I still feel a surge of pride that even in the most chaotic of moments, the HHS Style Marchers find a way to make their own fun.

"Liza, come on! It's the Time Warp!" Hillary shouts over the chorus while waving her arms over her head in full-on jazz hands.

I have an almost Pavlovian urge to jump in and pelvic-thrust right alongside them, but I need some quiet time. I have about twelve hours until our next rehearsal, and I plan to spend every minute of it trying to figure out how to save our performance—and our band.

"Y'all have fun, I've got some stuff to take care of," I shout back. "But please don't leave the floor, okay?"

"Don't worry, I'll keep everyone in line," Huck says, a devilish glint in his eye. He's got the bow tie from his concert suit fastened around his head, the bow askew on his forehead. He breaks into a very intense variation of the twist.

"Don't worry, *I'll* keep everyone in line," Hillary says, and I mouth a thank you to her before disappearing into our room.

I've got to strategize.

With the practice room switcheroo, it's obvious that the Athenas are planning to play dirty this week.

Which means we've got to get dirty right back.

★ ★ ★

By the next morning, the power still isn't working. On the plus side, the backup generators are grinding away and the ship is still seaworthy. So far.

Since the Athenas stole our practice space yesterday, I told the band to meet for our Saturday-morning practice in what should have been *theirs*. I scoped it out last night, and while it's not nearly as large as the one the Athenas took over, it's at least large enough for us to sit down in actual chairs and practice. Which is good, because we clearly need it. Forget the prize money; if we repeat last night's performance I wouldn't be surprised if the Sail Away Cruise Line *fines* us $25,000.

I push open the door to our new humble home, three floors up and down the hall from the big atrium at the center of the ship. The plaque on the door reads HIDEAWAY HALL.

"Hideaway *Hell* is more like it," I mutter to myself. I put my hand on the door to shove it open, but a tap on my shoulder stops me.

Demi is standing next to Mrs. Haddaway, who is wearing a vintage sailor suit and cat's-eye sunglasses buried in her curls.

"Liza, I'm glad we caught you," Mrs. Haddaway says. She nudges Demi with her elbow.

Demi grimaces, then rearranges her face into something approximating a look of apology. All I can see is the face she used when we were seven and had to apologize to her mother for using all her (very expensive) makeup for our circus extravaganza backyard show, where Demi played the ringmaster and I was a clown. It looks just about as sincere now as it did then.

"I'm sorry we stole your practice space," she says, somehow managing to hide the fact that really she's just sorry she got caught.

"Oh, uh, thanks?" I glance at Mrs. Haddaway, who I assume is responsible for Demi's sudden bout of contrition, because she's giving Demi a *look*.

"And you can have it back," Demi says finally.

"The Athenas will be happy to help you transport your instruments if you need help," Mrs. Haddaway adds.

Demi's mouth falls open, and I can tell she will definitely *not* be happy about that.

"Oh, that won't be necessary at all," I tell Mrs. Haddaway. I turn to Demi and give her a smile that I hope doesn't look *too* smug. "And Demi, I *so* appreciate your heartfelt apology. It means a lot."

Demi's nose wrinkles, and she pretends to scratch it with a certain middle finger.

Mrs. Haddaway doesn't notice, though, because she's too busy fanning herself.

"I'm glad that's taken care of," Mrs. Haddaway says, waving a sweaty curl away from her forehead. "Now if only they'd get the power back on. Those generators are just not doing the job on the air conditioning in here."

At the mention of the engine trouble, I freeze.

"Yeah, um . . ." I pick at the remains of my blue nail polish, trying to appear unconcerned. "Have you heard anything more about that?"

Mrs. Haddaway shrugs. "The captain mentioned at breakfast that they were looking at some surveillance video to find out what happened. They suspect tampering," she says, but she quickly goes from fanning herself to waving off that idea. "That just seems ridiculous, though. I doubt they're going to find anything on a video."

"Right, exactly," I say, my voice squeaking, and panic surging through my veins. If the captain looks at a video, what he's going to see is a bowling ball smashing into, well, whatever it is that's down there that causes boats to break. And from there, they're going to find *us*.

"Okay, well, we'll let you get back to your rehearsal," Mrs. Haddaway says, smiling. "And like I said, if you need help moving your instruments, let Demi know."

Demi shoots me a look that says *Do not let me know*. But Demi is now the least of my problems. All my mental energy is focused on the video. Will it show the band *tampering* by means of a certain pink bowling ball? What will happen if we get busted?

While Demi and Mrs. Haddaway make their way back down the hall, I shove the door open to Hideaway Hall. Inside I find what looks like a standard-issue conference room, the tables pushed to the edges of the room, all the chairs arranged scattershot across the middle of the floor. A few band members have arrived to set up early, but before I can tell them not to bother, a flying silver object whizzes past my face.

"Fore! I mean, duck!" Russ intercepts the baritone mute, cradling it in his arm like a receiver heading for the end zone. He fakes left around me and executes a pass toward Huck, who's sitting on one of the back tables examining Hillary's new typewriter tattoo on her shoulder. Huck's reaction to Russ's throw is to stare helplessly at the metal projectile headed right for his face, so Hillary reaches up and swats it away seconds before it careens into his nose. The mute lands back on the carpet and rolls into the leg of a chair.

"Dude, you saved me!" Huck wails. He flings his arms around Hillary's neck like she just threw herself in front of a speeding train for him.

"Down, boy," Hillary says, patting his head gently. "It was nothing. You're just indebted to me forever now."

I turn to yell at Russ as the mute comes whizzing back in a tight spiral. "Nice!" Russ calls. He raises his hands for another perfect catch, then wings it toward the clarinets, who are sitting in a circle sucking on reeds and cleaning their instruments. Ray, a sophomore trombone player, darts over at the last second, preventing the mute from colliding with Madeline's head. He grins and tosses it back.

Russ reaches around for another catch, so I throw my hands into the air and intercept, a skill I'm shocked I've absorbed from simply watching three years' worth of high school football games. He crosses the space between us in three long steps, arms out like he's going in for a hug, or —

Not a hug. A tackle.

In a flash I'm on the ground.

"What in the fresh hell?" I shout, but my words are muffled by a gray Holland High Athletic Department T-shirt and a very muscled chest.

Russ just laughs and attempts to pull himself off me. "Sorry. Instinct." He puts his hands flat on the floor next to my ears and lifts himself in a push-up, the smell of detergent and spicy deodorant filling my nose.

"*Eeeiii!*" I screech as he lifts himself off me. My gold hoop earring, a gift from Grandma Sanders when I started high school, is caught in the sleeve of his T-shirt. I worry that my ear might actually detach from my body, so I grab a wad of his shirt and pull him back down. He lands with a thud back on top of me.

"My earring," I say into his chest. "Hold still." I reach up and unclasp the hoop, remove it, then shove him off.

Russ rolls to his feet. He offers his hand to me, but I smack it away and pull myself up. I glance around the room to see that, per usual, all eyes are on me, except for the french horns, who are already whispering behind their hands while they throw glances at Russ and me.

"Sorry, boss," Russ says. He gives one of those corn-fed-farm-boy *aw shucks* shrugs. "My training kicked in a little there."

I feel an instinct kick in, too, only mine involves my foot and his ass.

"I don't know if you realize this, but this week, you're not

67

a football player," I say, my voice rising like steam from a kettle. "You're not the quarterback or All-American or Captain America or whatever the hell else you fancy yourself to be." My words send Russ's all-star grin melting right off his face. "You are here because you were screwing around, and now you're being punished. You're here to *work* for me, which is ironic, since all you've done is *cause* work for me. From the moment we stepped onto this ship you've acted like a prize jerk."

Someone behind me snorts. I spin around, feeling as if my anger is going to sizzle out through my eyeballs. "And you guys! You're just as bad! It's like you don't care whether we win or lose. Like it doesn't mean anything to you, when it means *everything*. It means *everything*!" My voice is rising as fast as my blood pressure. Everyone is staring, even Russ. The expression on his face has morphed past embarrassment into something else. Shock? Terror?

The room is silent. Huck is staring at me like I've gone bonkers. Hillary clears her throat.

"Dude, when did you get so obsessed with winning?" she says. She gives me a look that tells me I've gone full loon. "It's spring break. You need to chill out."

"Seriously, Liza, what's going on?" Huck's voice is low, cautious—and suspicious.

As much as I want to explain, I can't. I won't tell them—any of them—how close we are to losing the band. I *need* them, which means I need to keep quiet.

I press my fingers to my temples, where a monster headache is beginning to throb.

"I'm sorry," I say, grasping for an explanation, anything that might make sense. "I'm just, um, really . . . not feeling well. Maybe it was the coconut shrimp . . . or the mango shrimp . . . ," I sputter, hoping no one will realize I didn't actually eat any of those things.

Everyone is still staring at me as if I've lost my mind. Without another word, I turn and bolt for the door.

"Guys, meet back here for our afternoon practice time, okay? This practice is over," Huck calls, even as I hurtle into the hall. Then: "Liza, wait!"

But I don't wait. I zigzag down the hall and up the stairs to the mezzanine, dashing past the gallery full of surf gear and miniature plastic replicas of the *Destiny*, up another set of stairs and past the casino, where a bunch of blue-haired ladies are hunched over the slot machines shaking plastic cups of nickels, and at last burst into the sunshine on the main deck. The sun is high and bright in the sky, and I have to blink and shield my eyes to keep from seeing spots. When I drop my hand, Huck is standing in front of me, staring me down, panting slightly.

"Nice try," he says, leaning against the railing of the ship, the open water over his shoulder. His voice is light, but his sunglasses are crooked on his nose, one end of the neoprene leash hanging down onto his chest. "Do you want to tell me what *that* was about?"

Once again, I have no excuse to give him. I *never* yell like that. Raise my voice? Sure, who doesn't in a group of sixty teenagers? Use my stern, grown-up voice? Of course. But yell? Never.

I don't lie to my best friends, either.

My braid feels too tight, like it's going to pull my hair straight from my scalp. I reach up and pull the rubber band out of the bottom, running my fingers through my hair and shaking my head into the wind. The breeze catches it, blowing it into my face and out over the ocean.

"I told you. I'm just not feeling well." I place a hand on my stomach, hoping that will convince him. It's not even that much of a lie. Increasingly, I feel like I might throw up.

He makes a face. "If you're gonna yak, please do it over the side," he says. Huck is a champion babysitter, but he's never been good with vomit. It's a good thing neither of us drinks, because I'm pretty sure I can't trust him to hold my hair back.

"I'll be fine," I say. "I just needed some air." I take a step toward the railing and look down at the waves churning against the side of the ship, one hundred feet below us. The water is so deep and dark it's almost black, little whitecaps cresting on the waves. By now, we must be hundreds of miles from the shore and even farther from my house back in Tennessee. The view is certainly different from the one I see when I'm leaning over the back deck of our house, where my backyard gives way to trees, which break to show off the gently rolling foothills of the Smoky Mountains.

"At least this is better than climbing the hills of San Francisco with a perky blond secretary," Huck says, nudging me with an elbow.

"She's an associate," I say. But Huck is right. Dad wanted me to spend spring break with him in his shiny new condo in San Francisco. His email went on and on about the views of the Golden Gate Bridge and how we could get chocolate milk shakes at the Ghirardelli place. Of course, the "we" there would be me, him, and his new girlfriend, Kimberly, a pretty young associate at his law firm. I didn't have the heart to tell him that everything in that equation—except for the chocolate milk shakes—sounded like my version of hell.

Huck sighs and leans next to me, staring out over the ocean. "Look, I know you're under a lot of pressure, what with school and the parade of potential future stepmonsters and this newly cultivated need to win, but acting like a crazy stressball isn't doing anyone any good. What can I do to get you to relax?"

"I don't know," I say, allowing irritation to creep back into my voice. Hillary basically said the same thing. If only they knew that I *can't* relax. "Can you make sure that Mr. Curtis doesn't turn psycho vigilante on the captain of this ship? Or go back in time and erase our horrible performance? Or prevent Russ from turning this cruise ship into a reenactment of the *Titanic*? Better yet, maybe you can figure out a way to keep the captain from watching the surveillance video that's probably going to show us vandalizing the ship?"

Huck pauses, using his fingers to stroke an imaginary beard.

"The time travel issue is, well, difficult. Video? I'll mull. And making sure that Mr. Curtis stays distracted . . . hmmm," Huck says. He grabs a bunch of my windblown hair and gives it a little tug. "That I can do. But you'll need to meet me by the pool if you want to make it happen."

"Are you serious?" I stare at him.

He shrugs a shoulder, fake-modest. "I already have an idea. It won't solve *all* our problems, but it'll be a start." Huck pulls me into a bear hug.

"What would I do without you?" I say, my words partly muffled by the green fabric of his T-shirt.

"Be a lot crazier, that's for damn sure," he says. He pulls

back and stares into my face like a naturalist observing some kind of endangered species. "So what do you think? Are you in?"

I know setting Huck loose is a risk, but we're at that point where it's time to go all in. So I take a deep breath and plaster on a smile. "Let's do it," I say.

Huck slaps me on the back. "Attagirl. Now go change into your suit. Meet me on deck in five. My plan commences in ten."

CHAPTER 7

As I make my way down to the Laguna, the largest of *Destiny's* three outdoor pools, I pull the towel tighter around my waist like it's my own personal cloak of invisibility. It's bad enough that we've lost another practice opportunity, but I also acted like a hormonal lunatic and yelled at all my friends. I'm hoping a moment of lounging by the pool will help me get control of life and the band, and maybe, possibly, get me back to my normal self. I do *not* like being spazzy, panicky, out-of-control Liza.

I walk onto the pool deck, scanning the crowd for Huck. The pool is packed, maybe because the backup generators on board mean the ship's AC seems to be on its last legs. The deck is dominated by forty or so fellow performers and their chaperones, lounging on the purple beach chairs or splashing around in the oval-shaped pool. Near the back of the ship— The prow? The stern? I've already forgotten what was written in the promotional materials—a small band of men and women are playing shuffleboard, visors holding back their gray hair, oversized sunglasses taking up most of their tanned, wrinkled faces. There's a crowd gathered around a makeshift tiki bar with a cerulean awning at the far end of the pool, and waiters in crisp white uniforms are bustling around the deck delivering brightly colored drinks filled with fruit and umbrellas. Next to the tiki bar is one of the ship's many buffets, covered by a row of navy-blue umbrellas.

I haven't eaten anything since breakfast, and suddenly I'm ravenous. I don't see anyone I know in the line, so I scoot over and join the end of it while still searching for Huck. When I get to the front, I see it's mostly tiers of cheese and crackers, along with a large fruit salad in a crystal bowl. I reach for a plate and the gleaming metal tongs, then scoot a few pieces of cantaloupe aside and start plucking the big, fat strawberries out of the bowl, placing them on my plate.

"Morty, she's takin' all the strawberries!" a scratchy-voiced lady croaks to her husband. Her eyes look massive behind her thick plastic glasses, like they might jump out and land on my plate. She nudges her husband hard, sending a few crackers tumbling off his plate and onto the deck. She points at me with her fork. "See that? She's takin' all the strawberries! Little missy, you can't take all the strawberries."

"Don't listen to her, my dear." Another voice, this one smoother and heavily accented, floats down to me. I look up to see a tall, thin woman, her graying hair swept up in an elegant french twist, a summery orange-and-yellow silk caftan hanging off her slender frame. She winks at me. "Life's short. Eat the strawberries."

"Thanks," I say. I glance back triumphantly at the cantankerous old lady and her husband, Morty. She's still giving me the evil eye. I pop a strawberry into my mouth and smile.

Okay, not the classiest thing to do. But sheesh, lady. Who made you the strawberry police?

The tall woman transfers her plate to her left hand and reaches out to me with a tanned, french-manicured hand. Her palm has the smooth, waxy feeling of parchment paper. When I let go, I can smell her lavender lotion. "I'm Sofia. Would you mind, darling, helping me with this extra plate?" She reaches for a glass of iced tea and gestures to another plate on the table piled high with cheese and crackers. "Hands full and all."

"Sure," I say, and take her plate in my free hand. She sets off through the crowd and the sea of chairs, moving with easy confidence, like a cat. She stops at an empty high-top café table, where she rests her plate and glass and gestures for me to do the same.

"Do you have a minute to chat? I love a little girl talk," she says. She must be at least sixty, but her demeanor makes her appear years younger. Her smile carves deep dimples into her cheeks, the sparkle in her eyes practically infectious.

I don't see Huck, so I figure why not? Sofia's voice is soft and lilting, and I can feel it sending a wave of calm right over me. "Sure, I'd love to," I reply.

"Oh, good! So tell me, darling. Are you here with your family?"

"No," I reply, tasting another one of my own strawberries. They're perfectly ripe and sweet, like they've been sprinkled with powdered sugar, and I'm glad I took plenty. "We don't do much traveling as a unit anymore." I don't know why I blurted that out, but seeing Sofia arch an eyebrow makes me hastily add, "I'm on a class trip with my high school band, actually. We're playing in the showcase."

"Oh, that's wonderful! Ramon and I will have to come see you perform," she says, and winks. She's so nice, I wonder how I can tell her not to bother. I'd hate to assault her ears the way we did the audience last night. "We're here celebrating our wedding. His first, my fourth."

I can't hide my surprise.

"Oh dear, don't look so scandalized!" Sofia laughs. The sound is loud but delicate at the same time, like the sound of glass shattering over a tile floor. "What did I say? Life's too short not to eat the strawberries . . . or fall in love!"

Her joy is contagious. Before I know it I find myself laughing along with her. She stacks three pieces of Brie on top of a cracker, then pauses before taking a bite.

"But, darling, you're not here to spend your time with an old woman," she says, her voice light and playfully scolding. "Go now, be with your friends. But don't forget what I said."

"Eat the strawberries," I say, raising my plate to her in a toast.

"And fall in love! Don't forget that one," she says, a knowing smile on her face.

But I have to forget that one. I don't have the brain space for love right now. In fact, I rarely have the brain space for love, other than the occasional fictional character. Between school and band and dealing with my parents, it's a wonder I have time for friends. Which is what makes it so convenient that the people in band *are* my friends. And what makes it all the more important that I not lose them.

When I scoot back from the table, I spot Huck near the shallow end of the pool. He sees me at the same time.

"Liza! Over here!" He's lounging in a pair of red vintage swim trunks, his signature fedora (at least for this week) atop his dark hair.

As I move through the crowd toward him, I spy Andrew and Clarice sharing one lounge chair and reading aloud from a tattered copy of *The Prisoner of Azkaban*. Michael, Ben, and Nate are all taking turns doing some kind of flip where they launch one another from their interlocked hands. A few other band members are lounging under the clouds, flipping through magazines and sipping Cokes. Seeing them provokes fresh waves of embarrassment about how I acted earlier, and I drop quickly down into the chair next to Huck's.

"What's with the muumuu?" he says, and I realize I'm still wearing my towel like a cape. "You trying to go incognito?"

Huck is on his back, squinting up into the sky, which is starting to get gray. It doesn't matter, though. Huck has no need to work on his tan. His skin glistens in the heat, and I'm simultaneously jealous and overcome with desire to apply sunscreen. I reach for the tube I brought out with me. Of course I applied liberally before leaving my cabin, but I'm the girl who always misses a spot and winds up with some kind of wonky burn, even if it does look like that storm Mr. Curtis was talking about might roll in.

"I wish," I say. I squeeze a quarter-sized dollop of sunscreen into my palm. "I acted like a total lunatic in front of all my friends, who are also the people I'm supposed to be leading." I rub sunscreen onto my knees, which I often forget until they've burned red as summer tomatoes. "Oh, and don't forget that when we performed last night, we sounded like a bag of cats in a dryer. Not that it matters if the cruise mechanics figure out we broke the cruise ship—I'll be remembered forever as the drum major who broke the band."

"Oy with the drama." He flips over in his chair, lowering the back so that it's flat, allowing him to lie facedown for an even tan. With his change in position, I can see that four chairs down is Lenny, his nose scrunched up as he studies the back of his camera. Sofia's words echo through my mind. Those strawberries *were* damn good. . . . Maybe falling in love isn't such a bad idea. Okay, maybe not love, because who has time for that? But maybe a serious case of *like*. I definitely have time for that.

"Holy crap," I mutter, and quickly adjust my chair to flat so that I can lie down and hide behind Huck. The last person I want to see is the hottest guy on the entire boat.

Huck cocks an eyebrow at me and then follows my gaze to Lenny. "I can't believe that kid is related to Curtis. I mean, for serious?"

"I kissed him," I say, the words coming out before I can suck them back in. "Lenny, I mean. Not Mr. Curtis."

Huck lets out a squawk that makes him sound like a parrot caught in a hair dryer. He props himself up on his arm and gapes at me. "*You kissed him?* Where? When?"

I wave my hand frantically to shush him. "We were twelve. It hardly even counted. It was at performing arts camp."

"Who knew?" Huck says, grinning. "Liza, a twelve-year-old temptress."

I ignore him. "But he walked me to my room yesterday and I think . . ." I pause, wondering what I think. Since he came on board, he's been finding little excuses to talk to me, bringing up our old camp days. Then again, we haven't exactly spent a lot of quality time together. "I think I might . . . have a little crush . . . just a *tiny* one. . . ."

Huck leans across the space between our lounge chairs. "You like him!" he crows with accusatory glee. "You totally like him! You want to take him out into the woods at band camp!"

"Shhh!" I glare at him, even though I can't help but smile. "What is wrong with you?" I shake my hair off my shoulders. "Anyway, it doesn't matter whether I like him or not, or whether he likes me. I have to focus on the competition."

"Liza and Lenny, sitting in a tree . . . ," Huck singsongs. I reach out and whack him.

"So weren't you saying something about a plot?" I say pointedly, desperate to change the subject. I check one of the shoulder straps on my suit to be sure I'm not burning. Last summer I went to the beach and fell asleep with both hands resting on my stomach. For four weeks I had perfect white handprints pasted over my otherwise scarlet skin. You only make *that* mistake once.

"Liza, I got more plot than a Stephen King novel. And we're starting with Curtis." Huck points to the tiki bar. Mr. Curtis is there, dressed in a banana-yellow polo and long black swim trunks, the first time I've ever seen him out of his uniform. He's managed to tame his hair (and his collar), but he's still frowning, and his eyes dart periodically between the pool, the sky, and the ocean, as if trying to anticipate the most likely source of our demise. He's sipping some kind of neon-colored frozen beverage topped with a cornucopia of brightly colored fruit and umbrellas.

"You want to spike his drink until he's too drunk to notice how badly I'm screwing up?"

"Think bigger," Huck says, pointing back toward the bar, "and less felonious. Observe."

I turn back to Mr. Curtis. At first I don't notice anything unusual, except for his insane fashion choices.

"What am I looking for, exactly?" I say, beginning to grow impatient.

"Shhh." Huck leans forward, clearly enjoying himself. "Just keep watching. Trust me."

After another moment, something clicks, and I notice that Huck's right: every time Mr. Curtis's eyes sweep over a certain woman, they pause, and his expression turns momentarily gooey.

The woman is wearing a black sarong over a fire-engine-red halter suit. It's a far cry from the hoodie and ball cap ensemble she was sporting when we arrived. She raises her cat's-eye sunglasses up to push back her blond curls. The gesture causes Mr. Curtis to cough, choking on his drink and dribbling it down the front of his shirt.

"Mrs. Haddaway?" I squeak.

"Make that *Ms.* Haddaway," Huck says, leaning back in his chair, satisfied. "She got divorced over Christmas."

Aside from being the Athenas' faculty advisor, Tanya Haddaway teaches home ec, a class no one takes anymore except the girls who are too stoned to sit through an art class and the athletes looking for a hookup or an easy A. I'm pretty sure she spends all her time down in the home ec room making her vintage re-creation dresses on the ancient sewing machines, wishing desperately that she were teaching the class circa 1958.

She's nice, but a little strange. Actually, in another life, she could have totally fit into the clarinet section.

"And you want to play matchmaker *why*?" I glance between Huck and the potential lovers at the bar.

He shrugs. "You said you wanted to keep Mr. Curtis out of your hair, didn't you?"

He has a point. "And how do you propose we make that happen?"

"You'll see, *amiga*." He winks at me, then calls out, "Hey, Russ, how about some dodgeball?"

Russ is acting as a human jungle gym for a group of kids, who are taking turns climbing up onto his shoulders and cannonballing off into the shallow end. I catch a few sunning moms watching him lift their children, his broad shoulders shaking with laughter at their excited squeals. At Huck's suggestion, Russ ushers his new friends back toward the steps and grabs for one of the colorful, spongy foam balls floating lazily around the pool. His game-winning smile cranks up to a thousand watts.

"Seriously, Huck?" I say through clenched teeth. Russ immediately sets me back six steps in my path toward relaxation. I feel a bubble of anxiety growing in my stomach. Not only is he a giant pain in the ass, he'll never have to worry about someone cutting *his* bus fund. The band gets cut and what does the football team get? A bigger weight room.

"We need the power of a crowd," Huck says. He stands up from his chair and deposits his hat back where he was sitting, placing his sunglasses safely inside. "Everyone likes Russ." Before I can correct him, he adds, "Besides, who's going to believe that *I* want to play dodgeball?"

Huck's not wrong. He's faked nearly every illness on WebMD to avoid gym class. As far as I know, the kid's never actually run the mile. Last year, he was struck down by strep throat, avian flu, and rickets, an illness I'd never even heard of. Neither had Coach Morrison, apparently, because Huck sat out a whole week for that one.

"Dodgeball!" Russ bellows, and all eyes swivel to him. He raises his hand to point to a little girl, who tosses him the purple ball she's holding. He wades over and, with the ball cradled in one arm, lifts her out of the pool with the other. She giggles and skips away. Then Russ wings a sopping wet ball at Andrew, who after only one and a half semesters of high school gym has already developed catlike reflexes when it comes to flying objects. In a flash, he's under the water. The ball sails through the space he just occupied and lands on Britt Marsh's tanned back with a loud, wet thwack. Britt spins around; her mouth, which is usually belting out soprano parts with the Athenas, forms a surprised O. As soon as she realizes Russ is the culprit, her surprise turns to laughter.

"Dodgeball! Who's in?" she calls to the rest of the Athenas. A few roll their eyes, but they fall in nonetheless. I have to admit, Huck's instincts about Russ were spot-on. He knows how to mobilize a crowd.

Huck stretches and cracks his knuckles over his head. "You in?"

"Dodgeball?" I eye Russ, who's dividing up teams in the pool as a bunch of skinny, giggling airheads—Demi's friends—ogle him. "Uh, no thank you."

Huck shrugs and jumps in. When the few grown-ups in

the pool realize they're paddling through a makeshift dodge-ball court, they make a quick retreat toward the bar. The moms usher their kids off to the kiddie pool at the far end of the deck. The teams separate to their respective ends of the pool, and the bright blue Sail Away logo on the bottom of the pool is designated as the line of no return.

Russ raises the ball above his head, and for just one second—one teensy, tiny microsecond—I notice how nice his smile looks against his tanned skin, and the broadness of his shoulders and arms. I quickly look away. Russ is way too annoying to be hot, and I can't let his good looks distract me. After the practice-room switch, I'm still not sure he's not a double agent for Demi and the Athenas. I need to keep my eye on him.

"Game!" Russ shouts out, the verbal equivalent of a starter's pistol. Brightly colored balls whiz through the air at high speeds. Players leap, splash, and dive, shrieking and yelling. Missy is cowering behind one of the burlier members of the Mechanicals, who's pretending she doesn't exist. Demi seems to have worked her way toward the edge of the pool, where she's half playing, half posing for Lenny, who is snapping shots of the madness from his deck chair. I can't tell if he notices her or not, but I definitely do, and I don't like it one bit. I don't like that he has barely acknowledged my presence, either—he hasn't even looked my way.

Now that I've admitted my crush on Lenny, the truth of it is coursing through my veins, making me practically drunk on lusty thoughts. It's exactly why I avoid the love stuff, but now I'm too far gone to stop it. Dammit, Sofia. This better not throw me off my game.

I turn my attention back to Huck. He wades toward a forgotten green ball floating near the edge of the pool, dunks it, then sends it flying. Only it doesn't head toward the opposing team. Instead, it sails over their heads toward the tiki bar.

"Incoming!" Huck shouts, then disappears beneath the surface.

Mr. Curtis shouts and then launches himself in front of Ms. Haddaway, his arms out like a human shield. For a lifelong band geek, he has surprisingly good reflexes. The front of his banana-yellow polo takes the brunt of the hit. The ball bounces off him and lands with a soggy thump, leaving behind a darkening wet spot.

A mottled flush works its way up Mr. Curtis's neck. But before he can start yelling, Ms. Haddaway bursts into peals of laughter. She runs her hand over the wet fabric on Mr. Curtis's chest. This time, when his cheeks redden, I know he's not angry. She gestures to him and he nods. They proceed to retrieve their drinks from the bar and take a seat at a nearby table, deep in conversation.

Completely distracted . . . by *each other.*

I don't believe it. Huck's plan actually worked.

Thwack!

The sopping ball straight to my face causes me to nearly topple off my chair. I blink the water out of my eyes and wipe away the wet strands of hair now stuck to my forehead. Unlike Huck, my attacker doesn't have the good sense to duck and swim.

Russ is standing in the pool biting his lip, looking sheepish. The blood begins to pound in my ears. I can't figure out if Russ *enjoys* annoying me, or if he's too dumb to realize he's doing it.

Either way, I curse Principal DeLozier for the fiftieth time for sticking me with him on this trip.

I don't know if it's a breeze that picks up or the water dripping off the ball that's now resting in my lap or the throbbing hatred of our star quarterback, but I start to shiver like a drowned Chihuahua. Not my finest look. I cross my arms over my chest as if they can act as some kind of full-body shield.

"Here ya go, take this." I look up to see Lenny unzipping the blue track jacket he's wearing. He sheds it and passes it to me. "I don't want you to get cold."

I remove the ball from my lap. In the pool, Russ holds up his hands for a catch, but I drop the ball on the ground. It rolls under my chair. Russ's smile fades. Lenny only laughs.

"Thanks," I say. I take the jacket from Lenny and wrap it around my shoulders, even though it must be at least eighty degrees. "That's really cool of you."

"Please, as if I didn't spend the entire week at camp giving you my sweatshirt," he says with a playful grin.

"It was cold in that theater!" I say. I smile back at him, and he immediately raises his camera and snaps a picture. He lowers it and hits a button, checking the image on the display.

"That's a good one," he says, glancing down at me from beneath his hair. "You've got a great smile."

"Hey, sorry about that, Liza!" Russ calls from the pool. I see Lenny peer over my shoulder at Russ, so I quickly wave my hand at him to indicate *yeah, whatever* and *please stop talking.* I lean over so that I'm blocking out any view of Russ, and bring Lenny's focus back to me.

Suddenly, Demi is out of the pool. She marches over to Lenny, reaches back, and wrings out her long brown hair, which has the side effect of arching her ample chest directly toward him. His eyes dart to her, then back to his feet, and he shoves his hands awkwardly into the pockets of his shorts.

Undeterred, Demi loops her arm through his. I wonder if they've already met, or if Demi is just exercising some of her trademark confidence. And suddenly I get a surge of jealousy, and worse than that, the swinging vertigo sense of watching history repeat itself. Demi's got her eye on a prize, only this time, it's one *I'm* hoping to win. Two, in fact, because I plan to get Lenny *and* the $25,000 check. And unlike when we were kids, I'm not going to back down. Maybe it's my newfound commitment to crush the Athenas, but suddenly I don't want to roll over for Demi. I want Lenny.

But Demi isn't going down without a fight.

"C'mon, Lenny," she says. She arranges her lips into a tiny pout. "Hot tub time!"

Before he can reply—or protest—she drags him along with a surprising amount of force for someone whose hobbies include singing and dancing. Several of the dodgeball players climb out of the pool and follow, including Missy, Russ, Hillary, Jared, and a few of the Athenas. Huck pulls himself onto the deck after them.

"Come on," Huck says, and grabs my arm. His eyes settle on Lenny's track jacket, and he gives me a knowing look. "This time you don't have a choice."

"What? No way!" I try to dig in my heels, even as he hauls me to my feet, but the polished wood of the deck combined with the dripping bodies that went before us makes this impossible.

"Liza, listen to me. Curtis is occupied. He won't be in-

86

vestigating any time soon. Besides, the boat isn't sinking. And there's no performance tonight—we'll have all day tomorrow to get back on track in rehearsal. So could you just take a minute and relax?"

I'm about to respond that watching Demi fawn all over Lenny will *not* be relaxing, but just then, a flash of yellow catches my attention. Across the deck, Sofia and a man in a white linen shirt are leaning over the railing. There must be a higher wind up there, because her gray hair is escaping from her french twist and whipping across her face. She reaches over, plucks the straw hat off the man's head, plops it on her own, and smiles.

Take the strawberries. Fall in love. Surely I can have both, right? I want to save the band, but I also want to kiss Lenny again. I want that smile of his for myself. So I loop my arm in Huck's and follow the crowd toward the hot tub. For once, I'm going to let myself have all the strawberries I want.

CHAPTER 8

The words "hot tub" usually conjure up an image of a square fiberglass setup bubbling away in someone's backyard, or an embarrassing, booze-fueled YouTube video waiting to happen.

This? This is no hot tub.

Roughly the size of the shallow end of the ship's main pool, this hot tub is plenty large enough for the ten or so of us who are dropping into it. Perched on a private, elevated deck, it's the perfect place from which to keep an eye on the pool below without actually being seen ourselves.

An elderly couple in matching floral suits climb out as my classmates and friends step in, disrupting their relaxing afternoon soak. They're clucking quietly to each other, so the only words I can make out are "such a ruckus" and "act like ladies and gentlemen." I snort, wondering when Demi last acted like a lady. Probably around the same time Russ acted like a gentleman, and by that, I mean never.

Lenny moves into a corner, and Demi immediately slides in next to him. Missy gasps and gives a tiny hop when she sits down right in front of one of the powerful jets. Hillary takes a spot by herself off to the side, as if Demi's perkiness is a disease that's catching. Russ settles in next to Huck, who gives him a healthy side eye before scooting a little bit away.

I take a seat on the ledge and dip my toes into the warm, bubbling water, partly because hot tubs skeeve me out (seriously, it's like all those germs and skin particles are cooking in there, making some kind of disease-filled stew. No thank you!), and partly because I don't want to take Lenny's jacket off. I love the way it smells like whatever detergent his mom uses and his woodsy deodorant.

Once again, I look up to see Demi wrinkling her nose in my direction as if to say *Who invited you?* But Lenny ducks under the water next to her and emerges with his hair slicked back, immediately distracting Demi from the fact that there are band kids at her hot tub party.

"Truth-or-dare time!" she chirps. But her eyes are laser focused on mine, an eyebrow raised.

My stomach drops. I've played T-or-D plenty of times, but always with my friends, who I know won't judge or make me do anything that could seriously risk my life or my dignity. At band camp last summer, Hillary dared me to do a lap around the practice field in my underwear (which I totally did). But one look at Demi tells me a dare like that is just a warm-up for her. I'm having flashbacks to our childhood games of Trivial Pursuit, where Demi was completely brazen about "accidentally" taking a peek at the answer on the back of the card. There's no *way* a ten-year-old knows the date of the Peloponnesian War.

"I was thinking maybe you might want a friendly wager, Liza," Demi says, sugar dripping from every syllable. I recognize the voice as the one she used to use with our ballet teacher when she wanted an extra few bars of a solo. "Winner gets the loser's practice time?"

I pause. "How can you *win* at truth-or-dare?"

"Whoever fails to complete their dare or spill their truth loses," she says, her voice light while her brain is already concocting a winning strategy. I can't even imagine what that might look like, but the chance to win extra practice time is exactly what we need, especially after my epic meltdown today. And if we can win it while stealing some of the Athenas'? All the better. So against my better judgment (and deep history of losing to Demi at board games), I agree.

"I'm in," I say, leaning back against the warm bricks surrounding the hot tub.

Before Demi can speak again, Huck turns to Russ, one eyebrow raised.

"Russ," he says. "Truth or dare?"

Russ hesitates for a moment, glancing around the hot tub as if weighing the risks of either option. His eyes pass over me, almost stopping for a moment, before moving on to Demi and Missy. "Truth," he says finally.

"Boooo!" Missy says, giving him a thumbs-down, but Huck's face glows with a wicked expression.

"Why did you dump Demi?" Huck asks.

Russ's face goes white, and Missy gasps.

Demi splashes Huck. "As if! *I* dumped *him*," she says. She gives Russ a stern look. He glances at her, then back at Huck.

"She's right," he adds, and shrugs. A momentary chill

passes through the hot tub. Everyone is suddenly very interested in the jets or clouds or readjusting their suits. I expect to see Demi glaring at Russ, or even Huck, but when I look over, she's giving *me* the evil eye. What did *I* do?

After a moment of silence, Russ turns back to Missy.

"Okay, Missy, truth or dare?"

"Dare!" she yelps as Demi pokes her in the ribs just below her Tennessee Vol–orange bikini.

"Good girl," Demi coos. I have a flashback to the time in fourth grade when Demi staged a Miss America swimsuit competition in her backyard . . . in January. The thought makes me shiver, so I tuck myself farther into Lenny's jacket. Immediately, Demi scoots closer to Lenny.

"How about you—" Russ starts to say.

But Demi steamrolls him. "I dare you to score us some drinks."

My trouble meter starts beeping at a high frequency. I catch Huck giving me a look that says *Chill out, Liza,* so I keep my mouth shut and shift uncomfortably on the bricks surrounding the hot tub. All I need right now is to get caught drinking, or being around people drinking, since I don't actually drink. I mean, not that I *don't* drink. There's always beer at the band parties, smuggled in Nalgene bottles or hidden in neoprene sleeves disguised as soda. But I think beer tastes like bread-flavored spit, so I usually just volunteer to be the designated driver, giving me an easy out. Regardless, if we came all this way on a half-crippled cruise ship only to get disqualified for a pilfered margarita, I think I'd throw myself overboard.

"No problem." Missy lifts herself out of the hot tub as if there are paparazzi waiting to take her picture. Her long black curls cascade down her back. She gives a shimmy, I presume to shake off the water, but probably also to show off her petite body to everyone with eyes.

"Okay, while she's gone, let's do something fun," Demi says. She leans into Lenny. Now her chest is practically in his lap, and I have to look away so I don't barf into the bubbly water. Demi reaches into the mesh beach bag she's brought along and pulls out a small notepad. She roots around some more until she produces a handful of pens. "What we're going to do now is write the name of our number-one crush on a slip of paper. Then we'll put them in a hat and draw them out one at a time, trying to guess whose is whose."

She snatches Huck's fedora off his head and places it on the deck behind her, then starts tearing out scraps of paper and passing them around. I expect Huck to snatch the hat right back, or at least object, but he just goes with it. Britt starts scribbling away. I see Hillary glance around the circle before writing. Huck takes to the paper right away. Lenny scribbles, his cheeks going red.

I look down at my piece of blank paper. The group is too small; everyone will notice if I don't write *something*. But I also don't want to actually reveal my number-one crush. My eyes go to Lenny, who is handing the hat to Russ. He deposits a slightly soggy folded slip of paper into it. My stomach does a little flip.

As the hat gets closer to me, I give up and settle on Marcus Wellington, the name of a character in one of my mother's trashy romance novels she keeps hidden under her bed, so that I don't have to incriminate myself. I scribble the name and drop it into the hat after Hillary.

Missy appears back on the deck holding three half-empty

cups. One looks like a beer, and the other two are filled with slightly melted frozen drinks topped with soggy bits of fruit.

"Done and done!" she says, placing the drinks down on the deck.

Demi wrinkles her nose. "Missy, are those drinks *used*?"

"No one was using them *anymore*," Missy says.

"That's so gross!" Demi cries. She turns to Lenny. "Isn't that so gross?"

Lenny half smiles and shrugs. Huck and I trade a glance that says we are totally not shocked that Missy would be dumb enough to steal half-empty drinks from strangers. Russ sort of sinks farther down into the water, maybe to get a better angle on that jet. I'm surprised he doesn't take one of the glasses and pound it. I've heard the football team knows how to put it away.

"They were totally carding! What did you expect?" Missy huffs and drops back down into the hot tub.

"I think that's a dare fail," Huck declares, nodding at the glasses.

"Is not!" Missy snaps.

"Uh, it so *is*," Hillary says. She lifts one of the glasses, which appears to have a cigarette butt floating in it. "The dare was to score us drinks that we could, you know, *drink*. And unless someone is willing to down this *right now*, it's a dare fail."

"That's crap!" Demi says through clenched teeth.

"Looks like we get your practice time," I say, crossing my arms over my chest. I take the glass from Hillary and wave it toward Demi. "Unless you're willing to bottoms up?"

"No! No way," Demi says, her cheeks going red. She's starting to panic. She throws a pleading look at Lenny, like he's the referee or something, but he just shrugs.

"Russ told the truth, and you confirmed it," Huck says. "Are you saying he *lied*?"

All heads swing to Demi. But she's unruffled. She crosses her arms and raises an eyebrow. "Um, *no*," she says. "I'm saying Russ doesn't count as part of the band. Y'all still have a turn."

"Russ is absolutely with the band," I fire back. Demi can try to win on some half-baked technicality, but I'm not going to let her. "Principal DeLozier sent him on the trip with us. He wouldn't be here at all if it weren't for the band."

I glance over at Russ, shooting him my trademark *Do as I say* drum major look. And even though he hasn't spent an entire season responding to my commands, he still seems to catch my meaning.

"She's right," Russ says. "I mean, I'm definitely not with the Athenas."

Demi's nose scrunches up in a tiny flinch, a sure sign that a major tantrum is on its way. But she recovers, and immediately turns a sugary sweet smile in Lenny's direction.

"What say you, judges' panel?" she practically purrs.

"I didn't realize I was judging, but . . ." Lenny pauses and rubs his forehead. "It seems like they're right. The band won, fair and square."

Suddenly my stomach is doing a tango with my heart, because Lenny is standing up for me. Not Demi and her skimpy bikini and syrupy smile.

The celebration is short-lived, though. Russ gasps and points at the pool, where Mr. Curtis is making his way toward the stairs to the hot tub. "Incoming!" he says, and lunges for the drinks. Even though no one even thought to sample them, they're still incriminating. Russ gathers them, then leaps out of the tub, leaving a wake of water that washes over Lenny, Missy, and Demi. Lenny takes the chance to duck under the water and slick back his sandy hair, but Demi and Missy screech and jump up, as if they're not already soaking wet.

"Let's get out of here," Demi hisses to Missy, cocking her head toward the steps. She shoves Huck's hat at Hillary, then turns to Lenny. "You coming?"

She grabs his hand and threads her fingers through his, leaving me in awe of her boldness and totally jealous that she can pull it off. Lenny glances down at his dad, then nods, climbing out of the hot tub with Demi. Before he disappears, he turns and gives me a shrug and a half smile that seems to say, *What can you do?*

Russ is still frantically trying to solve the drink problem. There's no trash can on the deck, and if he tried for the one at the bottom of the stairs he'd have to walk right past Mr. Curtis carrying the evidence. He glances around for a solution and settles on the railing behind me, sending the drinks, cups and all, overboard into the ocean. He drops back down into the hot tub, sending a wave of water rushing onto the deck.

"Not bad, dude," Hillary says, giving a tip of an imaginary hat.

All eyes turn toward Mr. Curtis. But Mr. Curtis is gone, having bypassed the stairs and disappeared into the ship. Bullet officially dodged.

In the commotion, Huck pulled a serious disappearing act and is nowhere to be found. Which I take as my cue, because if Huck is fleeing a situation, then you know it must be bad. With Lenny dragged off by Demi (hopefully against his will?), there's no reason for me to stay here anyway, so I stand and stretch, feigning a yawn. "I think I'm going to get a nap in before lunch," I say.

Hillary climbs out of the hot tub. "I'll come with you," she says. She takes a towel from a nearby cart and wraps it around her waist, then tosses one to me, still carrying Huck's hat in her other hand.

The two of us make our way down the stairs and back into the ship. We walk in silence, but as soon as we're inside our room, Hillary squeals, "I can't believe no one said anything!"

"What?" I ask. She holds the fedora under my nose.

"Look what I have!" she says. She rushes past me and dumps the contents of the hat onto her bed. She starts unfolding scraps of paper and laying them out on the fluffy comforter. I can't help myself, so I wait to watch.

"Who's Marcus Wellington?" Hillary squints at the piece of paper.

"Never heard of him," I reply. She shrugs, lets the paper flutter back onto the bed, and returns to unfolding the rest.

"Holy crap," she mutters. Her eyes go wide as she stares at a tiny scrap of paper between her black-polished finger and thumb. She flashes it at me. The writing is small and messy, and the last few letters are spreading out in a damp ink spot from someone's wet fingers, so I have to get right up next to her to see it.

"What's it say?" I ask. I squint down at the writing and finally make it out.

Liza.

Holy crap.

My first thought is that Demi wrote it to screw with me, but the chicken scratch on the paper definitely came from the hand of a boy. And not Huck, either, who prides himself on his penmanship. The only logical conclusion is that another boy, one who isn't my best friend, wrote it. I close my eyes and try to reproduce the lineup from the hot tub in my head. Who else was there? I can't think of anyone except . . .

Lenny.

Lenny!

I bury my face in the sleeve of Lenny's jacket, which I failed to return when we left the hot tub. I breathe in the smell of it, of him, and imagine standing next to him on the upper deck where I saw Sofia, smiling into the sun, the wind in my hair, Lenny's arm around my waist as he leans in to plant kiss number two on my lips.

Take that, Demi. This time, *I'm* going to win.

CHAPTER 9

A couple of hours later, I'm following First Mate Kevin, leading a line of my bandmates as we wind our way through the lush gardens of the Poseidon Resort, a hulking structure designed to look like a coral palace sprung up from the sea. It rises twenty stories in the air, with various turrets jutting out, and is surrounded by lush palm trees, manicured gardens, snow-white beaches, and clear blue water. It's the first of *Destiny*'s ports of call, the shortest one, and we'll be spending the rest of the afternoon on the beach. We'll be sharing space with the tourists who chose the Poseidon and the island as their final destination, and we're under strict orders to stick to the beach and keep out of the luxury hotel.

Since we left *Destiny*, I've kept a close eye on Lenny to see if he'll give away any hint of his feelings for me, feelings that led him to put my name down on paper. But so far he's mostly hung back, his eyes glued to his camera, rising only to take a periodic snap of scenery. I don't blame him. Even though the Poseidon is painted a shocking, almost putrid pink, the building itself is pretty impressive, and the scenery is unlike anything I've ever seen outside of a postcard.

"All right, now keep in mind that all the same rules apply on the island that apply on the ship, so no underage drinking, and please remember what I said before about illicit substances," First Mate Kevin says as he walks backward like a tour guide through a cobblestoned courtyard with a marble fountain of a sea horse bubbling away in the middle.

"You ready to get high on life?"

I gasp as I realize that Lenny's snuck up behind me, and when I turn, I see that his camera is trained right on my face. He presses the shutter button, and the camera gives a mechanical *click-click*. He lowers it and takes a peek at the viewfinder on the back, his face cracking into laughter.

"Oh, man, you did *not* see me coming," he says, his smile flashing along with his gray eyes. I feel my heart melt into a puddle at the sight of him, but I try to play it cool.

I bat his camera down. "I liked it better when you were a theater kid," I say, raising an eyebrow at him.

"Yeah, but that wasn't really for me," he says with a shrug. "The older I got, the less I liked the spotlight. You can't get away with quite as much when all eyes are on you."

I chuckle at his joke, then point at his camera. "So how long have you been doing this?"

"Few years," he says. "My mom got me a camera when their divorce was final, not long after that summer. But I didn't really start messing around with it until high school."

"You on the newspaper staff?" I ask. Brentwood is famous

for their student newspaper, which is always snapping up state and national awards. But Lenny shakes his head.

"No way. Newspaper is dumb. You have to do what other people tell you to do, and that's not what art is about. Art comes from here," he says, tapping his chest over his heart, "not from here." He taps at his temple and rolls his eyes. "Besides, they're all 'Rah-rah, we're a team,' and I'm just not that guy."

"Yeah, but that can be cool," I say. "I mean, with band—"

"Nah, I think it's important that I be free. Just me and the camera. You know? Like when you're listening to music and it's just you and the tunes and you can really let yourself *feel* it."

I nod. I know that feeling. I feel it every time I'm on the field, standing on the platform on the fifty-yard line. Sometimes I just close my eyes and let the wall of sound wash over me, and I know it's exactly where I'm supposed to be. And even though there are sixty band members on the field in front of me and hundreds of fans in the stands behind me, I can for a moment imagine that it's just me and the music.

"That's awesome," I tell him. "I know sometimes when I'm conducting—"

"Ooh, hold that thought," Lenny says, then stops and jogs back a few steps. He squats down next to a potted plant and trains his camera on a brilliant purple blossom that's bending over into the walkway, trying to escape its pot of soil. He snaps away, pausing to peek at the viewfinder before adjusting something and snapping again. He's grinning to himself, and I can't help but mirror his smile. It's exactly the way I feel when we've worked our way through a hard spot in a new piece of music and finally gotten the measures down. That moment when it comes out perfectly, just as the composer wrote it, is as good as a cold chocolate shake on a hot summer day.

"Hurry up, guys, we don't have all day!" First Mate Kevin calls as he leads us under an ivy-covered arbor and out onto the white sand beach. The line slows as we have to plod through the sand, so soft our feet sink deep into it. I turn to make sure everyone is still with us, and a quick eyeball of the line tells me we haven't lost anyone. Lenny is catching up, but instead of making his way to the front of the line, he stops at the back, chatting with someone I can't see.

Out on the beach, the ocean is clear blue, with gentle white-topped waves slapping the sandy shore. Blue chairs and matching umbrellas dot the beach in pairs, and men in white shorts and polo shirts scurry around with trays of drinks and extra towels.

First Mate Kevin leads us to the left, away from the paradise of the resort beach, until we seem to cross an invisible line. On one side, luxury vacation. On the other, cruise ship carnival. No more matching beach chairs, no more attendants bringing fresh towels. As we file past a wooden cart, Kevin directs us all to grab a towel off the pile and find a spot on the beach.

Hillary quickly settles into a plot of sand and leans back on her towel, earbuds firmly in her ears. Huck takes the spot next to her, and I lay my towel next to him. I dig into my bag for a magazine, ready to soak up some SPF 30–protected sun. I keep my eye on Lenny, watching to see where he puts his towel. Even though Demi is hovering near him, he takes a place not too far ahead of me and pulls out his camera, scanning the horizon with the lens.

"Banana boats!" Jared shouts, pointing to a dock a bit down the beach where a line of bright yellow, inflatable rafts in the shape of bananas wait for riders. Out in the water, the rafts, pulled by Jet Skis, zip across the waves at dizzying speeds. "Who's in?"

Clarice and Andrew quickly rise to their feet, along with half the trumpets and all the percussion. Watching the inflatable yellow rafts career across the horizon doesn't do much for me, but when I see Lenny ask Nicole to watch his camera and then join the group making their way to the dock, I quickly hop to my feet and jump in.

"Liza, you sure about that?" Huck asks, probably thinking back to that time I tried waterskiing in the seventh grade. With my suit up my butt and half a lake up my nose, I vowed never to do any kind of speedboating again.

From the back of the crew heading toward the dock, Lenny turns around and cups his hands to his mouth while plodding backward through the sand. "You coming, Liza?"

Well, that settles it. My heart flip-flops at his invitation. How bad could a banana boat be? There are actual children riding on them, without parents or anything.

I grin at Huck, but call back to Lenny, "Yup! Coming!" Then I trot through the thick, soft sand to catch up.

"Too bad I don't have a waterproof setup," Lenny says as we make our way to the dock. "I could get some kickass shots out on the water."

"Are those expensive?" I ask, eager to keep our conversation going.

"Yeah, but I can probably work the divorced parents angle. You know how it is, pit one against the other, see who's willing to pony up," he says with a chuckle, and I have to laugh. I've never done that, but from the way my dad likes to throw expensive gifts my way, I can see how it could work.

On the dock, the line moves quickly as we board the boats in groups of four. One takes off and another pulls right up. I lean forward on my toes, trying to count to make sure I'm going to end up with Lenny, but everyone keeps moving and I lose track. It isn't until the next boat pulls up and Brianna, Missy, and Demi step on that I realize there's only one seat left. And it's for Lenny. He climbs on, but when he realizes there are no more seats, he turns to me.

"You want me to wait for the next one?" he asks, his hand over his eyes like a visor as he squints up at me.

If I were Demi, I'd be able to say no in a way that conveys, *Yes, absolutely, ride with me and we'll cuddle and fall in love.* But I'm not Demi, so instead I'm left standing on the dock watching the banana boat pull away.

"Guess we're up!" a deep voice booms from behind me. I spin on my heel to see that Russ has appeared and is ready to climb aboard the empty boat that's now pulling up.

When I don't move, another voice, this one even deeper, grunts from behind him. "You going, little lady?"

I lean around Russ to see our two banana boat companions, a couple in their seventies who look like they've spent every day of their lives covered in baby oil and sizzling in the sun. Their rough, wrinkled skin is approximately the color and texture of a leather saddle. Both of them have on heavy gold jewelry, the man's thick chain tangled in his mass of gray chest hair. And to cap off their *I'm trying to pretend I'm not actually seventy years old* ensemble, they're wearing matching leopard-print swimsuits: hers a string bikini, his a teeny tiny Speedo.

A look of sheer horror must cross my face, because Russ glances over his shoulder once, then twice in a classic double take. When he turns back to me, his eyes are wide, his mouth stretched in an O.

"How 'bout a Jet Ski instead?" Russ says, pointing at a row of them bobbing on the other side of the dock, each with only two seats.

Before I can tell Russ that I'd rather just stay on the beach thankyouverymuch, a shriek rips through the salty ocean air. I spin in time to see the banana boat streak past us, now up to full speed. Demi, who must have switched seats just before they took off, is now behind Lenny, her arms wrapped tight around his chest, her head thrown back as her dark-brown hair streams out behind her. She's several hundred yards away and careening across the ocean at an impressive speed, but I *swear* I see her shoot me a devilish smirk.

Without hesitation, I turn to Russ. "Let's do it," I say, shrugging on a life jacket from the rack on the dock. Russ grabs a jacket and climbs into the driver's seat, and I lower myself carefully behind him, double-checking all the buckles on my yellow-and-orange life vest. I look like an oceanic traffic cone.

"Not too fast, okay?" I say to Russ, putting a hand on either side of his waist to hold on.

"But that's the fun part," he says as he cranks up the engine.

"Seriously, Russ, not too fast," I tell him again. As we bob there in the water, inhaling the gassy smell coming from the idling engine, I'm having flashbacks to that summer at the lake. I didn't know it was possible to face-plant in a body of water, but I discovered the truth on that hot Saturday. I reach up and rub my nose at the memory of water shooting into my brain.

But just as quickly as they arrived, those images disappear, snapped out by Russ twisting the throttle with a violent jerk. We shoot away from the dock, bouncing on the waves as if we're riding a bucking bronco. I open my mouth to scream, but whatever sound comes out gets left behind as Russ takes a sharp left turn. A massive tower of spray rises up behind us as we skid across the water. I want to smack Russ, maybe even clock him right in the head in an effort to get him to slow down, but I'm too terrified to let go. Instead, I grip his life jacket so tight I wonder if I'll be able to draw blood through the foam.

We jerk left and right, several times catching air on the bigger waves, and I spend the whole time with my eyes closed, pressing my face against Russ's back, praying that I get off this thing alive.

I'm trying out one of those Zen breathing techniques I taught Nicole when I hear the engine sputter and slow. In just a few seconds, it cuts out completely, and we're left bobbing and drifting lazily across the surface of the water.

I open my eyes and see that we're several hundred yards off the shore, far enough that the whole of the resort is spread out before us. The gaudy pink of the stucco now looks soft and warm like a late-setting sun, and it complements the sparkling blue ocean around it.

"Pretty great view, huh?" Russ says over his shoulder. He shakes his head like a dog and sends a spray of salt water across my face.

That's when I realize I've been clutching the side of his buff upper body with a death grip.

Instantly, I let go. "What is *wrong* with you?" I screech, right into his ear. He jerks away, and the Jet Ski leans hard to the left. He twists at the waist until he's practically facing me, his brow furrowed.

"What are you talking about?" he asks, rubbing his injured ear.

"I said not too fast!"

"I wasn't going that fast," he says, his tone wounded. "You should have said something."

"I tried!" I cry. I finally take the opportunity to punch him hard in the arm, though he barely flinches.

"You were hollering," he says.

"Yeah, in *terror,*" I snap. "Take me back, *slowly* this time."

"I'll take you back, but not before you take a moment to appreciate this view," he says. He gestures back toward the shore, where I can again see how beautiful the resort looks, almost as if it's popped right out of my imagination, like an oceanic mirage. But it's not until I follow Russ's gaze in the opposite direction, out into the ocean and toward the horizon, that I see the real view.

The water is so blue it almost looks Photoshopped, and it's clear and smooth as glass. The turquoise of the water meets the baby blue of the sky at a point so far away that no matter how long my eyes search, they can't seem to pin it down. The fluffy white clouds dot the sky, scattering beams of sunlight onto the water. They glitter like diamonds. And after a moment, I notice something else, too. Something a few hundred yards away is disturbing the clear water. Up and down, up and down. And as I squint, I see that it's a group of dolphins, leaping through the water as they make their way across the horizon.

"Worth it?" Russ says, his voice barely above a whisper, even though it feels like there's no one around for miles.

"Yeah," I say, the word rushing out of me soft and quiet, like a prayer.

We sit there in silence for a few more minutes, watching the dolphins until they disappear, then staring up at the clouds as they move lazily across the sky. And only when our skin is completely dry from the sun does Russ twist back toward me.

"Ready to go?"

"Okay," I say, my pulse more than slowed from my earlier wild ride. But that doesn't stop me from reminding him, "*Slowly* this time."

Russ rolls his eyes and turns back to face front. Reluctantly, I place my hands back on his waist. The engine grinds up again, and we're off, though this time the speed is less NASCAR and more elderly mall walker. We're going so slowly, in fact, that I'm barely catching a breeze, and the hot sun high in the sky is searing into my exposed shoulders.

"Very funny," I say to Russ.

"Hey, you said slow," he says, his eyes focused on the shore.

"I'd like to get back sometime today, please," I retort.

Russ shrugs and kicks up the throttle slightly until we're motoring briskly—but not dangerously—to the dock.

We pull up right behind Lenny and Demi's banana boat. They've just climbed off and deposited their life jackets and are now making their way down the dock to the shore. I don't want to lose Lenny. I want to spend more time with him after our talk earlier, so I quickly stand, ready to launch myself onto the dock.

"Liza, wait a second," Russ says, reaching for my arm, but

I shrug him off. Only, without the engine running, the Jet Ski is far less stable. The motion sends it pitching away from the dock, and in my standing position, there's no way to maintain balance. I try to correct, but it's no use—I'm thrown headfirst over the side. My life vest sends me spinning underwater until my head pops up above the surface, my ponytail plastered to my face. I cough and sputter and splash until my toes dig into soft-packed sand. The water next to the dock is only about four feet deep, so I slowly stand up to catch my breath—and glimpse Russ, who is practically pulling a muscle trying not to laugh.

I feel my blood pressure rise, and I open my mouth to scream at him. But my fury quickly turns to terror when I feel something brush against my leg, then wrap around it. It's cool and slimy, and it's got a grip on me. Instantly, I forget all about Russ and the Jet Ski and the dock. I turn toward the shore and take off kicking.

"Jellyfish!" I screech through salty mouthfuls of ocean water. "Jellyfish!"

Despite all my kicking, the jellyfish doesn't let go. In fact, its grip only tightens. My screams quickly turn to cries as I start to emerge onto shore. I trip and get a faceful of sand, but ignore it as I spring to my feet. I dance from one foot to the other in a frantic attempt to shake the jellyfish free.

Russ, who climbed onto the dock and sprinted after me, drops to his knees in the sand to examine the creature.

"Get a stick! Get it off! Get it *off*!" I yell, my voice reaching the piercing pitch of a cartoon character. But Russ skips the stick and simply reaches for the white gelatinous glob with his bare hands.

"Careful, it'll sting you. . . ." But the words die on my lips as I spot the words THANK YOU FOR SHOPPING printed in red on the jellyfish.

No, not a jellyfish.

Russ looks up at my attacker, held between his thumb and forefinger.

"Liza, it's a plastic bag," he says in that gentle, soothing tone that's usually reserved for toddlers or mental patients. As much as it makes me want to smack him, there's only one thought that occupies my mind. I glance over Russ's shoulder.

Please don't let him be watching. Please don't let him have seen that.

But there he is, water glistening off his short strawberry-blond hair. Demi is doubled over with laughter, but Lenny is staring at his toes, a pained expression on his face.

He's embarrassed for me.

And I don't blame him. Not a bit.

CHAPTER 10

The bathroom in my cabin is tiny, maybe the size of a double-wide coffin, and my shower has steamed it up completely. Stepping out of the stall, I use the palm of my hand to swipe at the steam on the mirror. Not that it matters, because I'm not paying any attention to my reflection. My eyes keep flickering down to the scrap of paper I put on the bathroom counter, right next to the sink. It's starting to curl slightly from the humidity, but I can't stop staring at it. Lenny really likes me, and after yesterday, I know it for sure.

Okay, so I royally embarrassed myself with my jellyfish freak-out, but he didn't laugh. Not at all. In fact, after I managed to scrape together what was left of my dignity, we spent the rest of the afternoon on the beach, where he showed me all the pictures he'd taken so far on the ship. And there were a *ton*, so that was basically two hours spent side by side, huddled over the little screen on the back of his digital camera.

I could hardly fall asleep last night, replaying the entire day in my head.

Now I brush my teeth and gather my wet hair into a messy bun, then take the paper off the counter and dance out of the bathroom into the narrow strip of floor that separates my bed from Hillary's. Her bed is rumpled and empty, since she decided to squeeze in a quick stop at one of the small cafés on the Sunrise Deck in hopes of winning the Ship's Bounty, the award the seniors have decided to bestow upon the first band member to sample every buffet aboard the ship.

I root through my duffel until I find my favorite pair of dark denim bermuda shorts. I pull on a gauzy white tank top over them and, glancing in the full-length mirror on the back of the closet door, I give myself a little booty shake. I may have wet hair, a few odd tan lines from yesterday, and even a bit of a sunburn on the back of my neck, but I can't even care. Lenny likes me. *Me.*

But there's no time for dancing if I want to pass through the breakfast buffet before claiming our extra practice, rightfully won from the Athenas. With yesterday morning's practice botched, this is a chance to hopefully reroute our proverbial ship away from the iceberg of failure that was our first performance. I know we can do better. We *have* to, and it's my job to get us back on course.

I grab my watch, my folder of sheet music, and Lenny's track jacket. I *might* be planning to run into him to return the jacket and maybe, you know, fall in love and make out a little. But first, I need to get the band back on track for competition. Friday night was a total embarrassment. We've never played that poorly. Ever. And I don't plan on a repeat. Even after all the insanity (and, I'll admit, fun) of yesterday, I can't get the horror of our showcase performance out of my memory. Luckily, we had Saturday night off. But we've got another performance tonight. And I know we've got the chops to win this competition; I just need to get everyone's head in the right place. Including my own.

I hop on the elevator, carefully avoiding the young blond couple pressed against the back of the elevator . . . and each other. Their arms are wrapped around each other as they whisper and giggle. Normally such an obvious public display of affection would gross me out, but glancing at them has me imagining a delicious sunset kiss on the upper deck, Lenny's arms around me, clasped at the small of my back. He's taller than I am by a few inches, so I'll have to look up, maybe rise on my tiptoes to see into his clear gray eyes. *Sigh.* I hug his jacket to my nose and breathe in, catching the last of whatever detergent Lenny's mom uses mixed with Irish Spring and maybe a little campfire. The elevator pauses on the Empress Deck, the home of the most luxurious staterooms. The doors slide open, and a middle-aged couple tumbles into the elevator in a lovesick haze, alternately staring into each other's eyes and giggling, acting as if they're much younger than their graying hair would indicate. As I watch the reflections of the two swooning couples in the mirrored walls, I realize they look like before-and-after versions of one another, and it's an image I can't help but insert myself into. With Lenny at my side.

I'm pressing myself against the side of the elevator to avoid being sucked into their romantic orbit, when I hear another giggle coming from beyond the elevator doors. This giggle is a little more familiar, and it's mixed with a deep laugh that makes my stomach flip. I glance into the hall to see Demi wearing an oversized maroon hoodie with BRENTWOOD HIGH SCHOOL emblazoned across the front in big blocky letters. The sweatshirt is about two sizes too big and falls down over her hands. As she giggles again, she uses the excess fabric to swat at Lenny's chest while he leans over her, a wide grin on his face.

The elevator slides closed, leaving me to stare at my own reflection in the gold-mirrored doors. Or I *would* be staring at my reflection, if the image of Demi and Lenny grinning at each other weren't burned into my retinas like a screensaver left on too long. Suddenly that sunset kiss seems light-years away, and I grimace as Demi takes my place in my imagination. I look down to try to replace the image, and I see the track jacket in my hand, the smell of Irish Spring suddenly so overpowering I feel dizzy.

I reach into my pocket, but I left the tiny scrap of paper in my duffel back in my cabin. Without it, I have nothing to reassure me. All I have is the image of Demi and Lenny, laughing and grinning.

The elevator dings open again, but I'm just staring at Lenny's jacket, which suddenly feels like lead in my hand. I feel like such an idiot for thinking it mattered at all. The foul mood comes over me like hot syrup dumped on my head, weighing me down and running all the way to my toes.

"Uh, is this you?"

The male half of the swoony couple behind me jerks me out of my misery. Right, practice. I'm on my way. I fling my arms into the now-closing doors so I don't miss my stop. They jerk and pop back open, and I hurry off the elevator before I get another view of the honeymooners making out. At least I won't miss practice.

But as I make my way down the hall toward our practice room, a niggling thought won't leave me. I got one up on Demi last night, but now she's got some newfound free time. And what is she doing with it?

Once again, even though I managed to catch a break, it's turning around to bite me in the butt. I can't help but remember that one time in fifth grade when I beat Demi in our town's Fourth of July essay contest. That was the year that, on top of winning the hundred-dollar prize, the winner had to deliver the speech at the annual Fourth of July festival. Which meant that I had to sit on a dais in the town square, next to the mayor and half the city council, baking in the hot July sun at high noon, and then deliver my speech in front of a crowd of hundreds. I was so hot and nervous that I thought for sure I would pass out right there onstage. Some prize.

Beating Demi isn't always what you think it will be. Sometimes you just end up in a puddle of your own sweat and embarrassment.

Suddenly extra practice doesn't feel like such a victory. But I vow to push that aside and beat Demi where it really counts: in the final competition.

Most of the band is already in their seats, assembling their instruments, shuffling music, tuning up, or chatting about the variety of foods they speed-consumed during breakfast. I hear a long, low belch come from somewhere in the brass section, followed by a brief cheer and a flurry of high fives. I'm going to guess those are the pirates of the Ship's Bounty. At least they made it here.

I step up onto the podium in front of the rows and place my folder on the music stand, spreading out my music, prepared to start rehearsal. I pick up the baton and tap it on the stand, and everyone stops chatting or burping and turns to face me, instruments at the ready. I'll focus on the music, and when I'm done, I'll turn my focus to Lenny. Demi may be trying to work her magic, and it might even be doing the trick a little, but I'm not out yet. There's no way they have the chemistry we do. The passion and integrity he has when it comes to his art is the way I feel standing on this podium, a folder of music in front of me and rows of musicians waiting for my cue. She can't even begin to understand what that's like.

Game on, Demi, I think as I raise the baton.

The ship's cooling system chooses the one moment of silence to kick in, the air conditioning roaring to life with an almost human-sounding *whoosh.* Nicole practically levitates from her chair, her eyes darting around as if smoke is going to start pouring into the room at any second. Her abandoned chair tips back on its hind legs, sending the music stand behind her crashing into Amelia's lap, snapping her bassoon reed into splinters.

"Hey! That was a new reed!" Amelia whines, trying in vain to salvage the bits.

Nicole spins on her heel at the exclamation, her hip knocking over *her* stand, sending it into the one next to hers, which causes a domino effect of falling stands and fluttering sheet music down the front row. As I watch the white pages hit the floor, all of a sudden all I can see is red.

"Dammit, Nicole, get it together!" I snap. "Do you have any idea how much your neuroses are screwing us up? I don't know how you expect to survive Juilliard when an *air-conditioner* sends you over the edge."

The room goes silent. No one can believe I've snapped at Nicole over dropping her music. *Nicole*, who is our most talented and reliable musician. She *never* makes mistakes.

Nicole's face goes white, then red. At first I think she's going to cry, but then I realize the color is more the shade of fury. She snatches the music from the floor, the edge of it crinkling in her fist. She slaps it back onto the music stand, then rises so fast her chair tips over backward again, sending a second-row freshman flute player scooting back to avoid the shrapnel. For once, I don't see Nicole quivering. Everything about her is steely, from her stature to the daggered look she's giving me. Without a single word, she takes a wide step around the stand and strides past me, flute in one hand, case in the other.

"Wh-where are you going?" I sputter.

Nicole pauses and glances over her shoulder, eyes narrowed.

"I've worked my *ass* off for this band," she says, her voice sharp and steady as a chef's knife. "I don't need this, not from you."

"What does that mean?"

She glances across the rows of musicians. They've gone from a band to a silent chorus, their mouths agape as their eyes volley between Nicole and me. Her gaze settles on me, and suddenly all the steel is gone.

My tongue feels like it's swelling up in my mouth as I fumble for words, but nothing is coming out. *Her* mouth turns down as she gives me a look that's something close to pity.

"It means you need to chill. Also, I quit."

I hear Huck snort, and as I turn to shoot him a look of *Don't even start right now,* Nicole walks out.

Huck stands up and lays his oboe across his chair, then follows after Nicole, snagging my arm on the way and dragging me off the conductor's stand. I nearly trip over my feet as I try to keep up. By the time I have my footing, we're in the hallway, walking toward the stairwell door that's just closed from where Nicole disappeared through it.

"When Nicole Mauser is telling you to relax, you know you've taken a sharp left turn into crazy town," Huck says, still charging ahead.

"You know, Huck, I could use a little less commentary and a little more attention to your cues. You blew every single one back there." I can hear the words coming out of my mouth. I can tell they're mean and just making the situation worse. And yet I'm powerless to stop them. I *yelled* at Nicole. What is wrong with me? It's like I've been taken over by some body-snatching rage monster. It feels like PMS on speed, and I'm not a fan.

Huck stops midstride. He grabs my arms and whirls me around to face him, giving me a little shake for good measure.

"Okay, now it's *me* telling you to calm it down. You have officially marched off the field," Huck says. When I don't respond (because the rage monster has chosen this moment to shut me up), he lets go of me and takes a step back, sighing. "I'm going to find Nicole and try to fix this. There's no way she's *actually* quitting. But you need to go back in there and work on acting like the Liza I'm actually friends with. Because this version?" He gives me an up-and-down glance, his lips pursed in a frown. "This girl would be better off joining the Athenas."

I gasp, but Huck just arches an eyebrow at me, his expression simply saying *deal with it*. Then he turns on his heel and marches down the hall after Nicole.

I want to take off after him, and after Nicole, or maybe even up to the top deck so I can fling myself off, but I've got a roomful of people who are counting on me and a competition fast approaching. I can only fix the problem in front of me, and right now I need to get everyone ready to blow the doors off the ship's theater. I take a few of the deep, cleansing breaths I taught Nicole and banish the rage monster to a deep, dark corner of my brain.

I return to the rehearsal room, pausing with my hand on the door to take another deep breath. I push the door open and am pleased to find that they haven't revolted. No one else has quit. The trumpets are fingering their way through their part, while Molly, the clarinet section leader, is moving from student to student with a handheld tuner. In the back, the percussionists are adjusting their drum setup, making sure that every player has the pieces they need.

Watching them take care of business amid my hysterics, I feel that pressure behind my eyes that comes just before they well up. I take a deep controlled breath, willing any potential tears away. The last thing I need right now is to break down in front of my bandmates.

When I'm sure the tears are at bay, I climb onto the pedestal and tap my baton on the stand. In an instant, everyone is on the edge of their seats, instruments at the ready, eyes on me. I raise my hands, and the instruments rise with them. I count off the beat, and we begin. I force myself not to look down at the music. Instead I just watch them. Their heads bob along to the music as they make their way through the piece. Instead of freaking out that they're going to miss a cue, I sit back and listen as they hit them. All of them. It's not perfect, of course. Jared lets a cymbal roll go on too long. One of the saxophones is definitely sharp. And the trumpets are drowning out the french horns in the B section. But it's not the disaster I've been imagining, maybe even convincing myself that I hear.

As they move into the C section, I give myself a moment to remember why I love this band. Sure, they need shepherding to make sure no one wanders off before rehearsal, and they need monitoring to make sure they don't spend all their rehearsal time choreographing dance routines to Broadway musicals. But these guys can play. They know what they're doing. And instead of leading them through the music I know they can play, I've been stressing them out and strangling their talent. It's a rookie mistake, and the exact thing I was trying to avoid when I decided to keep the secret of the budget cuts. And it stops now. Huck was right. I'm letting Demi get to me. We've *never* operated like the Athenas, and we're not about to start now.

The rest of the rehearsal is one of the smoothest we've had, even though I have to pass Nicole's solo off to Rachel, the second-chair flute player. Without me breathing down their necks, the music flows. I make note of a few adjustments, but decide to save them for our next practice. If I've learned anything during this rehearsal, it's that sometimes you need to step back and let everything breathe.

As we pack up and store our instruments, everyone

chattering on about plans to hit the pool or the sundae bar in the karaoke lounge, I can't silence the one critical voice in my head that's telling me how much better everything sounded . . . without Huck. I love him, but he never met a key signature he couldn't butcher, and that's not taking into account the fact that a tone-deaf kid like Huck picked one of the hardest instruments to tune. His oboe is almost always squawking sharp or flat, and even though I was bitchy to have said it to him like that, he *is* always missing his cues. A sharp oboe played at the wrong time is like cats tap dancing on a chalkboard, and without it, the band's whole sound improved.

Just thinking it sends a sharp stab of guilt through my gut. It's completely treasonous to our friendship. There's no *way* I could ever do anything about it.

Then again . . .

Be a leader, Huck said, and maybe he was right. But being a leader sometimes means making choices, like taking a step back and letting everything flow . . . or deciding when someone *else* needs to take a step back. Someone like Huck. It's not like band is his only thing. He's always trying to juggle his roles in the musicals with rehearsals. I'd be doing him a favor.

Still, I can't shake the guilt that's growing from a pang to a full-on fireworks show in my stomach.

I need to talk this out. I've been so crazy these past few days that I don't trust myself to make this decision on my own. And being a leader also means knowing when to ask for help.

I knock on Mr. Curtis's door. It swings open, but my relaxed, perpetually calm band director is not the person who greets me. Instead, I find myself staring at a flowing red gypsy skirt over a vintage black bathing suit, wild blond curls falling over the face of Ms. Haddaway. It's clear from the terror that flashes across her face that she was expecting room service, not a student.

"Oh my! Hello, Liza!" Her voice jumps an octave or two as her hands rush to tame her curls. "Having a good trip?"

Uh, no, you see, I'm on the cruise from Gilligan's Island *while you're aboard the* Love Boat. But I know better than to let that one out of my head. Before I can formulate a more teacher-appropriate response, Mr. Curtis practically hip-checks Ms. Haddaway out of the doorway. He steps into the hall and pulls the door shut behind him. I notice an unusual tension in his shoulders, and his eyes are laser-focused on me, as if he's willing me to forget what I saw in there. *I wish.* Apparently Huck got one thing right. From the flush spreading across Mr. Curtis's cheeks, it's clear he's distracted from his surveillance-video mission.

"What can I help you with, Liza?"

Okay, so we're skipping right over the explanation as to why our rumpled home ec teacher is hanging out in his cabin. Fair enough. Frankly, I have no interest in getting any of *those* images stuck in my brain. Instead I talk to him about Huck's effect on the band's performance, managing to avoid explaining how we came to be in possession of extra practice time. I also leave out the part where our star flautist walked out of rehearsal and quite possibly the band.

He nods along with the story, arms crossed, a bit of his trademark sleepy Zen coming over his face. This is what I love about Mr. Curtis. When he's not panicking about death at sea, I can count on him to be a careful listener. And since his chief philosophy has always been *everything is gonna be fine*, I can usually count on him for a boost of positivity. He's fair and reliable, which is exactly what I need right now.

"So, I think I need to ask Huck to sit out the competition," I say, the words sitting on my tongue like lead weights. I feel almost sick saying it out loud, but it's the truth. I can't hide from it. "What do you think?"

Mr. Curtis gives one final nod. "Well, Liza, here's what I think," he says, and I feel the relief of a forthcoming solution wash over me. But before he can continue, the sound of squeaking wheels draws his gaze down the hall. A porter in all white is pushing a room-service cart, and when he sees Mr. Curtis, he breaks into a Sail Away Cruise Line signature smile and stops the cart right next to us.

"Delivery for Curtis?" he says. I glance at the cart, on top of which sits a silver bucket, a bottle of champagne, and two glasses. A single long-stemmed red rose lies on top of a crisp white napkin, and all I can think about is using one of the thorns to gouge out my eyes. It seems like the only sensible way to halt the avalanche of truly horrifying images that are now filling my brain.

Gross.

Suddenly the relaxed Mr. Curtis is gone, and the flush is back with a vengeance. He takes a step back, crashing into the door of his cabin. He reaches behind him and fumbles with the handle. The porter, who is probably trained to ignore such theatrics, pushes the cart through the door without a word, though the smile on his face betrays a hint of a smirk. Yeah, easy to laugh when it's not *your* teacher performing sexual Cirque du Soleil in your mind.

Double gross.

"Um, I think that sounds like a good plan, Liza," Mr. Curtis says, trying to station his tall frame in the door so I can't see the flash of red skirt disappear into his cabin bathroom. "I trust you to do what's right!"

The door slams, and I'm left standing in the hall with the answer I needed, but not in the way I needed it. And now it's on my shoulders to throw down the hammer.

Huck's plan definitely worked. Maybe too well.

CHAPTER 11

The grand dining room, with its gold-painted molding and floor-to-ceiling windows, is abuzz with chatter. All around us, tables full of diners are feasting on prime rib, pumpkin ravioli, and plump, bright assortments of fresh steamed vegetables. They're slurping spoonfuls of tomato bisque and passing heaping cheese plates while they replay their day aboard the *Destiny*.

All the tables except mine, that is. My normally boisterous band is curiously quiet, talking in low tones, mostly focused on the food in front of them.

I take a golden-brown roll out of the silver basket in the middle of the table and crack it open, steam rising from the center of the freshly baked bread.

"Pass the butter?" I say, nodding toward the plate topped with pats of butter molded into tiny seashells.

John reaches for the plate, his eyes purposely avoiding mine.

"Yes m—" he says, his eyes growing wide as the "ma'am" dies on his lips.

Seriously? John is my age. He tutored me before our last chemistry exam in Mr. Roop's class. And now he's ma'am-ing me? Huck was right. I've not only turned toward crazy town, but I'm also en route to becoming its despotic dictator.

A few seats down, I hear Hillary suppress a snort, and I lean past Huck to give her a look. She shrugs.

"Hey, dude, you did a scary-good impression of Demi at practice," she says. "You can't blame everyone for wanting to avoid the wrath."

I sigh. I've known them long enough to know that pretty soon this will morph into some kind of in-joke, and I'm okay with that. I deserve it. Until then, I just need to wait them out. And not explode again. Hopefully a strong performance tonight will ease that along.

As we finish our dinner, I notice the cruise director nodding at me from the small stage at the front of the dining room. I signal to everyone to finish up their meals and meet at the stage.

Of course, we're still down one flute player. Nicole refuses to speak to me, and I'm not sure I blame her. Huck says she went straight from rehearsal to the spa. She's had a hot-stone massage, manicure, pedicure, and mud mask. Huck claims she's not leaving until she's found inner peace or worked her way through the entire spa menu, whichever comes first. I know the fastest way to solve the Nicole-quitting problem would be to go to Mr. Curtis, but that would involve a whole lot of explanation I don't want to give. I'd rather wait her out and hope she finds peace in a mud bath. Until then, we can make do without her and her superior vibrato.

But as everyone takes their places, I notice another gap, this one in the percussion lineup. I call Ryan up with a crook of my finger.

"Where's Jared?" I whisper. We have only a few minutes before we'll need to start, and we're short a snare drum player.

Ryan looks pained. He glances around, as if hoping to find a hole to disappear through instead of telling me whatever he's about to tell me. "He was flirting with that blond girl from the Mechanicals. The one with the hair down to her butt?" As soon as he says it, I can picture Jared laying on the charm over dinner, and then disappearing through the dining room door just before the tuxedoed waiters deposited plates of cheesecake on the tables.

I can't send Ryan to look for him, though, because then I'd be down a timpani player, and half the percussion section would be gone.

"Do you think you can cover?"

"Uh, I can try," Ryan replies, but the look on his face says *Not a chance.*

I glance at my watch, a shiny gold gift from my father. Were it not for my obsessive need to be on time and our school's strict ban on cell phones on campus, there's no way I'd wear it. And as it tells me that we've got about five minutes before we have to start, it feels like a lead weight around my wrist.

I sigh. "Well, finish getting set up. We'll just have to hope he gets here."

"And if he doesn't?"

I look back at the band, thinking about today's rehearsal. I don't want to blow up and distract them from the kind of performance they had this afternoon. For the first time since we boarded the ship, I heard the band I've been leading all year. They just got their mojo back, and I don't want to send it running off again. I *have* to keep my cool. I take a deep breath and focus on the music we're about to play. "We'll just have to wing it, I guess."

Ryan nods, but he doesn't look like he believes me. His shoulders are tense, as if he's expecting me to reach out and slap him at any moment, making it even clearer that I can't lose my cool. He marches back to the percussion section like a soldier headed to the front. War is hell, and sometimes, so is band.

Before I can formulate a plan to recruit a new drummer on the spot, the lights in the dining room dim. I spin around to see the whole space lit by flickering candles, a romantic glow overtaking the room. The energy changes as couples lean into each other, the romance of the room jumping about ten notches. It's great for them, but as I turn back to my own stand, I realize I can't see a damn thing. And in front of me, fifty-eight musicians are squinting and leaning into their sheet music.

My blood pressure feels like it's spiking, the iron grip of anxiety closing tighter around my chest, when I notice a box of stand lights against the back wall. I take a deep breath to reclaim my calm. Tonight's going to be different. Tonight it will all work out. That's a thing, right? Just keep telling yourself something until it becomes true? I sure hope so, because it's the only strategy I've got at the moment.

I quickly send the box up and down the rows along with extension cords and power strips. I'm impressed by the speed with which everyone gets the lights clipped to their stands and plugged in. At least my reign of terror did have one positive outcome: they're awfully obedient right now. Ryan grabs the master extension cord and drags it to the outlet on the wall. I have about 0.2 seconds to wonder if the ship's backup generators, which are still providing electricity while we wait for whatever is broken to be fixed, can handle this.

Ryan shoves the plug into the wall, and I get my answer. The lights flicker on, illuminating the stands, then promptly click off with a snap and a hiss, a wisp of smoke coming from the outlet accompanied by the acrid smell of sulfur. Ryan yanks the plug, but it's too late. The fuse, barely hanging on from our first electrical disaster, has now totally given up the ghost. The stands are plunged into darkness, my hope for a good performance going with them.

In an instant, Huck appears at my side. He places a hand on each shoulder and leans in until we're nearly nose to nose.

"Look, I know I gave you the what's-up earlier, and you deserved it. But forget all that now, because it's going to be fine."

"Huck, no one can see the music! How is that going to be fine?"

"We marched an entire season, playing flawlessly, without music. We've practiced this enough that everyone's pretty much absorbed it. Just trust."

"T-trust?" I sputter, my breath coming short and gasping.

"Do you need me to slap you?"

And I actually have to think about my answer.

"This is probably not a good time to tell you that I just smashed my reed and my extras are in my cabin," Huck says with a sheepish grin. "But no worries, I'll just mime along."

Huck gives me a pat on the shoulder, then returns to his

seat, front row at my left. My brain is spinning. *Darkness. Miming. Trust.*

Okay.

I force all the words out of my mind except "trust." I step onto the platform, raise my baton, and count off a whispered "Two, three, four" in case they can't see me well. Then, with a collective intake of breath, we begin.

Just like the rehearsal earlier, everything flows. Tonight we're performing a medley of Disney love songs, which are usually a crowd pleaser. In this candlelit room, it seems like we're primed to be a hit, assuming all goes well. And just like this morning, it does. We start out with "A Whole New World" from *Aladdin*, a fairly easy opening that's heavy on our woodwinds. And as I direct, it seems like things are flowing even more smoothly than they did this morning. The woodwinds crescendo into a chorus, and I can hear the chattering behind us die down as diners turn their attention more toward us.

Without me standing over the band members, without the notes on the page distracting them, they're really listening to one another and connecting. They're not just playing, they're actually interpreting the music, and I couldn't be prouder.

Then we move into "Kiss the Girl," a fun tune that's heavy on percussion, which reminds me of our absentee drummer. I hold my breath and say a silent prayer that Ryan's able to fill in everywhere we need him.

My prayers are answered when a snare roll appears at exactly the right moment, and I glance back at the percussion to find that Jared's spot has been covered. Only it's not by Ryan, or any of the other percussionists. No, standing there behind the drum is a tall, broad-shouldered blond guy. I blink, but it's not a trick of the darkness. It's Russ. At first my heart leaps into my throat as I wait for the inevitable sonic train wreck he's certain to produce, but it doesn't come. His eyes are squeezed shut in concentration, his head bobbing along to the rhythm I'm directing. He fills in at all the right spots, with a few whispered cues from Ryan.

The music swells as we approach the final measures. The trumpets crescendo, the timpani rolls like thunder, and Russ executes a snare roll that's even tighter than what Jared normally does, though it does go on two beats too long. At the last note, I wave my hands to cut them off, and from the looks on their faces to the feeling of the smile stretched across mine, I know we all feel it.

There's just a split second of silence before the audience breaks into applause. Not the tentative, pitying kind from two nights ago, but real, honest-to-goodness appreciation. I even hear a whistle or two coming from behind me, so I gesture for everyone to stand, then I turn and lead us all in a bow.

We file offstage and through a side door into a kitchen storage area where our instrument cases are waiting, the energy practically carrying us off like a helium balloon. Everyone is grinning and chattering on.

Lenny is already there, perched on top of a snare drum case, a plate of chocolate cake balanced on his knee. The sight of him whips up a frenzy of mixed emotions, from lust to confusion, as I remember his giggle fit with Demi this morning outside the elevator.

As the band fills up the space around him, Lenny leaps to his feet and strides over. "My dad wanted me to keep an eye on the cases while you guys were performing," he says, shoveling a forkful of rich chocolate cake into his mouth. He swallows and grins, a bit of chocolate on his lower lip that I can't stop staring at. "I could hear you through the walls. Y'all sounded great!"

All thoughts of Demi disappear as I grin back at him, basking in his smile and his compliment. It means a lot coming from him, after seeing how talented he is with a camera. He's certainly got an eye, and I'd bet also an ear, for art. That is, until Demi is standing next to me, trying to edge me out of the circle with her hip.

"Hey, Lenny," she says, pretending I'm not on the planet, much less in the room. "Listen, we're going to get a little party going down in the karaoke lounge, and I'd love it if you'd join in. You game?"

Lenny opens his mouth to answer, but it's Jared who jumps in, having reappeared from his Mechanicals tryst.

"Hell yes, karaoke!" he says, his voice loud enough for the whole room to hear. "Karaoke lounge, guys! Put away your stuff and meet down there, 'kay?"

All around me, the chatter kicks into high gear as they put away their instruments with renewed enthusiasm. Hillary is already discussing which Journey song she and Ryan will duet on, while Clarice and Andrew are contemplating a *Grease* medley.

My fury at Jared for missing our performance melts away as I watch angry red splotches appear on Demi's cheeks. She's glaring at Jared, but it's too late to put that toothpaste back in the tube. Once again, the band is crashing her party. So take *that*, Demi.

But I can't let Jared completely off the hook, so as he starts to leave, I grab him by the elbow. "Hey, where *were* you? You totally screwed us!"

Jared looks sheepish. He sticks his hands deep in his pockets, his shoulders hunched up around his ears. "Sorry, Liza," he says, a blush forming in his cheeks. "I lost track of time. But hey, Russ sounded pretty good, right? I heard him on 'Kiss the Girl.'"

"His snare roll was two counts too long," I snap.

"Uh, he was kind of good," Ryan says, joining our conversation.

I remember the way everyone looked terrified of me at dinner, and I'm not eager to go back there. Instead I just give Jared a stern look and tell him not to miss anything else or I'll put his name on the list to do wake-ups this summer at band camp.

Huck skips up next to me, his oboe case tucked under one arm. "Demi's a beast, but you *know* I'm gonna shut that room down with my rendition of 'Sweet Transvestite,'" he says, throwing his other arm around my shoulder. "You coming?"

Behind me, the door swings open again, and in walks Russ, a pair of drumsticks in his hand. He gives me a look like he's not sure if I'm going to hug him or kick him, a look that is somewhere between a smile and grimace.

"Uh, yeah, I'll meet you there," I say.

Huck glances from me to Russ and back again. "Have fun with that one," he says, before darting after Hillary, asking who's going to lead the Time Warp.

Russ shuffles over but leaves a distance large enough to prevent me from smacking him. He looks like he's waiting for me to say something, but I'm not sure what he's up to, so instead I focus on organizing the stack of music in my folder.

After a moment of shuffling around, he finally taps me on the shoulder, a wide grin on his face. "I was kind of awesome, right?"

I have to laugh at him, standing there like a puppy who just dropped a tennis ball at my feet. And even though I'm not ready to trust him yet, I can't deny that he was good.

"Where in the *hell* did you learn to drum like that?" I ask.

Russ shrugs, a touch of pink appearing in his cheeks. "I dunno, I just sort of always banged along with whatever I was listening to. Picked it up, I guess."

I gape at him, a look of pure incredulity on my face. "You don't just *pick up* snare rolls like that," I say, hooking my fingers in air quotes.

"Okay, so maybe I have a pair of drumsticks hidden in my desk, and *maybe* I've watched a few hundred"—Russ pauses, glancing up at the ceiling as if he's tabulating—"thousand hours of YouTube videos."

I laugh. "Dude, you're good! Why aren't you in the band?" Russ raises his eyebrows at me. "Okay, well, I know why you're not in *the* band, but you should be in *a* band. You can actually play!"

"My dad doesn't think I should be taking time away from practice and conditioning. The man's got football scholarships on the brain," he says, tapping at his temple as he rolls his eyes. He shrugs his wide shoulders again. "I mean, it's no big deal. It's something I do for fun. But it was cool to play tonight."

I watch him as he hems and haws, but there's no mistaking the light in his big blue eyes when he talks about playing. It makes my heart feel like it's growing Grinch-style, and his grin is infectious.

"It *was* cool that you played tonight," I say, taking the last step to close the distance between us. "Thank you, seriously."

Russ flings his arm around me, pulling me in close in the most epic bear hug of my life. It's like a full-body high five, and I'm powerless to resist. In fact, I can't even protest, because my face is smooshed into the fabric of his button-down, which smells newly ironed.

"Anytime, boss," he says, his words disappearing into my hair.

The door swings open again, and Demi trips into the room followed closely by Lenny. Demi is giggling while Lenny moves toward a cardboard box marked TEQUILA in black, blocky letters. He's starting to pry open the lid when Demi gasps. They both spot us, sending Demi tripping into Lenny's back. Russ's grip on me loosens at the distraction, so I take the opportunity to shove off him and take one giant step backward. But it's too late. The pair of them are taking the scene in, wide-eyed. I want to shout at Lenny that it was just a friendly hug, I was just thanking Russ for saving our performance, but it's clear that both of them have already decided what it is they saw.

"Sloppy seconds?" Demi says, but her voice is dripping venom that actually stings.

"Shut up, Demi," Russ mutters, but I raise a hand to silence him. If he defends me, it's only going to make it worse. And anyway, I don't care what Demi thinks. I care what Lenny thinks. But as I watch his face, his expression is inscrutable. He glances at Demi, a little wrinkle forming between his eyebrows. Then he glances at Russ, and then at me. My brain spins trying to formulate an explanation, something, *anything* that will make this better.

Lenny's frown deepens, and then he takes three long strides across the room, takes my face in his hands, and kisses me.

As soon as it happens, my mind goes blank. It takes me a second to remind myself to take in what's happening. I'm being kissed. By Lenny. I don't want to miss it.

Freshman year, a junior saxophone player named Jake asked me out to a movie. About an hour in, he leaned in for a kiss that was all tongue, and *not* in a good way. But Lenny's kiss is all lips, pressed firmly against mine. They're warm and wanting in a way that reminds me of the photo of the sunset he showed me the day we were sitting on the beach. There's also an urgency there that sends my heart somersaulting across my chest.

I hear Demi gasp while Russ lets out a shocked "Dude!" When Lenny steps back, my fingers fly to my lips, as if to make sure they're still there. I run my tongue over my lower lip, tasting lime and something salty. I blink at him, my face a picture of nothing but shock, which quickly turns to horror as Russ's fist flies toward Lenny's face.

The two boys are almost the same height, but when it comes to muscle mass, Russ's athletic body is twice the size of Lenny's narrow art-kid frame. Watching Russ's arm extend toward Lenny's face makes me worry that Lenny might actually be about to die. I want to yell, to shout at Russ to stop, but I'm speechless and in shock.

Lenny sees the punch coming and takes a quick step back, the blow just glancing off his cheek. I can tell it was enough of an impact, though, because a red mark blooms just above his jawline, and his hand goes up to cradle the spot.

"Russ!" Demi shrieks at the same time I leap in between the two boys.

"What in the hell, man?" Lenny barks, still rubbing his jaw.

"Not cool, dude. Not cool at all," Russ says, spitting his own venom in return.

"Whatever, man, you're just jealous," Lenny says, flinging his other arm around Demi's shoulder. I see Russ's fists balling again. He opens his mouth to retort, but I raise my hand to silence him.

"I don't know what's going on here, but both of you need to shut up right now."

Demi, who's been shockingly silent this whole time, takes one look at Russ, then shrugs out from beneath Lenny's arm and bolts from the room. Lenny follows close behind, leaving me to wonder why he kissed me, but followed her. And then there's Russ, who responded to the whole thing by *hitting Lenny in the face*.

I can't really tell who the winners and losers are right now, but the fact that my lips are still buzzing from the kiss feels something like a win.

"Liza, I'm really—"

"Stop," I say, not even able to meet his eyes. I don't want my memory of Lenny's kiss to be replaced by Russ or anything he has to say. It already feels like it's fading too fast. My head is starting to hurt like I'm the one who's been punched, and I don't want to deal with any of this. "I don't know what's going on here, or what that was, but it was too much. All of it."

And with the heat of Lenny's kiss still on my lips, I grab my folder of music and head for the door.

CHAPTER 12

Huck or Hillary.

Hillary or Huck.

Or preferably both. That's what I need right now if I'm even going to begin to make sense of what just happened.

What *did* just happen?

I pause on the black-and-white tile of the atrium and close my eyes, and it all flashes back. Lenny. The kiss. Russ. Hitting Lenny. My hand goes to my lips, and at the same time I shiver, dueling feelings of happiness and horror coursing through me in equal measure. It's been happening ever since I walked out of that room, and I'm not sure if it's going to stop until I find my friends.

The atrium is cavernous and filled with people, and even though a massive blue-and-gold sign overhead littered with arrows directs passengers to the Punch Line Comedy Club, the Blue Note Dinner Theater, and Lucky Strike's Casino, there's no listing for the karaoke lounge. That's when I collide with a white-clad *Destiny* crew member. He glares at me but keeps muttering into the walkie-talkie he has pressed to his mouth. I hear something about poker and a fifty-dollar buy-in, and something else about Miguel screwing him. As soon as he stops talking, I take my chance.

"I'm looking for the karaoke lounge," I say, and he nods, one ear glued to the walkie-talkie. Apparently someone is talking through the static.

"The lounge? That red door across the atrium," he says, pointing. Then he double-times it across the floor until he disappears through a set of doors marked STAFF ONLY.

When I get to the red door he indicated, I push through and find myself hit with a wall of light and sound. The entire room is cast in a deep red glow that bounces off the many mirrored tabletops, as well as the ceiling, dance floor, and walls. A disco ball spins in the center of a starburst of lights, with blue and gold and green glinting off in so many directions I feel like I'm in a nightclub aboard the starship *Enterprise*. Cocktail waitresses in vintage-style sequined uniforms of hot pants and suspenders carry trays of drinks around that are made up of so many neon colors they couldn't possibly be food. They look more like martini glasses full of cleaning fluids.

Even though the room is designed to look like some über-trendy hot spot on the Vegas strip, the crowd is decidedly not cosmopolitan. The dance floor is crowded with what looks like the parents who just dropped their kids off at the Kidz Camp next door and were so excited to cut a rug that they didn't have time to scrub the zinc oxide off their noses or change out of their garish Hawaiian shirts. They bob and flail along to the techno track pounding from the overhead speakers, but it looks like only about half of them have caught on to the actual rhythm of the bass. The rest are so far off tempo that they look like they're having some kind of group seizure, with sweat flying across the dance floor at such a rate I worry someone's going to slip and break an ankle.

"Can I buy you a drink?"

I turn to see a middle-aged man sporting a comb-over that starts just above his left ear. He's holding up his ship credit card between two fingers, trying to affect the high-rolling celebrity persona that the nightclub is meant to evoke. I swear to God, if this man says *pop some bottles* to me, I'm stomping on his foot and running until I hit the ocean.

Instead, I settle for the truth. "I'm sixteen," I reply, shouting over the techno beat.

"What?" he asks, leaning closer so I can smell whatever cheap body spray he purchased at the drugstore before coming on this trip.

"Sixteen!" I shout back, directly into his ear. "I'm sixteen!"

He jerks back from me and takes one giant step in the opposite direction, his card clattering to the mirrored dance floor. He scrambles to pick it up, muttering something that might be "I'm sorry" or might be "Oh my God." I can't tell over the music.

I don't wait to find out. I spin on my heel and bolt for the exit, not slowing until I'm through the swinging saloon doors and back into the cavernous atrium. I grab the first staff member I see.

"Excuse me, can you tell me where the karaoke lounge is?"

She points across the atrium. "Down the Havana Hall, on your left past the piano bar."

I thank her and set off. It doesn't take me long to find the piano bar, its tinkling ivories and soft blue glow oozing out of the glass doors. And just a bit farther down the hall I find the karaoke lounge. I push through an identical set of glass doors just in time to hear someone hit the third key change of Whitney Houston's "I Have Nothing." And from the way the voice screeches and veers sharp, I can tell they're right. I grimace and press my fingers to my ears in an effort to dull the cacophony, then scan the room for my friends. I spot Huck and Hillary in a red velvet banquette in the corner along with Jared, Ryan, Molly, and Nate, a pitcher of something electric pink in front of them.

I make my way over, trying to figure out how I can discreetly get Huck and/or Hillary away from the group so they can help me figure out what happened with Lenny. There's no way I'll be able to work this out in front of the others, or with the soundtrack of the worst Whitney Houston impersonator in the world blasting into my ears.

"Hey, guys, whatcha drinking?" I ask, then cringe. I didn't want to sound like a mom the moment I walked up.

"Pitcher of Shirleys!" Hillary says, sliding a heavy-bottomed glass across the table at me. "Extra grenadine and double cherries, of course."

I pour myself a glass and slide into the end of the booth next to Molly. A quick look around the bar, which is fairly crowded, shows that while the band showed up to Demi's party, Demi did not. Neither she nor any of the Athenas are anywhere to be found.

"It was weird," Molly says, as if sensing my observation. "We got like, three songs in and the next thing I know, Demi is marching in here like a tiny dictator. She whispered something to Missy, and within minutes they were gone. Which is fine by me, because there's only so many girlie pop songs I can listen to in one night."

Molly downs the rest of her drink and slams it on the table like we're at a bar in the old West. She turns to me. "You look like hell," she says in the deadpan voice she uses no matter what the subject. From anyone else, the statement would sting, but somehow from Molly I don't mind because (a) she's never actually been mean a day in her life, and (b) it's probably true.

"Just tired," I say, and surprise myself by actually yawning. I catch Huck cocking an eyebrow at me from across the table. I try to make eyes at him, eyes that say *You will never believe what just happened. Please excuse yourself so we can talk about it.*

But even though he's my best friend in the world, we have yet to master the critical best-friend ESP. Instead he pulls a binder of music off the back of the booth along with a pencil and a little slip of paper. "Whatcha singing, Liza?" he asks. He flips through the laminated pages. "Are we going Broadway tonight? Or something more classic eighties?"

On any other night I'd be pulling the book across the table and searching for my signature songs (usually something twangy and country, with notes that fit my upper alto voice), but I don't think I can do it tonight. There's still a lump in my throat from the earlier excitement with Lenny and Russ, along with random zaps of electricity that shoot up my spine every time I remember Lenny's lips on mine. There's no way I could get through a Dolly Parton classic with this level of distraction, and even though it's just karaoke, I'm not about to get up there like a tone-deaf reality show contestant. I take music seriously, thankyouverymuch.

"Liza?" Huck asks again, his pencil poised over the slip of paper. "Or you could just join Hillary and me. We're up soon for 'Friends in Low Places.' You *know* that'll get the whole bar singing along."

I nearly choke on my maraschino cherry. "You're doing Garth Brooks?"

Huck winks. "Hey, I'll do whatever gets the crowd on my side," he says.

The music echoes its final chords, and from the booth behind the stage, the karaoke DJ thunders on the mike. "Next up, Hillary and Huck," he says in a smooth, velvety baritone. "Hillary and Huck, where you at?"

Before Jared and Nate can scoot out of the booth, Huck is up and across the table. Hillary chooses to take the below-ground route by crawling out from underneath. She pauses before taking the stage.

"You coming?" she asks me.

I glance up at the stage with the warm spotlight pointed down on it. Huck is already bounding up to the center and pulling a mike from its stand. He executes a perfect Elvis hip swivel that has the crowd hooting and hollering for him.

I shake my head. "I think I'm going to head back to the room. I'm really tired," I say, and then yawn again. "You'll be back soon?"

Hillary's eyes narrow a bit as she studies my face, and for a moment I think the friend ESP might have worked. But then she breaks into a grin. "Not before I do 'Roxanne'!" she says, then flounces to the stage, the black flowy gypsy skirt she wears for performances trailing after her.

The opening notes of an acoustic guitar twang from the speakers, and Huck lifts his mike, transforming his accent into a perfect Southern drawl as he starts the opening lyrics.

Hillary joins in on the chorus, and it takes only one line before half the bar is singing along. I take that as my cue to go, before I get sucked into a conversation about how terrible I look, which will only lead to me pouring my heart out about how confused I feel. I need to hold it in until Hillary gets back to the room. Then we can really talk.

I try to stay awake long enough for her to get back. I need to know why Lenny followed Demi after he kissed me. Because he wanted to let her know he was sorry he likes me and not her, right? He just wanted to make sure she wasn't too hurt. Because he's nice, but he likes me. Right?

There's no sun coming through our tiny porthole when I wake up on Monday, just a mask of gray and beads of rain pounding at the thick layers of glass. I sit up from bed and find that my head is spinning, as if I spent the previous night sharing that handle of tequila with Demi instead of hiding in my room. When I put my foot on the floor, the whole room tilts slightly. Only it's not a hangover, it's real life. The storm we've been promised has rolled in overnight, and the boat is now pitching side to side like an oceanic seesaw. And my stomach is rolling right along with it. I also can't shake the image of water pouring through a hole in the bottom of the ship, ready to capsize us at any moment. This trip is quickly becoming a metaphor for my life: a slowly sinking ship.

I place my other foot on the floor, hoping to find some sea legs, when the previous night washes over me like a twenty-foot swell. The kiss. The fight. The argument. Images swim through my brain, and I feel like I'm sinking. I can't make sense out of any of it. And definitely not with my stomach doing the hula.

"Ugh." My stomach gurgles, followed by a hiccup and a burp.

Hillary's bed is empty, and I guess that answers the question about whether or not sunrise yoga happens when the sun hasn't exactly risen. I'm torn between being glad she's not here to see my misery, and bummed I can't hash things out with her.

Rising out of bed now, I wobble my way over to her duffel and dig around past vintage T-shirts and tangles of costume jewelry. Underneath her copy of The Hobbit, I find what I'm looking for.

"Jackpot!" I cry, her box of seasickness patches in my hand, and then groan as the ship dips, sending me onto my butt and my stomach into my throat. I fumble with the box, unwrapping a patch and slamming it onto my arm with a smack. I stick a spare onto my hip for good measure. I can't afford to spend my day in bed, and I'm definitely going to need some extra fortification if I'm going to deal with what happened last night. A set of facts I'm still not sure about, and won't be until I find my friends.

Lenny walked in to see me hugging Russ, which must have made him jealous? So he kissed me, the only high point of the whole scene. This, of course, royally pissed off Demi, which made Russ defensive. So he hit Lenny, either to defend Demi or to defend me. Either way, he's clearly trying to make *Demi* jealous to get her back.

Oy. My head is spinning again.

I close my eyes, holding on to the image of Lenny leaning in, his lips reaching mine, and then work hard to press the pause button on my mental DVR to avoid the rest of the scene. All I want to remember is that moment when my breath caught in my throat and my heart pounded to the beat of a John Philip Sousa march. Russ may have stopped it quickly, but from even that brief moment I can tell that Lenny is a good kisser. His lips weren't too slobbery, but weren't too dry either. The pressure was wanting, but not like he was *wanting* to swallow my face, and the way his lips parted slowly just before Russ shoved him away leads me to believe that he knows what he's doing in the tongue department.

I curse Russ aloud for keeping me from knowing for sure.

I cover my eyes with my hands to make the room darker and try to reimagine the moment. Instead of a kitchen storage room, we're standing on the upper deck with the wind in our hair and the stars overhead. Demi's somewhere else, and Russ has been dumped overboard. It's just us and the night and one perfect, long, uninterrupted—

Someone knocks on my door to a lazy triplet beat, and as much as I want to scream for him to go away, I know it's Huck out there. Huck, who holds the key to a stellar final performance, if only he'll move his chair from the stage down into the audience. I hate to do it, but I know I have to. I have to bench him for the rest of the trip. And even though that sucks, at least it's one thing I definitely *can* take care of.

I shuffle out of bed and open the door, barely pausing to

greet him before I turn and hurl myself back onto the bed. I roll over onto my back and fling an arm over my face, but not fast enough.

"Good lord, you look like death at the dawn of the apocalypse!" Huck says, taking one giant step backward, a gesture I appreciate since his neon yellow T-shirt and swim trunks are burning my retinas.

"Urgghh," I half groan, half gurgle, and Huck springs into action.

I hear the bathroom sink running, then Huck appears with a damp washcloth that he lays across my forehead. The relief is instant, and I sigh. The cool washcloth is already doing wonders for my condition. My stomach is still rolling, but I no longer feel like it's trying to escape.

"You know we have to cancel practice for today," Huck says, his voice soft, preparing for the inevitable explosion. Only I don't have the strength for a fight right now. I manage to groan some kind of protest, but Huck holds up a hand. "Liza, it's not just you. This storm has half the band praying to the porcelain god, and if we made the other half try to stare at music on a page, they'd be ralphing too."

I want to fight. We're on a roll with yesterday's practice and last night's performance. I don't want to lose momentum, because at this rate we might just win that prize money. But a crack of lightning and an ensuing clap of thunder have me gasping and grasping at my stomach until all I can do is nod.

"Why don't I spend the day trying to soften up Nicole, who, despite all her nerves and hypochondria, apparently does not suffer from motion sickness," Huck suggests, his voice wry.

"She's on her third seaweed wrap down at the spa, so she may be ready to talk."

"How?" I groan into my pillow.

Huck reaches for the spiral notebook on my bedside table and pulls the pen out of the spine, scribbling a note. "I'll post this on the door of the practice room," he says. He holds up the sign, which reads PRACTICE CANCELED DUE TO PROJECTILE BARFING. When I try to protest, he cuts me off. "*And* I'll go door to door to make sure everyone gets the message."

At the mention of talking, I remember why I wanted to talk to Huck in the first place, and my stomach rolls again. I must have moaned, because I hear Huck scurry to the end of Hillary's bed, farther from me and any potential projectiles.

"I can't believe you're still sitting here, what with how much you hate barfing."

Huck searches my face for signs of puking, and apparently still finds a bit of green, because he nudges the metal trash can closer to the side of my bed with the toe of his neon-green flip-flop.

"Let me be clear: if you start to retch, I'm for sure bolting to the bathroom and cranking up the faucet so I don't have to listen. But you're my best friend, and best friends at least *try* to prevent each other from horking into a trash can on spring break."

There's another knock, this one much less musical.

"Speaking of," Huck says, moving for the door, "that's probably your ginger ale, which I already ordered because nobody knows you better than me."

"True story," I say.

A porter dressed in white stands in the doorway, a silver-domed tray on his raised hand. He deposits the tray on the bed-side table, uncovering it to reveal a white china plate topped with a tower of saltine crackers, a crystal glass, a miniature silver ice bucket with matching silver tongs, and two cans of ginger ale. It's definitely the most elegant stomach treatment I've ever received.

The porter leaves, and Huck settles in on Hillary's bed, fluffing the pillows up behind his back. I take a cracker off the plate and nibble the corner. I don't know if it's the company or the crackers, but I notice that my stomach is settling down. It's more of a waltz than a cancan in there now, which I appreciate. I take a few deep breaths, testing out my newly steeled stomach. Huck leaps from the bed.

"I'm not going to barf, Huck," I say, cracking open one of the cans with a satisfying hiss. "I think the patch just kicked in."

Satisfied, Huck settles back on the bed, leaning on his elbows, a grin spreading across his face. "We were awesome last night! It felt good, didn't it? It was awesome to hear us all working together. Well, some of us more than others, since I was faking it. But it was like, everything I feel about the band being this awesome tight-knit family totally translated into the music."

I take a deep breath and prepare myself for what I have to do. "Yeah, it was great, Huck," I begin. "Listen, there was something I—"

"I had totally forgotten what a high it is to be part of a performance like that," he says, either not hearing or not listening to what I'm trying to say. "It felt really good. I can't wait to do it again at the competition. We've totally got this. We'd just lost our mojo a little, but it's back, baby!"

I listen to him babble on about the highs of the performance, and I can't help but agree. I also can't help but feel my chest swell with pride, tampered only by the guilt dancing around in my gut. Huck is right. The band *is* a family, and he's very much a part of it. What would we be without our colorful, conniving Huckster? Kicking him out now would be like punting a puppy.

"I know it doesn't feel like it *now,* but the cruise is actually really awesome," he says. I peek out from underneath my washcloth and see him rolled on his side, his head propped up in his hand, a wide grin beaming across the room at me. "We owe you huge for hooking us up."

If there was any doubt, it's gone now. Huck stays. He has to. And as soon as I tell it to myself, my stomach feels a whole hell of a lot stronger. I sit up and adjust the pillows beneath my head.

"Now, I almost forgot to show you." He reaches for the mini messenger bag he's been toting around the ship, lifts the flap, and pulls out a shiny golden microphone. I recognize it immediately. How could I forget all the times we bopped around on Demi's canopy bed, belting our little hearts out to our favorite Disney tracks? When Demi won the state junior talent show and was presented with medals instead of trophies (a serious faux pas in Demi's mind), her mother had the microphone made and presented it to her daughter as a birthday present that year. Demi has treated it like a talisman ever since. After joining the Athenas freshman year, she deemed it the group's lucky mike, waving it around at every performance and competition, probably hoping to blind her competitors with the wonder that is Demi.

I sit up straighter in bed, a bite of cracker catching in my throat. "Where did you get that?"

A devilish grin appears on Huck's face, and now I'm not sure I really want to know.

"Demi should spend less time shoving her C cups at Lenny. Then maybe she'd notice that I snuck into her room totally undetected while housekeeping was working on her bathroom," Huck says, spinning the mike in his hand with such enthusiasm that it skips off his palm and makes for the floor. My heart leaps into my chest as I remember the yelling that occurred any time the microphone hit the ground. Huck snatches it from the air just before it lands on the rough carpet of my cabin, and I settle back onto my pillows, still on high alert. "She didn't even hide it. Can you believe that?"

I really can't. I've always imagined Demi traveling with a mini safe for her most prized possession, but according to Huck, storing it next to her lacy underthings is protection enough. Usually.

"So I'm thinking we send her a ransom note. We could even do an audio version. Hillary could splice together lyrics from a bunch of their performance pieces so that the final piece demands that they drop out of the competition in exchange for her *precious*," he says, affecting a sinister Sméagol voice, wiggling his imaginary claws at my face.

Forget yelling. Ransoming Demi's mike would spark an all-out war that would certainly involve casualties. There's no way this can happen, and I tell Huck as much. But when I reach for the mike, he snatches it away, holding it high above his head. And between his height and my tender tummy, there's no way I'm jumping for it.

"Huck, we *cannot* deal with your shenanigans right now," I say, my voice cool and steeled. I arch an eyebrow at him and shoot him my best look of *serious business*. "Do you really want a repeat of last year's ETRs?"

Huck's eyes immediately drop to his toes as the memory of last year's East Tennessee Regional Marching Band Competition floods back to him, and to me. That was the one where Huck decided our performance needed a little extra flash, so he added a fistful of glitter to the boxes that held the white feathery plumes that sit atop our hats. Unfortunately, as soon as we started marching, the glitter started raining down into our instruments—and our eyeballs. The tubas, vision obscured by glitter, nearly marched right into the woodwinds, sending the entire band down in a game of musical dominos. It was a disaster.

I reach for the mike again. Huck scrunches his nose in frustration, but he hands the mike over quickly enough that I can tell somewhere deep down inside he knew there was no *way* I'd let that happen.

The mike in my hand completely stills my stomach, probably because it feels like there's a lead weight settling in there.

"What are you going to do with it?" Huck asks, his eyes sparkly, his brows arched as he no doubt pictures a variety of nefarious activities.

"I'm going to return it," I reply. "Stealthily."

Huck looks like he wants to offer up some suggestions, but before I can tell him I'll be doing it *alone* thankyouverymuch, there's a third knock at the door. Feeling better, I start to rise from the bed, but Huck holds up a finger at me.

"Stay," he says. He checks the peephole, then leaps back, whipping around to face me. "It's Curtis!"

The mike suddenly feels like it weighs six tons and is getting heavier with each knock on my door. I quickly shove the golden mike under my pillow, and then lean back on it to keep it from rolling out onto the floor.

When I nod at Huck to indicate we're good to go, he opens the door. Mr. Curtis is standing there in something closer to his standard uniform, though there are hints that Huck's plan is working: instead of khaki pants, he's in khaki shorts, these with a few smudges on the left thigh that are probably from various tropical cocktails. There's also a pink plastic lei hanging around his neck, one side oddly mangled.

"You're not sick too, are you?" Mr. Curtis says, his eyes going from the tray of crackers back to my pale face.

"I'm actually feeling better, sir," I reply, sitting up and willing some color into my cheeks. "Huck was helping me out with some stomach settling."

I see Mr. Curtis's eyes go quizzical as he glances over his shoulder at Huck, who's grinning, and I pray my band director won't bring up our conversation last night. I make a mental note to update him on my decision.

"Good to hear. Because Ms. Haddaway and I were, um, talking," he says, a slight flush creeping into his cheeks. I see Huck make a gagging motion from behind him, and I have to stop myself from reacting. "We think it's time the show choir and the band did a little team bonding, and we have just the thing."

I force my face to remain still and fight the urge to eye-roll, grimace, or mirror Huck's gagging motion. Teacher-enforced team bonding is awful in the best of circumstances, but team bonding with the Athenas? I'd rather wrestle an angry tiger while covered in raw steaks. Plus, if our teachers knew anything at all, the last thing they'd do is force us into competition with Demi. Talk about something I definitely *don't* need. My focus goes to Huck, and I allow my eyes to narrow slightly. Clearly his plan has backfired. The teachers were not supposed to be working together *against* us.

Mr. Curtis doesn't notice the tiny daggers I'm shooting at Huck, though. He's too busy snatching a cracker from my plate and clapping his hands in self-satisfaction. Our task? A shipboard hula-hooping competition scheduled for after lunch. Participation? Not optional. Fun? To be had by all, apparently. When he finishes his spiel, he looks at me, eyes glittering from an overdose of the home ec teacher persuasion. *Gag.*

"Sounds good," I reply, because it doesn't appear I have any other option.

"Great! Well, I'll let you get ready," he says, making his way to the door. He turns and gives me a jaunty tilt of his head, a ridiculous gesture that looks completely out of place next to his usual lazy smile. "Hit the deck, as they say."

The door swings shut behind him. "More like walk the plank," I mutter to Huck.

CHAPTER 13

The rain has subsided over the course of the morning, but thick gray clouds still cover the sky as far as the eye can see. As Huck and I emerge onto the shiny wooden deck, we're assaulted by a reggae mash-up of steel drums and bass booming through strategically placed oversized speakers. The crew of the good ship *Destiny* has decided that without the sun, it's their duty to bring all the color in the world to the upper deck. There are multicolored tiki lights strung up on anything stationary. The umbrellas have all been draped with swaths of brightly colored fabric, and for some reason, there are shiny metallic Mardi Gras beads hanging off everything, from deck chairs to buffet tables to the cruise passengers wandering around the deck. And there are crew members wearing as many rainbow leis as will fit around their necks as they skip through the crowd "lei-ing" the guests and cheering. Combine that with all the guests who, despite the clouds, are committed to their multi-colored bikinis and swim trunks, and the overall effect makes the upper deck look like a life-sized candy bowl. It's an odd hodgepodge of Caribbean, Polynesian, Hawaiian, and New Orleans that shows that First Mate Kevin either doesn't understand or doesn't care a bit about cultural correctness.

The frenetic sounds of steel drums pause as First Mate Kevin's voice crackles and whistles through the speaker. "We won't let a few clouds get in the way of our destiny," he chatters, his voice filled with double meaning. But for anyone who missed his pun, he hooks his fingers in the requisite air quotes. "And that destiny is, of course, *fun*! To get this funfest started, we've got a special treat in the form of a little intraschool rivalry we need to take care of. Would the Holland High Athenas and Style Marchers please grab your hoops and join me up on the stage!"

I glance over toward the ship's railing and give myself just a moment to imagine what it would feel like to fling myself into the sea. Huck clears his throat, nudging me with his shoulder.

"The executioner beckons," he says, stepping aside and gesturing for me to lead us to what I'm sure will be one of the most humiliating and miserable experiences of my life. Hula-hooping? In front of a crowd? Against the Athenas? God, the indignities just keep piling up. But I can fight only so many battles, so I fall in behind Ryan and Hillary, who have come out of the crowd to join the band in our death march toward the stage.

"Who in the what, now?" Hillary says over her shoulder.

"Just go with it," I reply. "Please." If this is what it's going to take to distract Mr. Curtis from our various shenanigans so far this week, then so be it. I'll hula, dammit. But screw the competition. Demi can have this one. I can't bring myself to care. I've got bigger competitions to worry about.

Hillary gives me a two-fingered salute and an "Aye, aye, Captain." When we get to the stage, there's a big wire bin full of multicolored hula hoops. I grab a purple one and climb up behind Hillary onto the risers that form the makeshift stage. The Athenas are falling into the mix too, and they look just about as happy about this forced fun as we do. It's a sea of scowls climbing onto the stage.

First Mate Kevin skips the stairs and leaps straight from the deck to the stage like some kind of coked-up gazelle. He lands, executes a wild spin, then faces the competitors.

"Band on my starboard side, Athenas take port!" he sing-songs into the mike, but when everyone just stands in a cluster blinking at him, he mouths "band" and points to his right. We all shuffle into place. I take a spot near the front, ever the leader, and ready my hula hoop on my hips, holding it out to the sides. I glance out at the crowd, an equal mix of whatever students aren't barfing their guts out and whatever oldsters have skipped their afternoon naps, those oversized eye-doctor sunglasses taking up practically their whole faces. I can see Mr. Curtis and Ms. Haddaway standing as close as they can without actually touching, matching grins on their faces as they watch education in action.

I scan the crowd once more, and just offstage I see a flash of buzzed strawberry-blond hair. Lenny is hanging away from the crowd on the starboard corner of the stage, his camera poised to capture every embarrassing moment for eternity. I feel a phantom twitch on my lower lip, the memory of the kiss flooding back. Without thinking, I raise my hand to my lips, sending one side of my hula hoop clattering to the deck. I look to see if Lenny noticed, but I can't see him, because a tall, broad-shouldered blond guy is blocking my view.

"Russ, what are you doing?" Demi snaps, asking the very question on the tip of my tongue.

"I'm with the band," he says, as if *duh*, and I don't have the energy or interest to get in the middle of the argument. Those two can have each other. Sooner rather than later would be ideal.

Demi shoots me a withering look and says, "You won't beat me. You never will."

And now I care about hula-hooping. I care very much. Any plans to let Demi take this one are gone. Because I'm a *great* hula-hooper. Demi's about to be very sorry she made us spend hours in her backyard practicing circus tricks. She may be a great juggler, but I kick *ass* at hula-hooping. I'm going to win this. And when I'm done with that, I'm going to wipe the floor with her and take home the $25,000 check at the end of the week. *This time* I'm *the winner, Demi.*

This contest is no longer some kind of miserable detention. Now I can't *wait* to start. I hold my hula hoop in my fingertips, balanced at my hips, ready for instructions. My waist feels itchy and twitchy, ready to get this show on the road.

"Okay, rules! When your hoop hits the floor, you hit the deck!" First Mate Kevin gestures a thumb toward the crowd. "I'll be calling out challenges to shake things up a little, as if there won't already be plenty of shimmying!" He pauses for laughter, but since he didn't give that instruction to everyone in front of him, the only response is the shuffling of feet and the sound of whipping wind from another far-off (but growing ever closer) storm. Ever the pro, First Mate Kevin gives an enthusiastic nod and charges on. "Okay, then. DJ, crank up those funky beats!"

At that, the silence is filled with a hip-hop-reggae remix from hell. "Hula!" he shouts into his mike like a dictator of fun, causing the speakers to shriek in protest. In a whirl of activity, multicolored hoops start to spin. Almost immediately, about a dozen band members and two Athenas are out. They were standing too close to one another, and when they started, their hoops bumped each other and bounced to the floor.

"Hit the deck!" Kevin calls, taking far too much glee in the failure of teenagers. But I guess when your job is to be an over-caffeinated camp counselor at sea, you take your kicks where you can get them.

The first song wraps up, leaving just a brief moment of silence before a more frenetic remix begins. I adjust the swirl of my hips to match the new beat, which basically allows me to completely zone out. I've got this. While I imagine myself to be anywhere else, the rest of the brass and half the percussion section lose their hoops, along with a fair number of the woodwinds. We may be able to march, but I clearly should have been handing out hula lessons at practice. Jared, who I know for a fact has excellent rhythm, is barely hanging on to his hula hoop with some kind of full-body spasm. It lasts about six more counts before he loses the hoop, and he looks genuinely disappointed. The Athenas, who are no strangers to coordinated hip shimmies, are faring much better. Three songs in and half the band is gone, but only two Athenas are out. I can't worry, though.

I plan to be the last woman standing, so whatever's going on around me doesn't matter. I keep swirling, the hoop spinning to the beat. It only takes one to win, and I plan on it being me.

As the fourth song cranks up, the crowd starts to look elsewhere. There's only so long you can watch a bunch of strangers hula-hooping, so Kevin takes the opportunity to "crank it up a notch." He instructs us all to spin in a circle *as* we hula, which fells about half the remaining band members and a third of the Athenas. When Kevin doesn't tell us to stop spinning, Huck gives up and lets his hoop clatter to the deck. He shrugs an apology, but I don't care. I'm still here, and I'm not going anywhere. I crank my swirling up to double time as a small act of defiance, my hoop whizzing at a dizzying speed.

When that song ends, First Mate Kevin halts the spinning and barks at everyone to stand on one foot. I bend my leg slightly, just like we do on the field, to keep my knees from locking and maintain my balance. I'm still in rhythm, so I have no problem with it, but nearly all the rest of the band members are gone. In fact, as I glance around, I realize that only Russ and I are left standing, holding it down for the marching band. His hula-hooping isn't nearly as fast or coordinated as mine, and in fact he's having to execute a sort of full-body swirl, his upper half moving in one direction while his lower half moves in reverse, to keep his hoop going. His eyes are narrowed, sweat forming at his brow, as he gives the same focus to this as he does to calling plays. The quarterback is on deck, and I let myself forgive him, just for now, for hitting Lenny.

Things are getting tight on the Athenas' side as well. Missy's hoop falls almost immediately. I see Demi glare at her and mouth something in her direction that I can't make out. I don't have time to figure it out, because Evil First Mate Kevin has another instruction.

"Hop!" he says, his voice practically cracking with the enthusiasm.

Demi glares at Russ and me, and we glare back, all of us seeming to dare the other to go first.

"C'mon, kids, you heard me! Hop!"

And so we do, each of us bouncing just once. And surprisingly, all three hoops keep spinning.

"Keep hopping!" Kevin shouts, and the crowd is finally on his side. They're shouting and cheering, a few of them bouncing along with us as we continue to bob on the stage. When Demi realizes that the spotlight is on her, she flashes a wide smile at the crowd. Suddenly her determined shimmy takes on a more seductive swirl. She looks like she's not just competing, but performing. A whistle rises from the crowd, followed by another. Her grin grows wider, and that's when I see it. The hoop, which has been riding just above the strings of the cherry-red bikini poking out of her board shorts, is now riding a little bit lower. Demi realizes the slip just a moment too late to get it back, and the hoop falls.

She freezes, a look of abject horror crossing her face, her eyebrows knitted together in fury. On the band's side of the stage, Russ and I have realized we've won before First Mate Kevin can screech it to the crowd. We let our hoops fall, and the crowd, which now includes all of my fallen bandmates, starts cheering. But my eyes go immediately to Lenny. He's just off the side of the platform, clapping and cheering, his head bobbing in an *Oh yeah!* nod. Then he reaches for his camera, which is hanging around his neck, and raises it to snap a moment of victory. I grin right at the lens, imagining him looking at this picture later, and I'm so lost in the vision that I don't notice Russ rushing in from my left. I don't know if he's going for a hug or a chest bump, but either way I miss the cue entirely. I start to tumble backward, and Russ's strong arms encircle me, keeping me from bouncing off him and instead wrapping me up in another fiercely tight hug.

"Oof," I grunt, the air escaping from my lungs with a squeeze of his arms. I try to get my breath back, taking in the fresh and homey smell of his detergent and deodorant on the tissue-soft tank he's wearing.

"Winners!" First Mate Kevin yells, scurrying up the stage and grabbing Russ's and my hands and thrusting them over his head, *Rocky*-style. "And now it's time for your prizes!"

At the mention of prizes, I can't help but get excited. Maybe some kind of monetary prize? At this point, even fifty dollars would help get the band closer to keeping it together. I grin in anticipation as First Mate Kevin turns to one of the high-top café tables off to the side of the raised platform. It's not until the tiny plastic trophy is shoved into my hand that I realize just how wrong I was. The golden replica of the *Destiny* sits on top of a black plastic base, and a small plaque on the front reads DESTINY HULA HOOP CHAMPION!

I shake my head in confusion, blinking at the plastic trinket. Seriously, all that for *this*?

I look up at Russ, who doesn't seem to care one way or another about the trophy. Victory is victory, and that's one thing he's used to on our state champion football team. He throws his arm around my shoulder and hoists his tiny trophy like it's the Stanley Cup.

My eyes go to Demi, who looks furious. And then she leans over to the tall, tanned figure next to her, who is no longer chanting my name. She rises up on her tiptoes and whispers into Lenny's ear, her lips brushing his cheek as she pulls away. He studies Russ and me onstage with a confused look on his face, and when I glance back at Demi, she's snaking her arm through Lenny's and throwing me a venomous smirk. I pull myself away from Russ, but it's too late. They make their way through the crowd together.

The wind picks up and I have to shield my face from my out-of-control hair. The sky has gone from a dull gray to a menacing dark slate, with black clouds bruising the sky. It looks like it's going to open back up at any second, and before I can change my mind, I grab Russ and yank him offstage, through the crowd, and around a corner to a bench outside the sundeck. We're alone, except for a white-clad crew member who's taking down the surrounding umbrellas in preparation for the second round of storms the ship's captain is expecting. When he doesn't leave, I decide I don't care. I pull Russ down onto the bench next to me.

"You have got to stop this," I say, trying to mask the quaver in my voice. I'm angry, but I don't want him to know. I don't want him to ask any questions, I just want him to leave me alone.

"Stop what?" His face is a blank page. I can't tell if he's playing with me, or if he's genuinely oblivious. Either option infuriates me.

"The hugging. That's twice now, just in time for Demi to stare us down. I don't need to be pulled into your drama."

Russ glances out at the ocean, which is now so dark it looks like it's not even on the same planet as the crystal-blue water from the other day. He runs his hands through his wind-tossed blond hair. He squeezes his eyes tight, as if the view is too much. Then he opens them and turns to face me, his big blue eyes boring into mine with such force I nearly lean back. "I swear to God, Liza, I have no idea what you're talking about."

My resolve falters only for a moment. For the first time in my life, I charge on, saying the thing I know I'll want to say later, when I'm alone and regretful that I've rolled over.

"I know you still like Demi!" I say, the power of the truth fueling my fire. "And you're using me to make her jealous, so you can get her back."

Russ blinks once, twice, his eyes blank. Then his brows knit together, his nose wrinkling in total confusion. "What?"

"You still want Demi, and you're using me to get back at her. Just stop it. It's messing everything up and giving people the wrong impression."

He takes a step back, his head cocked to the side. "People like Lenny?"

At the mention of his name I feel a catch in my throat. I don't even want to imagine the damage Russ could do if he knew Lenny liked me. "Just stop using me," I say, my tone final. I want to end this conversation. Now.

But Russ doesn't take the hint. He shakes his head, studying me like I'm a mental patient. "You think *I'm* using *you*?" The words hit me like a glass of ice-cold water tossed at my face. I jerk back, blinking at him, and something flashes across his face that I can't read. His face softens, but his words don't.

"Open your eyes, Liza," he says.

"Shut your mouth, Russ," I reply. I stand up and brush past

him with my shoulder, but he barely moves. He's practically a stone wall of muscle and frustration. I ignore the feeling of his rock-solid chest and go straight to the ship's railing. I lean over and look down, past the lifeboat waiting on the side of the ship, straight down to the swirling gray water below. Behind me, I hear him pivot, but he doesn't come near.

"I can't believe this," he says. "Seriously, I can't believe it."

I turn to see him shaking his head at me, a look of something—Disgust? Anger?—across his tanned cheeks. I can't tell what it is, but it infuriates me. He's acting as if the idea that Lenny could like me is about as normal as me growing wings and flying back to Nassau, which really hurts. I didn't think we were friends or anything, but I definitely didn't think he thought so low of me.

I watch the dark clouds race across the sky with the whipping wind in what would be a really impressive photo. And that's when I remind myself that Russ is wrong. It's not crazy to think that Lenny likes me. Because he does. I knew it when I was twelve and he kissed me behind the curtain, and I knew it when I listened to him talk about his photography and sat on the beach looking at pictures. We have a connection that's based on something other than popularity and hotness, which is something Russ could *never* understand.

"Just stay away from me," I reply.

Now it's Russ's turn to look like he's been slapped. His eyes widen, and then his face goes blank. "Whatever," he says, throwing his hands in the air. "I give up."

Russ turns and walks away, his usual lazy gait gone. His shoulders are tense, and I see the muscles of his arms flexing.

I look back down at the water, where whitecaps are forming

on the ever-darkening waves. Suddenly my stomach is rolling again. I turn and bolt in the opposite direction, taking the long way through the ship back to my cabin.

When I get back to my room, I rip off my two seasickness patches, leaving angry red welts that match the feelings coursing through me. I slap on two new patches and swallow a Dramamine for good measure. And because my head is now pounding at the base of my skull as if it's about to rocket right off my shoulders, I take the Tylenol bottle out of Hillary's bag and wash two down with the remainder of the flat ginger ale on my bedside table.

When I go to fluff up my pillow, my eyes fall on the little golden mike trophy Huck stole from Demi. I totally forgot about it, and now I get a moment of sick satisfaction imagining all the ways Demi is going to freak out when she finds it's missing. But that only leads to dread over what she's going to do to me when she finds out I have it. Crap. I've got to get it back before she realizes it's gone.

CHAPTER 14

When I planned this cruise, I had lots of ideas about how it would go. I'd hoped we'd win the twenty-five grand to save the band, first of all. After that, we'd stuff ourselves silly off the buffets scattered around the ship. Huck and Hillary and I would hang out on deck, making one another laugh until our sides hurt. Maybe I'd even get a sunburn. I guess I knew it wouldn't really be that easy, but I never imagined it would be this hard.

Because breaking into Demi's cabin to return her stupid lucky mike that Huck stole? Yeah, that was not on the list.

I've tucked the mike into my purple satchel, ready to return it without anyone noticing I ever had it. I make my way up to the luxury suites. At her room, I try the door, but in a totally not shocking turn of events, it's locked. I don't know what I was expecting. Why did I think I could pull this off? I should have brought Huck. This is stupid.

No, what was stupid was Huck stealing the mike. Of course, I'm the one who turned him loose in the first place when I sent him to take care of Mr. Curtis. Another plan that seems to have backfired.

I hear a squeaking followed by a shuffling and, not wanting to be caught standing outside Demi's door, I turn and bolt down the hall just as the maid rounds the corner with her wheeled cart, overflowing with fluffy white towels and bins of tiny shampoos, soaps, and foil-wrapped chocolates.

I stop just around the corner and lean against the wall so I can work to quietly catch my breath, willing my heart to slow down to a dull thud. I peek back around the corner to see the maid stretching the key card attached to her belt to unlock the door to the cabin next to Demi's. She takes a fat stack of towels off the top of the cart along with a handful of chocolates, then shoulders her way through the door. This couldn't be more perfect. Demi's room will be next.

I crouch there, my ear in the direction of her room so I can know just when to strike. Only now it's not the squeaky wheel of a maid's cart that gets my attention—there's a scurrying and a panting coming from somewhere near my feet. I glance down and see a little dog, about the size of a small cat, with long white hair fluffed up and sculpted in a way that tells me its owner spends more time on its hair than I do on my own. A small tuft of fur rises off the top of its head, held in place by a red ribbon with a heart-shaped rhinestone in the middle.

As soon as it sees me, it sits up, grinning at me with a crooked underbite.

"Shoo!" I whisper at little Fido, waving my hands over its head. "Go on!"

But the command doesn't do anything other than make the dog cock its head at me and start to whine.

"Hush!" I say, my whisper growing more frantic. "Go on!" I lean over and wave a little closer.

"Miss Gloria!" A thick, gravelly voice echoes down the hall, and the dog hops back up onto all four legs. It spins around in little hopping circles. "Miss Gloria, come now!"

It takes me a moment to place the voice, but a peek around the corner at the greasy-haired, ample-bellied cruise director confirms it. Mr. Ferengetti is leaning against the wall, a phone pressed to his ear as he jangles Miss Gloria's leash in his other hand.

I fling myself back around the corner and out of sight, my eye on the dog to make sure she won't smoke me out.

"Yeah, it's that shoddy maintenance schedule," Mr. Ferengetti mumbles into his phone. "I *told* them they needed to be doing more frequent inspections, but what do I know? I've only spent my entire adult life on these damn boats."

There's a pause, and I lean closer to the corner just out of sight, trying to home in on the conversation.

"Yeah . . . yep . . . of course . . . it's about taken care of, should be no problem. We'll be back to full power soon. . . . Uh-huh, bye."

I hear the jangle of the leash once more. "Miss Gloria, I said *come!*"

The dog gives me one last look that I swear says *You were lucky this time, missy*, then sprints off after her owner. The sound of her tinkling collar fades in the distance, replaced by the telltale squeaking and shuffling of housekeeping.

I reach into my satchel, which is stuffed with all the little last-minute necessities a drum major usually needs. There's a bottle of slide grease for the trombones, some pencils for marking music, a whistle, and some cough drops. And down at the bottom, fuzzy with lint, is a small roll of masking tape that we use to secure music to stands if the wind is high.

I tear off a three-inch piece of tape, sticking it to my index finger in preparation.

I peek around the corner just in time to see the maid swipe the lock on Demi's door with her key card. Propping the door with her foot, she turns to count out a tall stack of towels, then leans her shoulder into the door. As soon as she's through, I dart down the hall as fast as my legs will carry me. The plush carpet running down the middle of the hallways muffles my steps, and I have to hold my breath to keep from huffing and puffing.

I make it to the door just before it clicks closed. I place my hand on it to stop it, then pause to make sure the maid isn't right there. I peek through the crack and see the back of her uniform as she struggles to carry the stack of towels through the room, muttering to herself in a language I don't recognize. I probably have less than a minute before she finishes, at which point she'll come back into the hall and catch me red-handed, so I quickly pull the tape from my index finger and gently, quietly place it over the latching mechanism on the door. I stick it vertically, so once the door shuts, there will be no evidence that anything has kept it from locking as it should.

I run my finger over the tape once to ensure it's going to stick. I hear the water turn on in the bathroom, which means the maid is done depositing the towels and I may have only a few seconds. I place my hand flat on the outside of the door, letting it close with barely a sound. I give it a quick nudge, and sure enough, it gives behind me. The tape is working.

I hear footsteps coming, so I pivot on my heel and bolt back down the hall, passing my hiding spot and going all the way back to the elevator. No need for the maid to see me at all. I don't want to wind up in a lineup somewhere, a bright light in my face while she picks me out as the one who was around just before the room was broken into.

I stand by the mirrored elevator doors and count by tens to a thousand before I start making my way back to Demi's cabin. With my pounding heart and my full-body jitters, I'm afraid I look like I'm strolling through the hall with a live wire in my jeans.

With a quick peek to make sure no one's watching, I push through the door, letting it shut behind me.

I glance around, taking in how the other half lives when they travel VIP. The door opens into a small sitting room, which is the size of my entire room six floors below. Instead of that flat, industrial hotel carpet, this cabin has dark, shiny wood floors with a rug so fluffy and soft it looks more comfortable than my bed back home. The back wall is all windows and french doors that open up onto a balcony overlooking the ocean.

My cabin only hopes to be this cabin when it grows up.

There's an open door to the right, through which I can see a corner of fluffy white bedding. I tiptoe across the wood floors and back to the bedroom, which looks designed to give the illusion of a Cape Cod beach cottage. The whitewashed walls are accented by wainscoting and dark-stained trim, with glossy white beadboard on the ceiling. A sleek, silver nautical light fixture hangs from the center of the room, right above a bright white king-sized bed topped with a mountain of blue silk pillows. Dark end tables and a dresser match the trim, and a matching wooden deck chair sits out on the balcony.

I'm so busy admiring the room that I completely forget why I'm here in the first place. But when I hear the beep of a key card in the door, all the blood rushes to my head, leaving me frozen in place for a split second. Before the door swings open fully, I race over to Demi's open suitcase and shove the golden mike into the mesh pocket holding her underwear. Then, like a cartoon dog about to be caught stealing from the pantry, I dart mindlessly around the room. I hear Missy's voice getting closer to the bedroom; her high-pitched cackle is like a warning siren that screams *Hide!*

At the last second, I launch myself into the tiny closet in the corner, slide the door shut, and sink to the floor behind an oversized white terry-cloth robe, another item we don't have down in our cabin. I'm starting to think Demi was right when she said we were in steerage.

"I *so* did not pack for this weather," I hear Missy moan.

I hear someone rustling through a suitcase, and I pray that Demi doesn't notice that the mike has been moved . . . and that this is the last of Huck's stunts for this trip.

"Seriously. I can't believe this. I mean, what if we end up having to hang out in our cabin for the rest of the week?"

My butt sinks into the plush carpet that lines the closet floor, and I have to roll my eyes. Yeah, forced to hang out in a luxury stateroom with a flat-screen TV, Jacuzzi tub, and twenty-four-hour room service? What a hardship. *Hate that for you, Demi.*

"I think I'll wear *this*," Demi says, and from the tone of her voice and Missy's squeal, I'm guessing she's holding up Lenny's Brentwood High hoodie.

"God, he is so smokin'," Missy purrs. "But I thought you said he kissed Liza."

At the mention of my name, my breath catches in my throat and I have to struggle not to choke on it. I lean back into the wall and work on not moving a single muscle.

"I *said* Lenny was just trying to make me jealous," Demi snaps, her voice crackling with the same electricity as the lightning out over the ocean.

I feel a torrent of rage course up and down my spine. Once again, I have to sit here and listen while someone acts like it's totally unheard of for a guy to like me. First Russ, now Demi. If it weren't for the precarious position I'm in, crouching in Demi's closet, I'd burst out and give her the same what-for I gave Russ.

"I mean, come on. Why else would Lenny kiss Liza?" Demi continues. I ball my fists at the way she says my name, like a guy would have to be blind with a head injury to want to kiss me. "I know he's into me. It's like I told Russ when I dumped him. Life's too short for mediocrity."

I gag at the sound of the phrase, one that came straight from Demi's mom and was oft-repeated in her house.

"Why did you dump him again?" Missy's voice goes up into a squeak at the end, and I wonder if she wishes she'd kept that one to herself.

Demi pauses, and I lean closer to the door so I won't miss the answer. "It doesn't even matter," she replies quickly. "Because Lenny is *hot*."

I hear the door to the bathroom slide open. The water goes on full blast, and Demi's words are muffled by the spray of the sink. When the water shuts off, I hear Missy midsentence.

". . . *so* obvious Russ is jealous. He's like, totally drooling every time you walk by."

"Toootally." Demi drags out the word, her voice distant, probably coming from the sitting room. I lean into the crack of the closet door, but I can't hear anything else except the click of the TV as the channels flip.

I guess it's going to be a bit before I can make my escape. Luckily this carpet is *really* soft, and the robe makes a nice pillow. So I settle in and allow myself to zone out, a heavy fog settling over my eyes. Wait . . . why am I so tired?

And that's when I remember the Tylenol I swallowed right before this whole little mission. And the Dramamine. And the seasickness patches. Those don't make you drowsy, do they?

About one second later, I pass out.

CHAPTER 15

I wake up with a terrible pain in my neck and drool crusted down my chin. But that's not the most horrible thing facing me right now. No, that honor goes to an actual *face*. A tan one, perfectly smooth save for one freckle underneath a blue eye that's partially obscured by a lock of sandy-blond hair.

Russ's face.

I sit up with a start, nearly cracking my head on his chin. He leaps back in surprise, tumbling into the opposite wall of the closet, the other terry-cloth robe falling off the hanger and landing in a puddle on his head.

"Didn't I tell you to leave me alone? What are you doing here?" I yelp, then quickly cover my mouth with both hands, because the words sound weird coming out. Sort of thick and heavy, which is how my tongue feels right now. What is happening?

Russ yanks the robe off his head, leaving his hair standing

up from the static, which sends me into a giggle fit I can't control.

"Yup. Heard you loud and clear, boss," he says, adjusting his oversized frame to the tiny square of floor in the closet. "And I could ask you the same thing."

I have to stop and think, because the shock of the wake-up and the fog of whatever I took have sent the reason I'm sleeping on the floor of Demi's closet completely out of my mind. I have to close my eyes and block out Russ and the buzzing in my head before it comes back to me. It takes what feels like hours but is probably only a few seconds, but then I recall Huck holding the golden mike, that devious grin on his face.

"Ugh," I moan, and rub my eyes with the heels of my hands. My tongue sticks to the roof of my mouth, and I stumble to form any more words.

"Are you drunk?"

"I don't think that was Tylenol" is all I can mutter by way of explanation, but I trip over the word "Tylenol," and it comes out sounding like "Lylenylenol."

"Holy crap, you're *stoned*?" There's a look of total disbelief on Russ's face, his eyes wide as he chuckles to himself.

"*No!* Gooooo away," I say, but the word "go" hangs on for two counts too long, just like Russ's snare roll. In fact, it rolls around in my mouth until I'm sort of howling the word, and I break into another giggle fit.

Russ rolls his eyes and climbs to his feet, bumping his head on the overhead shelf in the closet. He stumbles back out into the bedroom. "I really don't get why your default setting for me is somewhere between suspicious and furious," he says.

"Because I don't trust you," I snap at him. I rise to my feet ready to get the hell out of here, but as soon as I'm up, I'm down again, my vision tunneling to black in an intense head rush. I collapse into a heap on the floor of the closet.

"Need a hand?" Russ asks.

"No, I do *not*," I say. Since standing didn't work out for me, I decide to give crawling an attempt. I rise to my hands and knees and slowly start to ease my way on into the bedroom. But I don't get far before I accidentally stick my hand into a high heel, which sends me tumbling down face-first onto a pile of laundry. When I sit up, there's something bright pink and covered with rhinestones wound around my arm, so I shake it hard to get it off. Whatever it is gets flung over my head. I turn to see Russ coming out of the closet with a heavily padded bra draped over the top of his head. He reaches up and pulls it off, dropping it to the floor, and I dissolve into a hiccuping case of giggles from which I fear I will not recover.

But as my giggles finally wind down to little gasps, I realize that I really can't stand up. And crawling through the ship back to my room isn't going to be an option. In fact, the only option may be standing in front of me, a blood red blush spread across his cheeks as he tries not to look at the rhinestone-adorned bra that was very recently on his face.

"Um, do you think you could maybe—*hiccup*—help me?" I ask.

Russ rolls his eyes and shakes his head, but he steps forward and offers me a hand, which I take. With a surprising amount of muscle, he drags me effortlessly to my feet.

"Ooh!" I groan, dancing from foot to foot, giving my legs a series of hokey-pokey-style shakes. "Pins and needles!"

"Smooth," he says, unable to suppress a smile.

I mean to tell him to shut up, but I only get as far as "shut" before I sort of lose my train of thought. "Why you here?" I mumble.

"I came to get back my sweatshirt that Demi's been holding hostage since the breakup. Demi wasn't here, but I found this in the door." He holds up a balled-up piece of masking tape between his thumb and forefinger. He arches an eyebrow at me, as if to say *you wouldn't know anything about this, would you?*

A crack of lightning illuminates the dim room, and an epic rumble of thunder follows closely behind it. Through the window, I can see that the sky is covered with a thick coating of heavy gray clouds and the ocean is nearly black, save for the cresting whitecaps. The wind roars, and I feel the boat pitch slightly. Between the sleep still holding me in its clutches and the pins and needles that haven't left my legs, I start to collapse. Russ takes one giant step toward me and catches me before I can land hard on my knees.

He moves to my side, throwing my arm around his shoulder and securing me with one strong arm around my waist. His hand rests right on my hipbone, holding it firmly like a handle, and I'm surprised at how small and delicate he makes me feel.

When he squeezes my hip, I stiffen and try to walk ahead of him, but he tightens his grip around my waist, his other hand reaching up to hold mine around his neck.

"Liza, just relax. Let me help you," he says. I want to hip-check him into the wall and run away, but the fuzz in my brain is spreading to my legs, so I sink into his side, letting my steps fall in with his. "See? Just like that. Not too bad."

"Lots of marching practice," I reply, my eyes drifting closed as I lean into him.

We make our way through the suite and to the front door. Russ lets go of my hand and pulls the door open, giving a quick glance down either end of the hallway. Then he props the door with his foot and grasps my hand again.

"Ready?"

"Yup," I reply, but it comes out as more of a hum.

I lean back into Russ as we start down the hall, focusing half on my breathing, and half on my steps. My legs are starting to wake up again, but they're still not ready to deal with what high winds and rolling seas are doing to my balance.

We get about thirty feet when I hear chattering coming down the hall. A short, elderly couple wearing matching souvenir sombreros turns the corner and comes toward us. As soon as they pass us, I reach up and pluck the sombrero off the woman's head and plop it atop my own.

"Cool hat!" I giggle, gazing up at Russ from beneath the brim. I hear a gasp behind me, and Russ looks horrified. He takes the hat off my head and leans me against the wall.

"Wait here," he says, and I roll my eyes as he turns to chase the couple down the hall and return the hat. But I don't need Russ. No way, I don't need him at all. I need a lot of things right now, but Russ is *definitely* not one of them.

So I push off the wall to make my way, but my legs aren't quite ready to move without assistance. I throw my arm back at the wall to hold myself up, then start moving slowly, one foot in front of the other. I'm going, dammit. Away.

And then my foot crashes into something on the floor. I look down to see a room service tray in the hall. One plate has some strawberry tops on it and a dried river of syrup, along with a stack of forks and knives and various crumbs. But the other has half a belgian waffle. Totally untouched, unless you count the missing half, and that's when I realize that between the nausea and the hula-hooping and the felonies, I haven't eaten. And I'm *starving*.

I drop down to my knees and reach for the waffle, my mouth watering as I imagine the crisp vanilla bite I'm about to take.

"Stop!" Russ's voice booms down the hallway, his steps thundering toward me. He grabs me by the elbow and jerks me to my feet. His face is a mask of horror as he glances from me to the discarded plates. "What are you *doing*?"

"I'm hungry," I whine, giving a little stomp of my foot.

"Okay, well, how about we get you some food that hasn't been, you know, *eaten*," he says, barely containing the disgust in his voice.

"Hey, don't look at me like that," I say, the words tripping out of my mouth. "I know you drank an entire cup of queso dip when you joined the football team."

"Yeah, but no one else had had their fingers in it before I did that," Russ says, chuckling at the memory of the fairly mild hazing the football players inflict on one another. "Where's your room?"

The question comes at me like a quadratic equation, and I'm no good at math. I squint at the ceiling, and start calling out all the numbers I can think of. "Six . . . three . . . two . . . second floor . . . eleven . . ."

A giggle echoes down the hall, and a deep voice follows it. "That sundae bar was really quite impressive. I don't know how you're walking after chocolate, caramel, *and* strawberry sauce."

"Crap," Russ mutters, and the fuzz in my brain recedes slightly. Because I recognize that voice, and thanks to my unfortunate run-in down in his stateroom, I recognize the giggle too. It's Holland High's newest couple, Mr. Curtis and Ms. Haddaway.

"They can't ssseee meeee," I hiss, the tension in my voice scratching at my throat. Unfortunately, even a shot of adrenaline from the fear of confronting a teacher isn't enough to have me walking and talking normally. There's no way I'd get out of that interaction without some kind of punishment.

Russ readjusts his hand around my waist and pulls me close, this time a smile playing at the corner of his mouth. "Okay, detour time, then."

We make it to the elevator. When the doors slide open, Russ drags me in and lets me lean against the back wall. I try my best to avoid catching my reflection in the mirrors that make up the entire interior of the elevator box, but the only way to do that is to focus my attention on Russ's reflection instead. He's wearing a pair of khaki cargo shorts that look like they're as old as he is, or at least like they've been through the wash a thousand or so times. They're fraying at the bottom, and there's the beginning of a hole at the corner of each cargo pocket. There are also paint splatters in several different colors at various spots. A loose-fitting red tank top shows off his tan skin as well as the lines of his muscular shoulders and arms, and there's a pair of cheap drugstore sunglasses, black frames with neon-yellow arms, perched atop his head.

His reflection breaks into a grin when he catches me staring, and I quickly move my focus down to the floor, where I count the anchors in the carpet. I'm at forty-seven (or maybe ninety-seven, I lost track) when the elevator stops on our floor, the doors sliding open with a mechanical ding.

Russ scoots back to my side, and when we step out into the hallway, I'm attached to his hip again, his arm holding me upright and close to him. But we're not on my floor. We're back on the upper deck, where the wind is so high that the place is empty. The clouds have dissipated, leaving a scattering of bright, twinkling stars across the inky-black sky. They're so bright and so big I feel like I could reach out and pull one out of the sky, and the sight makes me gasp.

"Liza, are you okay?"

"Wow" is all I can say, a word whispered into the night that disappears on the wind.

Russ leads me toward the edge of the deck, where a slight overhang from some piece of equipment shields us from the wind. There's a pair of wooden lounge chairs with plush blue cushions tied to them, and Russ carefully deposits me on one.

"What are we doing here?" I mutter, sinking back into what might just be the most comfortable chair I've ever sat in. Russ disappears for a moment, but when he returns, he sets up a bright yellow Wet Paint sign right at the corner where someone might wander around, hopefully ensuring our privacy.

Russ settles into the chair next to me, legs crossed at the ankles, his arms folded behind his head. I turn over onto my side, my hands folded under my cheek, and stare at him.

"Liza, you look totally wasted," he says, turning to look at me. "I don't know what's going on, but you can't tell me your room number, and I can't let you be seen like this. You'll get in crazy trouble. So we're just going to hang out here until you're more . . . with it."

"Okay," I reply. The wind changes direction, and suddenly I can smell his fresh, spicy deodorant. I take a deep breath, then turn onto my back to stare at the stars. "What's this place?"

"It's the Starlight Deck," he says. He gestures up at the palette of light above us. "Appropriate, huh?"

"Yeah," I say as I try to pick out a constellation. Even in an unimpaired state, it would be futile. I've never been able to tell one star from the other. They look as random as a toddler's sketches to me, and that's just fine. I know enough about astronomy to know that even though it all *looks* random up there, there's meaning and order to it. As I lie here, my brain feeling like it's rubbing against my skull with the current of the ocean, the thought comforts me. Those stars came together for a reason. They *like* each other. You know, like relationships. Two stars find each other because together they make something great, like the Big Dipper or whatever. And that's not *random*. It's because they both like sports or art or music. Or *Stuart Little*.

"Uh, okay," Russ says, his voice halting.

And that's when I realize that all that star stuff? Yeah, I said that out loud. So much for feeling more with it. I'm going to be sitting here for a while.

I shut my mouth and try to stay completely still, like maybe if I don't move he'll forget I said that stuff. Or I'll disappear entirely.

We lie there in silence, both taking in our own corner of the sky. From this high up on the ship, everything else seems very far away, and then, suddenly, very, very close. Too close.

Thoughts of the band and Lenny and Demi creep into my brain, and I don't want them there. Not now.

"Say something," I say, opening an eye a crack. I want a distraction, and Russ is the only one here who can give me one.

"About what?" He brushes a lock of hair that keeps blowing down onto his face out of his eyes.

"Whatever. Anything." It must be the drugs, because I open my mouth and hear myself asking, "What's the deal with you and Demi?"

"What do you mean?" he asks, but I can't respond. I'm suddenly overcome with something like drowsiness. "Uh, well, we dated for a while. It was fun, I guess," he says, pausing. I can feel him watching me, but I just stare at the sky. "I mean, she asked me out and I said yes because she's really cute, you know? And when she sings, she's amazing. Full of energy and light."

I nod. Even having seen her at her worst, I can't deny that Demi's a magnetic performer. It makes you forget everything nasty she's ever said. It makes you forget it's *her* up there. Whatever she's singing pours out of her and envelops her, until the song *is* her.

"And it was cool, you know, being a couple. Having someone to go to dances with or have around for holidays or whatever. But then I started noticing something weird. It was like I was her costar. She wanted to dress me. And she kept pointing out pictures of celebrities and telling me to get their haircuts. She actually made me an appointment at a salon and drove me there one night when we were supposed to be going to a movie. Can you believe that?"

Even through my drug-induced haze, I absolutely can.

That sounds exactly like Demi, and I snort at the image of her trying to kamikaze a haircut for Russ.

"First it was homecoming king and queen. And then it was all about getting nominated for prom court. And then she told me she wanted to campaign for the Mr. and Miss Holland High title. It's a stupid superlative in the yearbook! I mean, who even cares?"

"So then why did she dump you?" I ask, feeling my equilibrium start to return.

He's quiet, just staring at the sky, for a long moment. Then he takes a deep breath. "She didn't dump me," he says, his voice gravelly. "I broke up with her."

All of a sudden I'm as steady as a high-speed train. I sit up on my elbows, turning toward his chair.

"Wait, what?"

Russ sighs. "She was *really* pissed. Then she made me promise I wouldn't tell anyone that it was my choice."

"You agreed to that?" I ask, my face surely a picture of incredulity. "You let her tell everyone that *she* dumped *you*?"

Russ sits up and meets my eyes, his face soft and sympathetic. "I don't care what people think. I just didn't want to be with her anymore, so I let her have that one."

I gulp, turning his words over in my head. Suddenly I can see him sitting in the hot tub, shrugging as Demi declared that she broke up with him. And he just let her, because really, what *does* it matter? It doesn't. Not at all.

And as soon as the thought comes to me, I realize that while my brain is starting to clear, my exhaustion remains. I can barely keep my eyes open, and I settle back down on the chair, my eyelids heavy.

"When you remember your room number, just let me know," Russ says through a yawn, which spurs one in me. I reach up to the sky in a stretch.

"Yup, uh-huh," I reply, then let out the breath of the yawn. My eyes droop, but the image of the stars remains, and stays there until I drift off to sleep.

CHAPTER 16

The sound of waves lapping at the side of the ship six stories down, quiet and rhythmic, rouses me from a deep sleep. My eyes feel crusty, and I rub at them with my fists before finally cracking them open to see wide, bright beams of sunlight rising over the sparkling blue ocean. I take a deep breath and fill my lungs with warm, salty air, unable to contain the smile that's breaking across my face.

Sunrise . . . wait, sunrise?

I bolt up from the deck chair that served as my bed, bits and pieces of the previous night seeping into my brain with the rising sun. I was in Demi's closet. And I took something that was definitely *not* Tylenol.

And then I turn my head slowly to my left, holding my breath so I'm careful not to make a noise. And yup, there's Russ, one arm flung over his face, his chest rising and falling in a deep, slow rhythm. The longer I stare at him, the more comes back to me. He found me, completely impaired, in Demi's closet. He helped me get out of there . . . and something with a belgian waffle?

Next to me, Russ gives a sort of sniffle snort and rolls over onto his side, facing away from me. This is my chance.

I stand up from the chair slowly, making sure nothing creaks or squeaks, then tiptoe church mouse–like toward the door. With one final glance over my shoulder, my gaze going to the sliver of tan skin showing between his tank top and his khaki shorts, I push through the door.

I'll thank Russ later, when my mouth doesn't feel like I've been gargling moldy ocean water all night. I reach up to my hair to find it sort of knotted up on one side of the back of my head, and my reflection in the elevator doors confirms that I look as bad as the inside of my mouth tastes.

As the elevator glides down toward my floor, I lean my forehead against the cool glass wall, taking deep breaths to try to keep my body from staging a rebellion. If this is what a hangover is like, I don't know why anyone drinks. Ever.

Nothing—and I mean *nothing*—has gone right on this trip. Spilling my guts to Russ and falling asleep on the deck is just another symptom of whatever misery has overtaken my life this week. I can only be thankful that I didn't do or say anything totally stupid last night, and that nobody saw us. At least I got out of there in one piece, my embarrassment confined to Russ and that deck chair. And if what he said about the reason for his breakup with Demi is true, then he has no interest in being the center of attention.

It's entirely possible that I had Russ all wrong. And I don't know how to make sense of that in my still-hazy brain.

When I get to my room, I find the door propped and see Hillary on her bed, a multicolored gypsy skirt gathered around her knees as she paints her toenails a deep hunter green.

"Hey there, party girl, do I want to know where you were last night?" Hillary asks, capping her polish and flashing me a crooked smile.

"No, you don't, which is good because I don't want to talk about it," I reply. I don't mention the fact that I'm not entirely clear on the facts myself, and not sure I want to be. The details may be just fine where they are, buried in a deep, dark corner of my brain. I pick up the Tylenol bottle from her bedside table and shake it. "What I *do* want to know is what's in here."

"Oh, those are like, over-the-counter sleeping pills," Hillary says. "I don't really have insomnia, but sometimes I have trouble falling asleep. Those make me drowsy enough that I can finally drift off."

I put the bottle back down on the table with enough force that I feel it in my hand. "So it was definitely a good idea that I took three of them last night."

"Good lord, were you comatose?"

"Not exactly," I say, though I have to admit that once I was on that deck chair staring up at the sky, I did end up sleeping like a baby.

I quickly change out of yesterday's cutoffs and into a fresh pair, with a clean tank top and my marching band zip hoodie over it, then gather my hair into a high ponytail. When I look in the mirror, there are no dark circles under my eyes, and just a little red in my otherwise tanned cheeks. My life may be in shambles, but at least I look well rested. I rub on a smear of my favorite cherry-vanilla lip gloss, then follow Hillary to the upper deck for breakfast.

She moves to the nearest table, which appears to be the cold-breakfast area. The table is topped with heaping bowls of strawberries, pineapple chunks, fat red grapes, shiny apple wedges, and perfectly rounded melon balls. There's a massive crystal bowl of what looks like freshly made whipped cream and a small bowl of powdered sugar. By the time I get to the end, I have an entire fruit salad on my plate, topped by a dollop of whipped cream.

"Dude, save room. There's two more tables, and the french toast is a dream," Hillary says, nudging me in the ribs with her fork.

"This is all you can eat, right?" I reply with a wink. "Multiple trips, lady!"

"Ah, a professional," Hillary says. "I like how you think."

I gulp—behind her is Lenny. His strawberry-blond hair catches the morning sunlight pouring through the floor-to-ceiling windows and he's got a pair of sunglasses on, so I can't tell if he sees me or not. But the way he spins back toward the buffet when his gaze passes over me tells me that he's avoiding me. Whatever was there is gone, because I've managed to ruin it. Awesome. As if this day couldn't get worse. And it has barely started.

I hear a whisper coming from behind me, and I turn to see Brianna and Maya, two freshman Athenas, quickly direct their eyes from me to their plates, which are empty, save for a few apple slices and a handful of grapes. Brianna purses her lips to suppress a grin, and Maya drags her to the Athenas' table in the corner.

"What was that about?" I ask, my plate suddenly feeling way too heavy.

"Who knows," Hillary replies, barely paying attention to them. "They're probably just starving."

Something doesn't feel right, and the flutter in my stomach doesn't let me drop it. As I pass their table, I hear a harmonized series of giggles all suppressed behind perfectly manicured hands. My stomach has gone from fluttering to full-on somersaults. I scan the heads for Demi, but I don't spot her. I only see Missy at the end of the table, her eyebrows rising up to her hairline while her cherry-red lips form an O.

Something is up.

Hillary pokes me in the back with her fork again, and I realize I've slowed to a crawl as I try to listen in for an indication of what has the Athenas all aflutter. I double my pace to pass them and drop down in the first chair I see at the end of the band table. Hillary takes the seat across from me. Clarice and Andrew are next to me, their heads turned to each other, bowed over something in Andrew's hand. As soon as I sit, their attention whips to me, and whatever Andrew is holding disappears into his pocket. I see a flush of scarlet creeping up the back of his neck and winding its way around his ears. He can barely make eye contact with me.

Something is *definitely* going on.

Suddenly the entire table rattles as Huck flings his lanky body into the empty seat next to mine. "What is *up*?" he says. A butter knife skitters off Clarice's plate and lands on the wood floor beneath the table.

"Nothing," I reply. I try to spear a grape with my fork, but I miss and the grape shoots across the table into Hillary's lap.

She picks it up and flicks it back at me, but I just watch it whiz past my cheek.

Huck looks over at Andrew and Clarice, who are trying to pretend they're focused on their waffles and not on the conversation we're not having.

"Eyes on your own paper," Huck snaps, and they quickly slide their plates down three seats, still not making eye contact with me. "Okay, now for real. What happened last night?"

"What are you talking about?" I ask, but my voice cracks and croaks.

"Liza, knock it off. Everyone's seen the picture."

Picture?

All the blood rushes from my head, leaving my cheeks feeling icy cold. The pineapple in my stomach feels like it's made of lead. Or possibly a living creature that's now trying to crawl its way back up. I barely remember the events of last night, but what I do remember tells me that if there's a picture, it's of something embarrassing. Like maybe me eating off a discarded room service tray? Or me looking totally wasted hanging off Russ?

The memory alone turns my stomach.

Huck takes one look at me, and the playful grin melts from his face, replaced by a sort of wide-eyed seriousness. "So there's good news and bad news." He reaches into his pocket and pulls out his phone, with a large spiderweb of a crack spreading across the screen. He taps a few buttons, and the screen fills with a picture. At first glance, I breathe a sigh of relief. The picture shows an expansive, inky-black sky lit by an incredible half-moon that's hanging low over the glittering ocean. It's a pretty impressive picture to have been taken with a phone.

"Uh, okay, so is this the good news or the bad—" And that's when I see it. In the corner of the picture, just barely in the frame, is a sleeping form, cuddled up in a fetal position, brown hair spread out in a cascade of curls on the blue lounge cushion. The glowing moon casts a beam of light over the face, making it crystal clear, even if it's not the focus of the photo. And draped on the end of the deck chair is a blue-and-black Holland High sweatshirt, one sleeve extended so the viewer can read what's printed down the length of it: QUARTERBACK.

And the person sleeping peacefully, a slight grin playing at the corner of her mouth?

It's me.

The room starts to tilt to the left, and I have to place both my palms flat on the white tablecloth to keep from falling right out of my chair. Heat rushes to my cheeks, and I press my cool hands against them to block the rising blush.

"Please tell me that was the bad news," I whisper, "and there isn't anything worse."

"Well, that was bad. But not *that* bad. I mean, you're not naked or anything. You weren't naked, right?"

"Huck!" I say, and he nods.

"Of course not. So see? It could be way worse."

"How did you get that?"

"Uh, well, I guess that's the bad part. Now that we're close to Nassau, we've got cell service again, so the picture is . . ." He trails off, giving his phone a spin on the tabletop.

"Everyone got it?" My voice is coming in breathy gasps, and I can feel Andrew and Clarice staring at me, even from three seats away.

"Not exactly," Huck says. He clicks the screen, so the

picture disappears and is replaced by his home screen, a picture from freshman year of Huck and me dressed as Harry and Hermione. "One of the Athenas, probably Missy, texted it and it went viral."

I glance back around the dining room, where it suddenly feels like everyone I know is bent over screens and sliding phones across tablecloths. Even up in the buffet line, Jared is balancing a plate of bacon and eggs on one hand while scrolling through his phone with the other.

So that's why Lenny is trying to avoid me.

Of course he thinks I'm with Russ. Russ has done everything but fly a banner over the ship that says BACK OFF, LENNY! From his high fives and tackle hugs to the picture, it could make *me* think we're dating, when it's the last thing I'd want to do. But Lenny doesn't know that. And what's worse, he's got Demi in his ear telling him it's all true.

I take a deep breath, because unlike the photo going public, this is one problem I *can* solve. And I can solve it right now. I start to rise from my chair, but Huck throws his arm around my shoulder to keep me from bolting.

"The good news! You need the good news," he says. "While you were snoozing on the Starlight Deck, I talked my way into the crew's nightly poker game. Apparently the Sail Away Cruise Line has been a bit negligent when it comes to inspections and repairs. A jerry-rigged engine repair blew, requiring a visit from a repair boat with replacement parts. The engine is powering back up as we speak, which means full power should be restored by nightfall.

"And that's not even the best part," Huck goes on, his devious grin back. "I found out that more than half the ship's security cameras are fakes! Just for show, to make people *feel* safe. They're not even plugged in. The only ones that work are up near the luxury cabins and around the ship's railings. I guess so they'll know who to arrest if anyone gets thrown overboard."

I hear the words, but they don't mean anything to me. The security cameras are fake? Okay. How about the fact that thanks to a series of random and weird events that could only happen to me, it looks like I'm dating the star of the football team. Because *that* would happen. Seriously, Huck, security cameras?

When I don't respond, he spells it out for me. "Which means *if* the bowling ball did cause the engine problem, there's no way for them to know it came from us! We're free and clear, *and* we can get away with whatever we want!"

I nod, relaxing for a bit. "That's great, Huck," I say. "Good work." And then I steel my shoulders. I have to do it. I have to tell Lenny that Russ and I are in no way an item. It's going to be awkward and weird, but maybe then, he will stop avoiding me.

"Are you still thinking about the picture?" Huck asks, searching my face for signs of panic.

"Yeah, but it's going to be fine," I reply, my voice full of steely resolve. I see Huck cock an eyebrow at me, not expecting strength in the face of this moment. I rise from the table. Maybe I can get Lenny to sit with me, have a bite, and I can straighten this all out.

"I have to go," I say. I snatch my plate off the table and head toward Lenny's table. I keep my head down to avoid answering any questions and scurry off as fast as I can without looking like I'm making a run for it. With my head down, I won't see the sideways glances or the giggling, or the picture plastered on phone screens in cupped palms or hidden under tables.

Lenny's at a table by himself near a window, a beam of sunlight turning his strawberry-blond hair a rich coppery color.

As I walk up, I'm beset with a sudden urge to turn tail and run far away, but looking at his camera on the table, the old tapestry-style strap in a tangle next to his fork, I know what I have to do. If I stand any chance with Lenny, I have to make sure he knows I'm not with Russ.

"Um, hey, Lenny," I say, then clear my voice so it's not so rattling. "Can I talk to you for a second?"

He glances up at me, head cocked to one side, and I can see his gray eyes giving me the once-over. With one hand in my pocket, I cross my fingers and run a silent *please oh please* through my head.

"Yeah, no problem," he says, an easy smile spreading across his face that makes the tension dissolve out of me like air rushing from a balloon. "But do you mind if we do it later? I'm supposed to meet up with my dad."

"Oh yeah, totally, of course. Later is great. I'll talk to you later," I say, then bite my tongue to keep my nervous babbling from taking off in earnest. I give him a bright smile and step aside as he stands and winds his camera around his neck.

As I watch him disappear into the hall, I hope that it's a good sign, and that later I'll still have the guts to say what I need to say.

CHAPTER 17

With Lenny queued up for later, the next item on my list of things to make my life not so disastrous is to get Nicole back in the band. Our progress the other night was great, but I know once she's back, we really have a shot at that $25,000. Rachel, our second-chair flute player, is good, but she just doesn't have Nicole's expressive phrasing or her impressive vibrato. And those fine details are what we need to really impress the judges.

The Island Oasis spa boasts facials, mani-pedis, hot stone massages, mud baths, and pretty much every other bizarro treatment designed to help your skin glow and your Zen release. Between the stone water feature in the corner of the lobby, the copious potted palms, and the semi-soothing sound track of birds and crickets piping through a set of invisible speakers, I feel like I'm in a tropical rain forest when I enter looking for Nicole, who, as far as I've heard, has been basically living here.

I'm sure there are some people who must find this place sooth-ing, but I'm not one of them.

"Can I help you, ma'am?" a smiling attendant asks from behind the bamboo counter.

"I have a friend in there. Can I just look—"

The attendant, still smiling, shakes her head. "No entry be-yond this point unless you are here for a treatment."

I was hoping Nicole would just be sort of, I don't know, hanging out in the lobby, but no dice. It looks like I'm going to have to do some undercover work if I'm going to find her. I realize this is exactly what Huck was probably planning anyway when he suggested I go look for Nicole at the spa. He was hop-ing I'd "chill out" for a bit. Hoping the spa would do me some good. And you know what? Maybe he's right.

"I'd like a massage, please," I say, figuring if I have to, I'll just go with whatever is lowest impact. Maybe they have those ones where you sit up in the chair like at the mall. I could prob-ably deal with that. It'll give me a little more time to figure out what I'm going to say to Nicole, anyway.

Down the hall over the attendant's shoulder, I spot Nicole. She strides out of a frosted-glass door just off the lobby, clad in a fluffy white terry-cloth robe and those flimsy spa sandals on her feet.

"Nicole!" I say. I let my eyes gaze over her, from her newly highlighted hair to her tanned skin to the way she stands at full attention, tall with her shoulders back. For as long as I've known her, Nicole has carried herself low, curling her shoul-ders, rolling her back, and dropping her head, as if she's con-stantly running through a rainstorm and trying not to get wet. It takes her from five feet tall to practically garden gnome–sized.

But now, with her shoulders back and her chin up, she looks like she's grown a foot. Despite her diminutive stature, it looks like she's ready to strut the catwalk in Milan or stroll down the Champs-Élysées on a sunny spring day. I call her name again, but she either doesn't hear me or doesn't want to, because in a flash, she disappears through another door.

The attendant smiles and hands me an appointment card, then gestures for me to follow her. I stuff it into my back pocket and follow her down a pristine white hallway with soft glass lighting and the sound of gently rushing water coming from hidden speakers. She leads me into a small room with a massage table in the middle. Panels of silk hang from the walls, and lush potted plants peek out from every corner. She shows me where to put my clothes, then hands me a towel so fluffy it feels like it should have a marshmallow center.

"Just undress, drape yourself with the towel, and hop up on the table. The masseuse will be in in a moment with the menu."

The mention of a menu has my stomach growling. This morning's fiasco at breakfast kept me from the plate of waffles, and now all I can think about is food. Well, food, and the fact that my crush thinks I'm sleeping with someone else, and according to my friends, that someone else is the enemy. And pretty soon I'm going to have to tell him that's not happening, which is pretty much going to be me saying, *Uh, hi, Lenny. I'm not dating Russ. I'm telling you this because I like you. Do with that what you will. Ack.* Maybe I do need a massage. But the attendant is gone before I can ask what she means by "menu."

The door clicks shut quietly behind me, and I figure I

have only a few minutes before the masseuse comes in. The last thing I want is for her (or him!) to walk in while I'm half naked, so I set about undressing as if there's a million-dollar prize at the end. I shove my underwear into the pocket of my jeans, throw them on the wooden bench against the back wall, and then leap onto the table. I fling the towel around my front, tucking it under my butt so I don't feel quite so, well, *naked.*

But with the NASCAR pace at which I threw off my clothes, I'm left sitting naked on the table for what feels like forever. Of course there's no clock in a room meant for relaxation, but I can't help myself from counting off seconds. I shudder to think what this massage could be costing me, so instead I start passing the time figuring out how I can get this bill to go to Dad.

The door opens with a whispered whoosh of air, and my thoughts are put on pause by the masseuse, who looks like she travels with her own makeup artists and lighting director. The soft light bounces off her high cheekbones and full lips, and her ice-blond hair is in one of those twisty braids that looks as if it's effortlessly wound around her head, but that would take me thirty-six bobby pins, a can of hair spray, and three extra hands to achieve. A gold name tag pinned to her chest reads ILSA, a name as exotic as she is, and beneath it, in smaller type, BRUNNA, SWEDEN.

"'Allo," she says, her Nordic accent thick. "I am Ilsa. 'Ow are you?"

"Um, fine," I reply, wondering how long this small talk is going to continue. I kind of just want to zone out for a bit and then find Nicole, not trade meatball recipes with the Swedish goddess.

She flashes a grin that temporarily blinds me in the otherwise dim room. She walks over to a wooden stand and plucks a heavy piece of cardstock off the top. She hands it to me.

"Zis ees our manu," she says, and it takes me a moment to translate in my head. As soon as I see the listing on the page, I realize she means "menu." Each service is listed in a loopy bold script, and like a fancy restaurant, there are no prices anywhere to be found. Nor are there descriptions, only euphemistic titles like "Ultimate Bliss" and "Rejuvenated Relaxation."

I squint at the page as if maybe by looking a little harder, the thing will just talk to me.

"You 'ave question?"

I can feel the knot of tension beginning to retie itself inside me, so instead I shake my head and jab my finger at a title near the middle of the page. I get another dazzling smile from my masseuse, who directs me to lie facedown on the table (using gestures, thank God). I settle in as she adjusts the towel low on my back. Within minutes, I feel warm, firm hands working out the knots in my back.

Okay, *now* I get the spa thing.

Suddenly all sense of time or trouble is melting away like hot butter in a skillet as Ilsa digs the heels of her hands into my muscles. I take deep, cleansing breaths and focus on the sound of the water and the soft piano melody that seems to drift through the room like a fog. But my relaxation shatters as I realize the music is a piano version of a Copland piece we played in concert band last year. It was in our final spring concert, and we totally killed it. And Molly played a clarinet solo that totally *didn't* suck. I wonder if I could find the sheet music online somewhere and get it polished up tonight. I bet we could win with the Copland. I bet if I just run an extra practice or two . . .

"Turn over, please."

I open my eyes and stare through the hole in the massage table down to the spotless white canvas of Ilsa's sneakers. She wants me to do *what, now*? Please let that have been a misinterpretation due to her accent.

"Come now, turn over," she says, her words precise and clear for the first time since she entered the room. There's no mistaking it. And to avoid even a hint of any, she lifts the towel and gives my bare hip a nudge with the palm of her hand.

"Um, I don't think that's, uh, necessary?" I squeak, still firmly planted facedown on the table.

"You ordered full-body package. Ees time for you to turn over now."

Look, I'm not a prude.

Okay, I am a little bit. I just have no interest in showing all my business to a woman who looks like Anna Wintour custom-designed her in the *Vogue* offices. Why did I think this could possibly be a good idea? Why do I *ever* listen to any of Huck's suggestions?

"Could we maybe, um, skip—"

"Nonsense," she clucks. "Turn. I weel close my eyes if you are nervous. We keep towel, okay?"

I lift my head slightly and glance up at her to see that, true to her word, her eyes are closed. So quick as a flash, I flip over and jerk the towel back down over me, tucking it under my armpits and pinning it with my arms.

"Good?" I ask.

Ilsa opens one eye and peers down at me. She's a professional, so I can barely see the sigh she lets out.

"You need to relax, my dear," she says, but she doesn't push me further. She sets about massaging my arms, neck, and shoulders, and the Zen comes creeping slowly back. The massage continues for what feels like hours, but is probably only minutes. I may have even drifted off for a moment. I'm so concentrated on breathing in the warm air and letting it out in deep, cleansing breaths.

Before I know it, the massage is done. I open my eyes to prepare to climb off the table, but Ilsa is coming at me with what looks like a tongue depressor covered in chocolate pudding. I shrink back even though, plastered to the table, there's really nowhere to go.

"Ees mud mask. Part of service," she says, and before I can protest, I feel the warm goop splat on the side of my cheek. She plops a matching dollop on the other cheek, and one on my forehead, then begins smearing it across my face until I'm covered in a thick coating of mud. She takes a steamy warm towel and wraps it around my face with only a small opening for me to breathe out of. Then she covers my whole body with an airy white sheet, pulling it right under my chin. If I were claustrophobic, this would surely send me over the edge, as the weight of the mud and towel makes me feel like I've been sunk deep into the bayou.

"I leave you now. You relax," I hear Ilsa say, though her words are slightly muffled by the towel. I hear the door open, and the lights in the room dim by half. Then the door slides shut, and I'm alone.

The door opens, and even though I wasn't counting seconds, I'm surprised Ilsa is back so quickly. But then I hear a shuffle and a throat clearing that is decidedly *not* female. I tense, then realize that almost every inch of my skin is underneath a sheet and towel, and what's not is covered with about a quarter-inch of rock-solid mud.

"Listen, I'm sorry to barge in," I hear, and even though I can't see his gray eyes or strawberry-colored buzz cut, I can picture them along with the camera that's perpetually around his neck. *Lenny!* "Look," he goes on. "I feel like I've done everything totally wrong, and I just wanted to clear a few things up."

His voice sounds slightly edgy, yet still confident. I hear some shuffling that tells me he might be pacing in front of the door a bit. Whatever he's about to say, he's practiced, but is still nervous.

"I really acted like an ass the other night with that kiss. I'm sorry, I don't know what I was thinking. I should have just been honest and told you that I liked you. Instead I got nervous and was playing stupid games or whatever."

A sharp intake of breath shoots through my lungs. I try to move my mouth, but the mud has formed a hard crust around my lips. I want to reach up and help crack it, but the same towel that's covering my hands is covering my very naked bod.

"You're the one I like. It's *you*, okay? And I should have just said that right away."

There's a long pause where I realize he's waiting for me to say something, only I'm still incapacitated by mud. And even if I weren't, I'd have no idea what to say right now. But I hear some more shuffling, this time a quick foot-to-foot, and realize I'm leaving him hanging in the worst possible way. I have to let him know that it's okay. That I like him, too. That the kiss was fine. Great, even, but frankly I'd like another try at it. I try to make something like these words come out, but the only sound that escapes me is a soft groan as I try desperately to break the mud mask.

"Okay, well, uh, I know this is probably super weird, or whatever," Lenny says, and my heart practically stops. *Don't go!* "I'm going to let you think about it, I guess. Just find me if you want to, um . . . I don't know. If you like me too."

The last words come out all in a rush, and then I hear the door open and close again. There's no shuffling, no throat clearing, and no more heart-stopping romantic declarations. Lenny's gone.

Now that the room is empty, I'm not worried about flashing my rack to a few bonsai trees and a water feature. I sit straight up off the table, letting the sheet fall to my waist, and reach up for my face. The towel that Ilsa wrapped there is still warm, so I use it to break the mud mask and scrape off some of the larger chunks. Dark-brown dust and pieces of hard mud rain down into my lap, and I shudder to think of what's still on my face. I don't care, though. All I can think about is getting to Lenny as soon as possible before he decides to change his mind.

I reach for my pile of clothes and jerk my underwear out from the bottom, throwing one leg through, then the other. But both legs wind up in the same hole, and I go down like a prize-fighter, knocking a warm pot of yellow wax all over my clothes. I try to pull them out of the way, but it takes effort, as the wax begins to harden as soon as it leaves the pot, turning my clothes into a gross preserved specimen.

"Ugh," I groan, dropping the heavy pile back onto the

wood floor. With no sign of any fancy robes or souvenir T-shirts around the room, I have no choice but to take the towel draped over my lower half, wrap it around my body, and secure the little Velcro tab on the front. I give myself a quick glance in the mirror to make sure none of my, er, *bits* are trying to make an appearance, but the towel is doing a pretty good job. It covers more than my swimsuit, and as long as the Velcro holds, I should be fine.

I run out the door. My bare feet skid on the floor as I start down the hall, and I have to take short steps to keep my towel from flying open.

"Lenny!" I shout, finally getting back the power of speech. I shuffle past open doors of empty spa rooms, palm fronds pricking at my bare arms. "Lenny!" I call down one end of the hall, but it's empty. Then I turn in the other direction, nearly taking out a bamboo cart piled high with towels. A tall figure is turning the corner toward me.

"Lenny!" I shout again, but as the face rises to meet me, I see that it's not Lenny. This guy is taller and much more muscular, with an even, dark tan. I can see moisture glistening off skin that's stretched taut over rounded shoulders, tense biceps, and a rack of abs that looks like it stepped right out of a Calvin Klein ad.

Definitely not Lenny.

"Liza?" Russ asks, his hand going down to the towel knotted at his waist. His face is a puzzle of confusion, and I realize that I'm standing in the hall in a towel with untold amounts of dried dirt decorating my face.

Not my finest moment. Not that I care. Not about Russ, anyway. He's the reason I'm in this mess, him and that stupid picture. I straighten up, adjusting my shoulders back, and plaster a look of cool disinterest on my face.

"I was looking for Lenny," I say, practically daring him to say anything.

Russ draws back a half step and cocks his head at me, trying to read my tone. He stares at me for a moment, then nods over his shoulder. "He went that way," he says, his tone tentative. But I don't have time right now to explain to him all the ways he's screwed up my trip, so I just leave him to his confusion. Serves him right after all.

Before he can say another word, I stride past him, giving him a wide berth as he rides the opposite side of the hall. After a few seconds, I hear a door open and shut. When I glance over my shoulder, Russ is gone, and I'm back on my mission.

I need to find Lenny.

CHAPTER 18

With the power back at full capacity, the ship's air conditioning is working overtime to catch up, and the chill in the air has my bare skin covered in goose bumps. Not that I'm noticing the chill, because the grinding of my mind as it turns the last few minutes over and over is warming me like a furnace.

Lenny likes me.

Lenny likes me.

The words repeat until they fall into a rhythm, eventually picking up a bouncy little melody to go along with them. The notes singsong through my head into a thundering crescendo. *Lenny likes me. Lenny likes me! LENNY LIKES MEEEE!!!!*

Of course, there's a tiny bass line happening underneath my new tune, a low voice booming, *Wait, are you sure?*

Lenny likes me!

(*Wait, are you sure?*)

Soon it's like a duet in my head, each voice trying to top

the other, and I can't sort my thoughts. The melodies take on varying keys, becoming discordant and clanging until my brain sounds like a room full of six-year-olds learning to play the violin.

And then, as if my inner conductor has waved for a cut-off, the voices stop. There's a blessed silence in my head like a pause between movements, and the silence helps me realize that the sight of Lenny outside the door marked STEAM ROOM a few paces down the hall isn't a mirage. It's really him, in a pair of bright red board shorts, his lean and lanky limbs swinging as he disappears through the door.

My heart starts rolling like a timpani, and before the whole messy chorus can begin again, I tighten my grip on my towel and charge through the door after him. Once inside, the heat and moisture of the room closing in around me like a hug, I'm able to glance around. The wooden room, smelling strongly of cedar or some other overly fragrant building material, is silent and, thankfully, empty. The only spot of color is the red of Lenny's board shorts, sitting on a bench just in front of me. I can barely make him out through the steam, but I know for sure it's him.

"Lenny, I wanted to tell you that, um, you're right," I say. My voice falters a bit, but a healthy gulp of steam smooths it out, and I charge on. "We *do* have a connection. I feel it too, and I'm so glad you said something, because I don't know if I ever would have been brave enough to do it. You're this sweet guy who encourages me and is there for me and understands why I have this dedication to the band and music."

I see Lenny wave his hand in front of his face, as if he's trying to clear away the steam, but it doesn't do any good. There's still a thick curtain of white steam separating us. When he doesn't say anything, I take it as a cue to charge on.

"What I'm saying is, I like you. I like you a lot, actually." I take a step forward, but the thick steam doesn't abate. For a moment I actually wish someone would come in, just to prop the door and let some of that blasted moisture out of here.

Lenny must have the same thought, because he stands and takes a step toward me.

"What?" he asks, crossing the floor until he's right in front of me. The steam seems to dissipate, drifting down to the floor, allowing me to see his gray eyes and the way his hair is sticking up in a few wild directions. I can't help but let my gaze wander to his torso, which is surprisingly muscled for a lanky artist type. I count two, four, six abs, and I let out what I'm shocked to hear is a tiny sigh.

I want to meet his gaze, but I can't, because I'm afraid between the heat and his hotness, I might pass out dead. But the longer I stare at his well-defined chest, the more I want not just to look at him but to kiss him. I want another pass at what felt so awkward and rushed the other night. I want to get it right, without Russ and Demi and a fight. I want the kiss I deserve.

I take one tiny step until I'm inches from him, and then slowly let my gaze rise past his freckled shoulders, the thin piece of leather tied around his neck, and up to his sharp jawline. I stop before I get to his eyes, because I don't know if I can take another deep gaze into his eyes as gray as the ocean on a misty morning.

Instead I close my eyes as I rise up on my tiptoes to reach him. I'm not going to let this kiss just happen to me. I'm going to make it happen. I feel the buzz of electricity between our lips as I rise and lean, breathing in.

But I find myself leaning . . . *too far*. I should be there by now. We should be kissing. The crackles of electricity should be full-on lightning bolts.

But there's nothing.

I let my eyes flutter open and see that Lenny's taken one giant step backward, his eyes wide as dinner plates, his hands up in front of him like a cop ordering me to *halt*, a look that's equal parts horror and confusion on his face.

Which is exactly what I do, teetering on my toes for a second before my heels slam back down onto the floor with a teeth-rattling thump.

"Uh, I'm sorry, I think—"

"Oh my God," I say, the words barely escaping in a whisper. I cover my mouth, like maybe I can hide what just happened behind my fingers. But from the way Lenny's eyes are darting around the room, his feet shuffling on the wood floor, I know there's no taking back what just happened. It just *is*. "What is happening?"

"I think you might have gotten the wrong idea?" Lenny fumbles at an explanation, but it's not anywhere near sufficient. His face is crumpled and slightly pained, like he's been sucking on a warm lemon.

"Then why did you come over here?" I ask, waving my hands in the now-empty space between us.

"I don't have my contacts in. And with all the steam and you in that towel, I couldn't really tell who you were," he says. He gives a tiny shrug that sends a matching fissure into my heart. But before I can wince in pain, I realize he's right. I'm in a towel.

I'm *naked*, and I just tried to jump him.

Oh. My. God.

"Wait, was that, um, *you* in the spa?" Lenny asks.

The question hangs between us like a lead balloon, then smacks me hard in the gut. I hear an audible rush of air escape me. *Who did he think it was?*

As if he can hear my inner monologue, he grimaces. "I thought it was Demi."

"Demi." Her name sticks in my mouth.

"Yeah, uh, I thought it was her. She's, uh, the one—"

"Okay," I say, cutting him off. I don't want to hear him say it. I don't think I'll be able to take *that*, on top of the mountain of embarrassment now resting on my head. I wish the weight of it would just drive me through the floor to the deck below, so that I don't have to stand here and watch Lenny struggle through embarrassment and pity. *Pity.*

But the floor doesn't open up. A giant hook doesn't reach out and yank me out of the room. No curtain drops between us, no orchestra plays me off. It's just me, standing here taking in everything. Lenny likes Demi.

Lenny does not like me.

Lenny likes Demi.

Something isn't adding up. I try to run through the past few days, but there are so many mistakes, explosions (literally), and near misses that I can't sort fiction from reality. If that kiss was for Demi, then nothing is what I thought. And if Lenny didn't write my name that first day, then *who did?*

"But what about our kiss?"

"What kiss?"

"After the performance! You kissed me, and then Russ—"
I say, though as soon as the words tumble out of my mouth I
know the answer.

"I don't know, it seemed like a good way to get Demi to
notice me."

My embarrassment morphs into a white-hot rage.

"If you want a girl to pay attention, you kiss *that* girl, you
asshole," I snap.

"Fair point," he replies, one eyebrow arched.

"Why does everyone have to play games?" I mutter.

"Because sometimes they work," Lenny says with a shrug.
"I mean, that picture certainly did the trick."

At the mention of the picture, my ears perk up. "What do
you mean?" I ask.

"That picture of you all cozy with Russ. That got Demi
over Russ right quick."

Wait, what?

Watching him say the words has a strange effect, like suddenly the Lenny I knew is dissolving into this whole other guy.
He's not the sweet, artistic boy cheering for me from offstage.
Now he's this creepy dude snapping pictures and kissing people
and trying to woo *Demi*. The inside of my mouth turns sour,
and my face crinkles to match, as I realize what he's saying.

And what the real truth is. Russ didn't take that picture.
And neither did Missy.

Lenny did.

Maybe it's the twinkle in his eye, or the twitch in the corner
of his mouth that's working its way into a smirk. Maybe it's the

already painful memory of me standing on my tiptoes, kissing air while Lenny backs away in horror. Maybe it's just a snowball of anger and embarrassment and misery that this week has become. Maybe it's all that and more, because I feel my hand rise up to my shoulder and then swing, *hard*.

Lenny sees the slap coming and ducks. My hand whiffs over his head, my balance going with it as I teeter over on my left leg. I put my hand out to catch myself from splatting on the wood floor, and almost immediately feel my towel loosen. Without my left hand holding it to my chest, the fold is quickly falling apart.

Lenny, either trying to save me or my towel, reaches his hands out. I'm not letting this asshole anywhere near me, especially not when I'm three seconds away from standing there in my birthday suit. A girl can only take so much embarrassment before it's time to take control, and if I have to do that while standing naked, well, dammit, that's what I'm going to do.

I swat his hands away, and when he's off balance, I give him a shove for good measure. He compensates by throwing his body weight forward until we're pressed against each other in what might look like a romantic embrace, my towel between our chests.

I feel a light breeze on my rear end. I glance over my shoulder to see that my towel has risen in the scuffle, and my bare butt is now exposed to the wall behind me.

"Liza!"

No, not the wall behind me. The breeze is coming from the open door, and standing in the entrance to the steam room?

One very tall, very rigid band director and one horrified home ec teacher, both standing there, mouths open in twin Os.

CHAPTER 19

At the sight of my band director—his own father—Lenny leaps backward, slipping on the moist floor and falling on his butt into a puddle. I manage to catch my towel milliseconds before it lands at my feet, adjusting it so all the important bits are covered and I'm left with the naked-at-school nightmare come to life.

"Mr. Curtis, I'm so sorry," I say. "I can explain—"

"Liza, get dressed," Mr. Curtis says, words I never imagined coming out of his mouth. His face is a total blank slate, which is somehow more horrifying than anger or disappointment. Like the calm before a storm that ends with me shipwrecked on Detention Island for the rest of my natural life. "Get dressed, and meet me back outside this door in five minutes."

I don't even give myself time to nod. I simply dash out the door and down the hall to the dressing room, where I find my clothes in a small laundry bag on top of a chair, still heavy and stiff with wax.

Mr. Curtis saw my butt.

Lenny likes Demi.

I made a total fool out of myself in front of like, 66 percent of the Curtis family.

What is my life?

For the first time I'm not just thinking about the band or my love life. I'm thinking about what my parents will say when they find out about this, because Mr. Curtis is most surely going to tell them. Dad is definitely going to open up the private school discussion again. He's been hounding me to move in with him, insisting he can get me into some ridiculously prestigious college-prep academy where I'll have to wear plaid and hate my life. But with the way things are going, perhaps leaving the state won't be such a bad idea. And with my latest foray into nudity on a school trip, my mom might actually support the decision.

I dress faster than that time my dad took me shopping at Barneys and a salesgirl tried to barge in while I was still in my underwear to make sure the dress was fitting properly. I do not do naked in public . . . not until today, anyway. I'm halfway back down the hall when I realize my shirt is on inside out, the screen-printed logo of my favorite Holland diner rubbing against my bare chest, my bra stuffed into the back pocket of my shorts.

When I get back to the steam room, Lenny is nowhere in sight. Ms. Haddaway is gone as well. It's just Mr. Curtis, leaning against the wall, his head down, his arms crossed tightly over his chest. At the sound of my footsteps approaching, he glances up at me, his eyes steely.

"Follow me, please," he says, his words practically frosting in the air. Gone is my most Zenlike teacher. There's no trace of his easy smile, and I'm pretty sure the next words out of his mouth aren't going to be "everything will be fine." Because after what's just happened, I'm not sure anything will ever be fine again. My body temperature plummets, my skin pebbling as an increasing series of chills zips from my fingers to my toes. I don't know what's about to happen, but whatever it is, one thing is for certain. I'm in trouble.

Mr. Curtis starts down the hallway, and I fall in behind him. I watch his navy canvas deck shoes as they stride across the well-worn carpet of the hallway, my heart pounding with each step. We wind down hallways, up stairwells, through the cavernous atrium at the center of the ship, where all around me my fellow cruisers are enjoying heaping plates of food and fruity drinks topped with umbrellas. A group of kids led around by a haggard-looking ship employee chase one another around the potted palms. A gray-haired couple of retirees are poring over a printout, debating water aerobics or shuffleboard, and a pair of Mechanicals suck face in the corner, their over-sized plastic hipster glasses tap-tap-tapping against each other with each head bob and tongue thrust.

I follow Mr. Curtis through one of the automatic glass doors at the end of the atrium. He steps out onto the deck and turns to face me, leaning against the railing. I step out after him, the door shutting behind me and abruptly cutting off all the noise of the atrium. There's no one on the balcony with us, just the sound of the ocean breeze and the waves as they rush past the hull of the ship.

"Liza, I'm very disappointed in you," he says. And though

the wind sends his hair flying about in all different directions, his voice remains steady. Measured. Almost sad. And that's the moment where I no longer worry about getting into trouble. That's the moment when all I can think about is how terrible I feel that I've let him down. Mr. Curtis trusted me. He had every reason to. He always has, and I've *never* let him down. Not until he walked in on me half naked with his son in a steam room.

"Mr. Curtis, I'm so, *so* sorry," I say. My voice catches on the apology and turns it into a sobbing hiccup.

"I'm afraid I'm the one who should be sorry, Liza," he says, his face suddenly melting into a look of distress.

Now I can't even hear the waves. All I can do is turn his words over in my brain. *He's* sorry?

"I should have known this was all too much for you," he says with a slight shake of his head. "You were in over your head. That's the only explanation I can come up with for your behavior this week. And that display back there? Completely unlike you."

"I—oh—uh," I stammer, because I really don't know what to say. He's right. It's totally unlike me. But I'm also not sure I want to agree that I was in over my head. I can handle this. I *will* handle this. "I just, um—"

"You've totally lost your focus, and I blame myself, frankly, because I should have been paying closer attention," he says. He crosses his arms over his chest and shakes his head again, as much at himself as at me. "I thought you could handle it."

The words stab me right in the heart, and I don't think I've ever been so ashamed. He's right. I came on this trip with one focus. Just one. Win the competition and save the band. And somehow, that turned into passing out in closets and sleeping on decks and running half naked through a cruise ship, wrestling with his son. All in the name of what I thought was love.

Lost my focus? I think I set my focus on fire and let the ashes sink to the bottom of the ocean.

"It's time for me to step in. Obviously there need to be some consequences for what happened back there," he says. I notice a slight grimace on his face and realize how awkward this must be for him. He doesn't know that I was in the middle of slugging his son. To him, it looked like we were in the midst of a passionate, semi-naked embrace. And who knows where it would have gone had he not walked in. He's probably imagining that I intended to give Lenny something *other* than a bloody nose and string of insults and profanities. But I can't protest, because honestly, this is the least of the ways I've royally screwed up this week. The punishment for semi-naked hijinks has got to be less stiff than the one for vandalism, breaking and entering, or drug use (no matter how accidental). And then there're all the ways I've screwed up the band, from yelling at them to losing our star flute player to the disastrous performance of the first night. This can't be as bad as the punishment for all that, right?

"I'll take care of the rest of the performances. You'll be spending the remainder of the trip in your cabin, save for meals and mandatory meetings," Mr. Curtis says, and that's when I realize that yes, it can be as bad. It can be worse.

"Wait, what?"

"You've been relieved of your duties. When we return home, you'll be serving some detention. Until then, you're grounded, so to speak." I can see that the words feel unusual coming out of his mouth, and I give myself a moment to wonder when the last time he punished a band member was. Not in my memory, that's for sure, though there is an old story about a bunch of seniors who got caught smoking pot in the woods at band camp when they accidentally set a patch of poison ivy on fire. Mr. Curtis yelled at them all night long, and the next day he made them stand on the sidelines in the hot sun all day, covered in calamine lotion, until their parents could drive up and get them.

I always thought that was just a legend, but looking at his stern face now, I'm starting to think it's true.

"But, the competition," I whisper. All the plans for the contest, the hopes of winning $25,000, the future of the band, are all crumbling before me in a giant earthquake of suck. I lost my focus, and now it's the band that's going to suffer.

"I'll be taking care of all the band business for the rest of the trip," he says.

I feel like someone has squeezed all the air out of my lungs, and I have to gasp to get my breath back.

Mr. Curtis pushes off the railing and steps past me, activating the automatic glass door and gesturing me through. In a total trance, my eyes barely focusing on anything, I step through it.

"Straight to your cabin and nowhere else," Mr. Curtis says, and I nod in response. I don't trust my voice not to crack into a million tiny sobs. My eyes are already in serious danger of overflowing. I just hope I can hold on until I get back to my room, where I can let the tears flow for real.

I'm just inside the atrium when Mr. Curtis puts a hand on my shoulder.

"And I'll take care of letting Huck know."

"Huck know?"

"I think you were right. His skills are just not up to par. He's taking the entire performance off track, so I'll ask him to sit out the performance tomorrow."

I can't even believe he's bringing this up now, when he's just benched me for the most important performance of the band's existence. He wants to talk about Huck's *skills?*

"Mr. Curtis, Huck may be terrible, but—" I say, ready to tell him that the band's not the band without Huck, but he cuts me off. Mr. Curtis puts a hand on my back, right between my shoulder blades, and gives me a firm nudge. The implication is clear: no more discussion, just me marching back to my cabin in defeat.

I take a few steps forward when a flash of neon catches my eye. It's Huck, stepping out from behind an oversized potted palm just outside the door. And from the way his eyes are slanted, his mouth turned down in a sharp frown, I know he's heard everything.

"Huck, I didn't—" But Huck just shakes his head once, hard, and then pivots on his heel. He charges through the crowd, zipping around the blond-headed twin toddlers engaged in a shoving match, and disappears into a crowd of people in swimsuits, towels wrapped around waists and tossed over shoulders. I take a few steps into the crowd, scanning the heads up on my tiptoes, but I can't see a trace of Huck's dark spiky hair. He's gone.

I glance over my shoulder and see Mr. Curtis, his eyes still on me. I have no choice but to trudge back to my cabin, defeated in every way possible. I've lost my crush. I've lost the band. And now I've lost my best friend.

CHAPTER 20

Pit of disaster. Yeah, that's basically what my whole life has become, one giant pit of disaster, filled with alligators and snakes and no best friend.

I pause at the railing and rest my arms and stare out at the clear blue water. The sun is starting to set, putting a slight chill in the breeze that sends a shiver up my spine. The water is turning a deeper, darker blue as the sun gets lower, painting the sky in sweeps of orange, red, and yellow. I feel like I could reach out and touch the spot where water and sky meet, but the longer I stare, the farther the horizon recedes. It runs from my vision, reminding me that I'm surrounded by hundreds and hundreds of miles of sky, on top of hundreds of thousands of miles of ocean.

And I feel small. Very, very small.

The whole time I've been aboard the *Destiny*, I've felt like I was on a floating planet. It's felt huge and unwieldy, overfilled with people and food and activities. But now, as I stare out at the miles of deep blue ocean and clear blue sky, the *Destiny* suddenly seems as big as a rowboat, bobbing in the unbelievable expanse of the world, so small that if you blink, you'd miss it.

I let my arms hang over the railing and lean down until my forehead is resting on the cool metal. I feel the pull in my hamstrings as I bend, and I let out a long breath to sink deeper into the stretch.

"You look like you need to relax, my dear. Has anyone ever suggested you try a cruise?"

I glance up and see Sofia—the nice older lady who stood up for me and my strawberries the second day aboard the ship—clad in her usual uniform of brightly colored, flowing silk. On her feet are a pair of mint-green foam flip-flops from the spa, and one look at the way she's glowing tells me that her trip there was much more relaxing than mine. As I watch her watching me, I can tell I'm doing a very bad job keeping all the bad feelings inside. Her eyes go wide, then narrow, causing her forehead to wrinkle.

"Oh dear, I see it's going to take more than a blue ocean and unlimited peel-and-eat shrimp," she says. She places a long, tan arm around my shoulder. I'm not usually a particularly huggy person, especially not with strangers, but when the heat of her skin and the weight of her arm hits my shoulder, I immediately lean into her, letting her wrap her other arm around me and pull me into a hug. I bury my face in the warm pink silk of her tunic and feel wetness—my own tears. I try to back away, afraid of leaving ugly marks on her elegant clothes, but she pulls me in tighter, her hand buried in my curls as she pats the back of my head.

"Darling, don't you worry about it a bit," she says. She shushes me and lets me wait there until I'm all cried out. And when I feel spent, when my shoulders have drooped and my bones feel like they've been replaced with spaghetti, she lets me lean away and holds me at arm's length. I wipe the remains of the tears from beneath my eyes and take a deep breath. I'm surprised to feel something like a smile begin to creep onto my face.

"Never underestimate the restorative power of a good cry, I always say." Sofia's eyes search mine for any more waterworks, but I think she's right. The tears are gone, and I do feel . . . well, not quite restored, but better. "Now that we've got that out of the way, do you want to talk about it?"

I take a deep breath, prepared to let it all pour out, but nothing comes. I don't even know where to begin. I boarded this ship with one anchor-sized problem in my suitcase, and now I need another bag to hold all the problems I've acquired. The band? The contest? Lenny? Russ? Demi? Huck? Nicole? Where would I even start?

"Okay, well, why don't I just offer up a bit of wisdom for you, and we'll see what sticks," she says. She turns back to the ocean and rests on the railing, her manicured hands crossed elegantly at her wrists, her fingers dancing in the breeze. She closes her eyes and breathes in a lungful of ocean air, her whole body leaning into it. A few strands of gray hair escape from her bun and whip across her face. I can still see the splotches of wetness on her top, left over from my tearfest, and even though I doubt there's anything she could say that could make me feel better right now, I still want to hear it.

She opens her eyes, but keeps her gaze focused on the hazy horizon glowing pink and orange.

"When I was young, oh, about a thousand years ago," she says with a slight laugh that sounds like wind chimes, "I spent so much time trying to control everything."

When she says *control*, I feel like someone's popped me right in the sternum. A tiny sigh escapes my mouth, and I lean down into the railing next to her. She gives me a sideways glance before returning her focus to the water and the sky.

"I felt like I needed to wring life right out, making sure all the troubles and problems washed away, leaving only the *right thing*, whatever that was. But you know what, honey?"

She turns to me, her steely blue-gray eyes now meeting mine with an intensity I've never seen in this woman whose whole persona seems to be one of complete relaxation.

"What?" I say, but the word comes out croaked, my mouth dry from the wind.

"The only thing that was wrung out was *me*." She taps the spot over her heart with one finger. "When you spend time worrying about mistakes, miscommunications, troubles, or *failures*," she says, her eyebrow arching in my direction, "you miss all the wonderful misadventures, the lucky accidents, and even the perfect little catastrophes that make life interesting. Take my life. Most people would think my four marriages are a sign of failure. At love, at commitment, at life. But I've experienced more love in my lifetime than most, and I have four children, eleven stepchildren, and sixteen grandchildren to show for it. Who says that's a failure?"

"That's great, and maybe someday I'll laugh about all this,

but that doesn't help me *right now*. I'm still left with all these problems and no solution."

"Maybe there *is* no solution. Maybe *that's* the solution."

Her words sink into me and raise the temperature of my blood to the point of boiling. What does that even mean? Is she seriously trying to Yoda me right now? No solution means I lose the band. It means my favorite teacher thinks I'm a trouble-maker and will never trust me again. It means my best friend hates me. What's she trying to do, get me to fling myself overboard?

Sofia reaches out and covers my hand with hers. "My dear, listen to me. No solution is freeing. It means there's nothing to be done," she says, and just when I'm about to let a rant of epic proportions rain down on her with the fury of the storms we've been experiencing on the ship, she raises a finger to shush me. "Nothing to be done, except move forward."

I let the idea wash over me. What would that mean, moving forward?

I'd have to stop freaking out over the band going on without me, that's for sure. Which, I guess, is doable. I mean, their best performance on the ship was the one where the lights were out and no one could see me. It was like they played better without me leaning over them, shooting them scary stares and waving my baton with perhaps a little too much intensity. If they turn in a performance like that at the competition, they might still have a shot at winning. It's like Huck said, everyone just needed to listen and trust.

Just like Huck said . . .

I feel the corners of my mouth twitch, then sprawl into a grin. I turn back to the railing and close my eyes, leaning into the wind like Sofia did. And as I take in a deep, salty breath, I know she's right. And I know what to do. It might not work, but it's a plan, and that feels good enough for now.

"I think I've said something right?"

I turn and fling my arms around her, burying my face back in her tunic. This time I don't leave tear streaks behind.

"Thank you, Sofia. You really did," I say. I take a step back and smooth out my tank top. Then I run my fingers through my hair, thick with salt and wind. "And I really want to stay here and hug you more, but there's something I have to do now."

She grins at me, the laugh lines carving deep in her cheeks, her eyes wrinkling in delight. "Of course, my dear. I do have a marriage to celebrate, after all. Fourth time's the charm, I believe they say?"

"Who cares what they say?" I smirk playfully.

"Now you've got it, darling!" She waggles her fingers at me to shoo me away. "Off with you! And when I see you next, I expect to see a fruity drink in one hand and a delicious smile on your face."

"Yes, ma'am," I call over my shoulder as I skip away.

I round the corner toward Huck's room, the folded piece of Sail Away stationery clutched in one hand and my baton in the other. I'm probably the first person in the history of the hospitality industry to actually use the stationery provided to write a real live letter. And I'm counting on this letter to help me follow Sofia's advice: move forward.

I'm thinking about the letter and the three drafts I went

through before I got what I have in my hand. An explanation. An apology. And a proposal. I'm hoping it works, because the band needs Huck right now. And perhaps I'm a little too lost in my thoughts, because I turn the corner right into what feels like a brick wall. I bounce back a step or two. My baton clatters to the floor and bounces off a brown leather flip-flop, along with the flapping thud of a spiral-bound notebook, the cover folded back so the pages flutter.

I haven't seen Russ since he stood in front of me half naked, glistening and muscled and . . . Oh yeah, that's when I was screaming Lenny's name, after he told me he liked me, but before I found out he thought I was Demi. Before I poured my heart out to Lenny, telling him he was a nice guy (ha!) who cared about art (not even!) and encouraged me (yeah, right!). Before I found out I was wrong about all of it. Not my finest hour. Not by a country mile.

Maybe it's embarrassment over my supreme dorkitude, or maybe it's the weird rolling in my stomach when I picture him bolting away from me, but for some reason I can't find words. I glance at him, a shockingly long way up, since he's a good foot taller and standing a little too close. As soon as our eyes meet, he looks away and sighs.

I still don't know what to say, and the disturbance in my stomach has turned into more of an earthquake. I have to work to keep the quivering internal. I bend down to retrieve the notebook.

I pick it up, a thick spiral-bound number with rumpled and ragged pages, the metal binding bent and coming out at the top. I thrust it at him, but before he can take it, something catches my eye. The top page is covered with a series of Xs and

Os, lines and arrows connecting them in a seemingly random pattern. At the top, a line of shaky chicken scratch spells out *Pro Right Option Left*. Not that that means *anything* to me. It doesn't have to. It's the handwriting I can't take my eyes off of.

And all of a sudden those things I said to Lenny are flying back to me. Only it's clear I said them to the wrong person. Because Lenny isn't the one who's encouraged me. He's not the one who understands dedication and leadership and teamwork. He's not the one who's the nice guy, who plays with kids in the pool and bounds around moving instrument cases.

He's not the one with the wobbly, boyish handwriting who wrote my name on the slip of paper during truth-or-dare.

It wasn't Lenny at all.

"You like me?" I blurt out. My eyes sweep from the words on the page up to Russ's face, which has managed to get even *more* tanned, his blue eyes staring right back at me. I gulp. My voice comes out a whisper. "Why didn't you say anything?"

His lips part slightly. He gives a sharp intake of breath, and I wait for the confirmation. The confession. He was the one who wrote my name that day. It's his handwriting I've been staring at each night before I fall asleep.

But he doesn't say anything. Instead he takes the notebook out of my hands, rushing past me like he's gunning for the end zone.

"Russ, wait!" I call, my voice cracking. I turn to call after him again, maybe even run, but he's already gone.

CHAPTER 21

The paper in my hand is already soft and worn. The edges are starting to fray from my grip, and the ink is fading ever so slightly. Only I'd notice, but that's because I've been staring at it, running my fingers over the text, rubbing the softening edges, for the last four days.

I feel my neck start to stiffen, so I flip over to my other side. Again. I've spent the last four hours lying here in this narrow bed, trying not to think about everything my brain won't stop thinking about. Lenny and Demi. Russ. Huck. The punishment that's awaiting me back at home. And the competition, which is set to begin in—I flip back over to peek at the clock— just under twenty minutes.

I should be making sure everyone's got their music, and double-checking with Ryan that his is in the right order. I should be confirming that all the clarinets have spare reeds soaking under their chairs. That the percussionists have all their components in the right order, and that Jared didn't ditch his snare drum for a girl. I should be making sure my baton is at the ready between the pages of my binder. I should be gathering everyone by section and getting ready for our pre-performance pep talk.

But I'm missing it. I'm missing all of it.

Okay, so those are all things that make *me* feel better before a performance. It's not like the band will grind to a halt without me over their shoulders every moment. It's not like Huck won't remember to do the important stuff, like count heads and tune everyone up. I know he can do it. It's just weird that it's not *my* job right now. That it's not my job anymore.

And even if I were up there with them, it's not like I'd have any idea what to say right now. *Hi, I'm an epic failure of a drum major, please don't follow my lead* hardly seems inspiring, not even if I try to say it with a little pep in my voice. And after the performance the other night, where they couldn't even *see* me and still gave their best performance ever, it's clear they don't need me.

But I need them.

I slide my feet back into my sneakers, resting at the edge of the bed. I take one last glance at the well-worn slip of paper, but there's nothing I can do there. Like Sofia said, *move forward*. I have mental space for only one thing at a time right now, and my friends win that fight hands down. So I shove the paper deep into my pocket, take my room key off the bedside table, and bolt for the elevators.

After an excruciatingly slow elevator ride, the doors slide open onto the Sunrise Deck. I follow the brass signs on the wall to the Grand Auditorium, where the competition is set to take place. But when I arrive at the heavy double doors that lead into the performance space, I realize there's no way I can go in. Mr. Curtis likes to stand in the back of whatever room we're performing in so he can make sure our dynamics are spot-on, that our pianissimo is whispering and our fortissimo is blowing the doors off the place. If I walk in, he's going to notice me right away and send me back to my cabin.

I rise on my tiptoes and peek through the round portholes in the door. I don't see Mr. Curtis, but I do see my bandmates filing onto the stage, instruments and music in hand. I see Jared and the percussionists setting up the timpani just offstage, ready to wheel it on after the Athenas perform. They're laying out drumsticks, tambourines, and triangles on the rolling cart that's topped with a piece of velvet my mom salvaged from an old set of curtains, which keeps everything from rattling on the cart. My stomach clenches when I see that the snare drum stand is crooked, causing the whole thing to list to one side, but Luke, a freshman percussionist, quickly adjusts it, smoothing over the top with his hand to ensure that it's level.

Down on the floor in front of stage left, the band is gathering by section, doing some quiet final fingering and mental run-throughs of sticky sections. I can't help but do a quick head count, and that's when I notice: one oboe is missing.

Immediately, I bolt down the hall, then crank a left, my sneakers skidding on the carpet like I'm in a cartoon. I get to a set of swinging double doors labeled BANQUET KITCHEN, ignore the line underneath that says STAFF ONLY, and push through. The kitchen is a bustling center of activity, and the heat hits me immediately. It fills my lungs like hot tar, and I have to stop for a second to get my breath back. In an instant, the back of my shirt is damp, and the little hairs that have escaped from my ponytail glue themselves to the back of my neck. I don't know how everyone in here isn't collapsed in a puddle of sweat. But the white-coated cooks don't seem to mind, or maybe they're moving too fast to notice. They're stationed all over, tending to boiling pots, pulling slabs of meat from hot ovens, and chopping heaps of vegetables with giant serial-killer knives. They dart from place to place, calling out things like "Hot hot hot!" and "Behind you, roast coming in!" The amount of activity is dizzying . . . and perfect. No one pays a second of attention to me, lest they burn a sauce or hack off a finger.

The smell of garlic overpowers everything as one prep cook in a corner attacks a whole bag of it, peeling off the papery skin and smashing the cloves with the flat of his knife. I suck in the smell, thinking of pasta night with Mom, when we turn the kitchen red with our vats of homemade sauce that always bubble and splatter over the entire kitchen, making it look like we've performed an autopsy. I make my way carefully down the main aisle of the kitchen, ready to leap out of the way of a cauldron of bubbling soup or a tray of some kind of roasted beast. When I get to the back wall, I scan in both directions, looking for the door that would lead to the backstage area.

I finally find it, in the back corner, when it flings open. A flash of gold sequins and a flounce of a high ponytail storm through. Demi is a picture of fury, from the way her mouth turns down to the way her fists are clenched at her sides. Just before she turns my way, I open the nearest door and step in.

The heat of the kitchen quickly gives way to an arctic chill. My breath comes out in puffs of white smoke. I've stepped into the walk-in cooler, and as my teeth begin chattering, I hope I'm not going to be in here long. I step to the back and plop down on a box labeled STEAKS, and figure that by the time I count to fifty, Demi will be gone and I can still make it out to watch the band. And hopefully I won't get discovered in the process.

That hope quickly freezes and shatters into tiny ice crystals as the handle on the door turns. I get a moment of reprieve when the cold air escapes and the warmth of the kitchen sneaks in, but that's gone right as the door shuts again. Demi has entered the walk-in cooler. However, she doesn't notice me, because she immediately turns and presses her forehead to the door. Her whole body shakes, sending tiny bits of light reflected off her sequins scattering around the room like a human disco ball. But she's not shivering.

She's crying.

Her shaking shoulders soon give way to a strangled sob, and her hands go to her face. She cries into them, and I'm instantly hit with a memory. We were nine years old. Demi was competing in one of those cheesy mall talent shows that her mom found on the Internet and signed up for. A low, portable stage was set up just outside the food court. The whole place smelled like a mixture of french fries and Cinnabon, and shoppers blithely bought new sweaters or sneakers or whatever else had brought them to the mall that day, mostly ignoring the parade of little kids performing dance routines.

I was sitting in the audience next to her mother, watching the dance routine Demi had practiced about a billion times, only something wasn't right. Her smile was so forced it looked like it was about to crack, and when she went into the double pirouette I knew she could do in her sleep, she wobbled on the first turn and fully crumpled to the stage on the second.

At the sight of my best friend in a heap on the cheap, carpet-covered risers, I couldn't help it. My mouth gaped open and I gasped. Demi's mother nudged me, and I quickly hid my shock, just before Demi glanced into the audience to see me. But even though I managed to get my smile back, Demi knew. She took one look at me, and we both knew that whatever was happening up there wasn't right.

Demi leaped back to her feet and quickly caught up to the music, jumping across the stage, shaking her hips. She finished up in an impressive split, her hands overhead and a triumphant (but fake) smile plastered on her face.

Demi stomped off the stage and went straight to a plastic palm tree in front of the Gap, leaned her forehead into it, and cried into her hands, just like she's doing now.

Back then, I followed her over to the tree and wrapped my arms around her until she dropped her hands and cried into my shoulder. But I don't think that's something I'm going to do now. I don't think it's something I *can* do now. That was so long ago, and so much has changed.

Instead, I settle for clearing my throat until Demi spins on her character shoes, her skirt flaring out around her hips. When she sees me on the box of steaks, her eyes grow as wide as dinner plates, then narrow.

"Great. Great! Just what I need," she sneers between sniffles. "*You.*"

I raise my hands at her, the international symbol for *hey, I come in peace.* "I was just sitting here. I have no idea what's going on," I say.

"Of course you don't, Liza," she says, punctuating the syllables of my name with a sharp cock of her head.

She starts pacing back and forth in the tiny walk-in cooler before continuing. "You're way too busy flirting with my ex-boyfriend. All week he's been following you around like a frickin' lovesick puppy, and you lapped it right up. Which, I mean, like, *what?*"

I would not have been more surprised if Demi had told me she cut off her own leg and handed it to the judges. "Demi, you have got to calm down," I say. I take a step toward her and grab her by the shoulders. "I wasn't trying to flirt with Russ. I didn't even *know* Russ was trying to flirt with me. And besides, I'm pretty sure he hates me right now."

She looks at me, tears pooled in her green eyes. She blinks once, hard, and they spill, leaving black tracks of eye makeup down her cheeks. When she opens her eyes, they're soft and resigned, and filled with sadness.

"So he just doesn't like me, then? He ditched me, just like you did?" Then tears spill in earnest, and her hands go back up to her face.

I take it back. I *could* be more surprised.

"Demi, what are you talking about?" I ask, careful to keep my voice soothing. "I didn't ditch you."

She drops her hands back to her sides, her eyebrows knit together in frustration. "You did! You were my *best friend*, and one day you just disappeared. You stopped coming over. You stopped sitting with me at lunch. You got yourself all those new friends, and left me all by myself," she says. She tries to swallow more tears, but ends up hiccuping.

I take a step back from her. I try to process what she's saying, but it just sounds so wrong. I didn't ditch her. She ditched *me*, by throwing herself into the rat race of middle school. She became this totally different person, with no time for me anymore. I was just dragging her down. And I tell her so. I tell her how *I* remember it, and I can tell from the way she shakes her head, confusion splashed across her ever-melting makeup, that she doesn't remember it this way at all.

"If you still wanted to be my friend, why didn't you just tell me? Call me? You could have come to sit with me at lunch any time you wanted."

"Liza, you had the *band*," she says, a note of disdain dripping from her overly lined cherry-red lips. Her stage makeup makes her look a bit like a mime, and every expression seems exaggerated.

I give her a dirty look, my lip curling when she says *band*. "Oh right, I forgot. The band is way too full of losers for you to deign to sit with us," I snap, crossing my hands over my chest and cocking a hip out to the side.

"That wasn't it at all!" she says, her voice breaking again. She reaches for an old cardboard box nearby, one with the corner peeling upward from moisture and age. She starts to pick at it, tearing the brown paper into tiny bits that rain down on her black character shoe. "Y'all had all these inside jokes. You were always having parties or sleepovers or whatever. I wasn't in the band, so I wasn't included. You pushed me out."

It's not the version of events that I remember. But the more I think about it, I can see it from her side. It's not like I made any attempt to invite Demi into my world. I just assumed she wouldn't be interested. And after a while, it all became a foregone conclusion. We weren't friends anymore.

Unless maybe we always were. We just both didn't realize it.

"I'm sorry, Demi," I say. I hear the words come out in a whisper, and then I say it louder: "I'm sorry." It feels good to say out loud. I still have a mountain of problems to climb, but somehow this feels like a good start.

We step back and blink at each other.

"So what, are we like, friends now?" Demi asks, giving me a tiny shrug.

I give myself a second to think about it, about all the time and distance, all the snubs and dirty looks, and even the occasional downright nastiness. There's a lot of good history there, but there's also a lot of not-so-good stuff in between then and now. I shrug, hands in the air.

"I don't know," I say. "I guess we could give it a whirl."

She sniffles and nods, her ponytail bobbing. "That could be cool," she says.

And just like that, my mortal enemy might just be my friend again. Without looking back, without pausing, just moving forward, like Sofia said.

"Okay, fine, sounds like a plan," Demi says. She kicks at the floor begrudgingly, but there's the start of a smirk on her face. She sticks out her hand like we're negotiating a mob deal, so I take it and give her a jerk toward me until we're enveloped in a hug.

As we step apart, twin smiles on our faces, I remember two things. First, we're standing in a walk-in cooler and it's *cold*. And second, the band has probably started already, and if I don't hurry, I'm going to miss it. I tell Demi I need to get out there to watch.

"Yeah, go for it," she says. She crosses her arms over her

chest. "I mean, we choked, so you might actually stand a chance!"

It's exactly what Enemy Demi would have said, but this time her hip cocks out dramatically, and there's a twinkle in her eye. Her nose scrunches up in a teasing grin, and I give her a light shove on the shoulder.

She steps aside and lets me reach for the door handle. But before I go, she tells me, "Don't give up on Russ. I'm sure he doesn't hate you. Russ doesn't hate, like, *anyone.*"

"No, I think I messed this up really good. I was too busy swooning over Lenny to realize that Russ was the good guy all along."

Demi wrinkles her nose. "Lenny? Gross. He's totally hot, but oh my *God* what an ass. He told me that picture he took of you was all about getting me over Russ, which, okay, breaking up with Russ sucked, but I don't want him *back.* And there's no way I'd go for a guy who thinks immature games like that are the way to go. Anyway, like I said, I'm sure you haven't scared Russ off yet. He's stubborn as hell."

I can't hide the smile that springs up on my face, and I immediately brace for the explosion. But Demi shakes her head at me.

"Russ broke up with me. He said we weren't right for each other. And deep down, I knew it was true," she says, and sighs. "I just hate to lose. You know that."

"Do I ever," I say, and she gives me a shove through the door.

"Maybe I need to pull a Liza and throw myself into my friends instead," she says, and I gape at her. *Pull a Liza?* That's a first, for sure. I watch Demi as her eyes sweep over the storage room, from the boxes of fruits and vegetables to the toddler-sized bags of sugar and flour. Then her eyes come back to mine. "Whatever, it's fine. You better go, or you're going to miss the band."

"Thanks, Demi," I say. She answers with a grin straight from our elementary school slumber parties.

We've got some work to do before we're back to braiding each other's hair and singing along to *Fame*, but I'd be lying if I said I wasn't looking forward to getting there.

I've missed my friend.

CHAPTER 22

I duck out of the cooler and disappear through the door Demi emerged from. As soon as the door closes behind me, shutting out the clatter and buzzing of the kitchen, I can hear that the band has begun. The smell of garlic lingers, but it's mostly replaced by the musty smell of the velvet seats of the auditorium and the floral notes of old-lady perfume wafting from the audience.

Most of the pieces we've already performed on the ship were pieces Mr. Curtis picked out, ones that we've practiced since marching season. But for the final competition, I vetoed his John Philip Sousa medley and picked a selection of movie themes. I knew the band would like playing them more than the bouncy, patriotic marches, which would mean a better final performance. When I step into the wings, they're already starting the *Pirates of the Caribbean* theme, which means they're almost halfway through the performance. I pause just before I reach the edge of the curtain and close my eyes, letting myself just listen to the music. The percussion on this one is pretty epic, and the boys in the back are working overtime to get their timpani rolls and bass drum beats. As I count along, picturing the score and tapping my toe, I'm pleased to hear that they're hitting every cue. The brass are also spot-on, evoking the rolling ocean and fast-approaching ships from the movie theme.

It's only when the cymbals crash and the instruments transition into the lilting melody of the *Jurassic Park* theme that I think to open my eyes and take a peek at the conductor's stand. I half expect to see Mr. Curtis in his polo shirt waving the baton, but he's not there. No, it's Huck waving the baton, eyes going from the music on the stand to the performers in front of him. He's marking every breath, every dynamic, every fermata, with this perfectly relaxed intensity. And the band is responding to every direction.

When they transition again, this time into the *Titanic* theme, a tall, smiling flute player rises from the first chair and tosses back her newly highlighted hair. She raises her flute and out comes the familiar theme that most of the time makes me cringe with the sheer amount of cheese involved. But Nicole manages to bring all the emotion back to it, and watching her play nearly brings me to tears, just like the song did when Demi and I first saw Leo sink to the bottom of the ocean during one of our slumber parties. I see why Nicole got accepted to Juilliard. Technically, she's perfect, but it's more than that. Her artistry is incredible, and the band is much better with her in it.

Huck, who's had his eyes closed for most of the flowing melody of "My Heart Will Go On," suddenly stiffens. His arms jump with a renewed intensity, and they transition into the final song of the medley. The trumpets tout the intro, then the bass drum joins in the march. My eyes go to the back row, where Russ has the mallet in his hand and a grin on his face. He's pounding along with the music in a way that tells me there's a bit of a nerd inside that jock after all.

The crowd sits up straighter at the intro to the *Star Wars* theme, which never fails to have audiences of all ages bouncing along. I take a peek at the judges, and I see a tiny smile on the man at the end of the row, his head bobbing along to the beat. It's the best performance I've ever heard out of the Holland High Style Marchers.

And leading it all is Huck. He's got them in the palm of his hand, the band and the audience both. From the pleased looks on the judges' faces, we might actually have this thing in the bag. I can't believe I spent even a second thinking he was bringing the band down. He *makes* the band, he just needed to find the right place for his talent. He's everything I'm not: relaxed, in tune with the music and the performers, and just having fun.

When they hit the final notes of the *Star Wars* theme, Huck keeps his hands raised for a brief moment. There's a second of silence as the audience holds their breath, then Huck drops his hands and they all thunder to their feet. My palms sting from the strength of my applause, but it's only a drop in the bucket of the admiration coming from the audience. The band rises and takes a deep bow, then another. Then Huck gives them a wave with his baton and they collect their music and start to move offstage, on the opposite side from where I'm standing.

I'm so proud of them I could burst, but I'm still not ready to see them yet. I don't want to ruin their moment of triumph with the mess of my leadership. I don't want their questions to distract from what they did out there. I want them to have that moment. They deserve it. Huck deserves it.

And I don't.

I lean back against the wall and close my eyes, letting my mind wander back over the performance, every high point and quiet moment. I can't hear a single mistake. I'm so proud that I start to feel a tickle in the back of my throat. I clench my eyes shut to keep them from welling up.

WHOOP! WHOOP! BEEP-BEEP-BEEP! WHOOP! WHOOP! BEEP-BEEP-BEEP!

The sound is abrupt, and loud—it cuts right through the Mechanicals, who have started their production of *West Side Story*. Emergency lights on the wall begin to flash and my eyes go toward the ceiling, as if I'm anxiously awaiting a message from our alien overlords.

And I half expect one when a crack of static and a squeal comes through some kind of shipwide speaker system.

"Attention, passengers," a voice drones, "please report to your emergency locations. Please report to your emergency locations."

The double doors of the auditorium fly open, and the audience starts to stream out. It'll only be a matter of time before my bandmates and Mr. Curtis show up, so I quickly wedge myself into the crowd and duck low as I follow the surge toward the emergency exits.

Up on the deck, at stations all around the pool, white-clad crew members with clipboards and checklists are directing the various student groups to their designated corners. I round the deep end of the pool, and that's when I see what everyone's standing in front of. It's the lifeboats, which until this moment have been covered with some kind of white material that makes them fade into the background of the ship. The covers are now pulled back, and neon orange life vests dot the rows of seating, just waiting to be filled and lowered into the ocean.

I glance around and realize the ship has been surrounded by these big hulking boats all along, just artfully disguised so people won't spend their whole time aboard thinking about what the boats signify: that the ship could sink.

Wait . . . is the ship sinking?

I see Russ standing by the pool and realize that now is my chance. I have to sort things out. I push my way through the crowd until I'm finally standing in front of him, staring at him in his white tuxedo shirt with his bow tie and his rumpled hair.

"Russ, I—" He dodges me, turning and moving toward the edge of the pool, but I'm not about to let him get away. I reach out and grab his arm, tugging until he spins around to face me. "Russ, I need to talk to you."

"What about?" He crosses his arms over his chest like he does during pep rallies, glaring with athletic intensity. I've always thought it looked silly, until that intensity was turned on me. Now I have to swallow the massive lump in my throat and steel my nerves for what I know has to come next.

"I was an idiot," I say, which feels like a good start. I see a tiny chink in his armor, since it was clearly not what he was expecting, and that buoys me to continue. "I was so busy following around this ridiculous idea of a crush that turned out to be totally stupid that I ignored what was right in front of me. I truly had no idea that you liked me, and to be honest, I had no idea that I could ever like you. But I do. And I can't believe

I was so dumb after all those times you saved me, like when I was hiding in Demi's closet and you helped me dodge Curtis, or when you punched Lenny, or when that jellyfish that wasn't a jellyfish was attacking me or whatever and you grabbed it."

As I babble, I can see Russ's eyes soften and the corner of his mouth start to twitch. By the time I'm done, it's all he can do to keep a straight face, especially when I get to the thing about the jellyfish.

"What I'm trying to say is that I treated you like crap, when all you've done this week is be nice to me. I was just too much of an idiot to notice. And for that I'm really sorry."

Russ stares at me for what feels like forever, his blue eyes now full of a different kind of intensity. I try to stand there, quiet, and wait for him, but it's excruciating.

"Like I said, I'm sorry, and I don't want to bother—"

I start to take a step back. The splash comes, and in an instant all sounds other than my own heartbeat vanish as I sink to the bottom of the pool, my sneakers acting as ballast.

Luckily, my underwater silence is short-lived. Another splash sends waves through the pool. I open my eyes and see Russ, still in his tuxedo, swimming toward me. Once again, I'm gazing into his eyes, which are full of concern. He's always been there to help me. How did I not see it all along?

Russ hooks his hands underneath my arms, and with one powerful kick, we explode toward the surface. We pop out of the water at the same time, and I gasp for a lungful of air, followed by some extremely sexy coughing and sputtering. He gives a few powerful kicks until we're in the shallow end, and when I feel my feet hit the bottom of the pool, I stand to face him.

"Liza, if you wanted to go for a swim you could have just asked," he says. He gives his head a shake, and his wet hair sprays water droplets across the pool as it settles back out of his eyes. A grin starts to cross his face and a drop of water rolls down his cheek, settling into his dimple. Without thinking, I reach up and wipe it away. The tips of my fingers brush his warm skin, and his smile grows. He tilts his head into my palm so that my fingers tangle into his hair. He reaches up and grips my arm, holding my hand in place, and I take one small step toward him, then another, until I start to sink into him. I reach my hand around the back of his head and tug, rising up on my tiptoes. He dips his head to meet mine, and our lips touch with an intensity that turns my knees to jelly. I start to sink back into the water, and Russ wraps his arms around my waist, keeping them firm on my back, holding me to him. The kiss deepens, our mouths parting. When his tongue meets mine, I gasp, then giggle, feeling his lips turn up into another smile.

I lose all track of time as we kiss. Maybe seconds, maybe minutes, maybe *hours* later, we break apart slightly. He reaches up and pushes back a wet curl that's plastered itself to my forehead. His finger leaves a trail of heat across my face, and I can't help but grin.

"*Wooo-hooo!*"

The chorus of hoots, hollers, and scattered applause rouses me from my moment of bliss. I turn to see my bandmates gathered at the edge of the pool. Ryan sticks two fingers in his mouth and lets out a piercing whistle, while Huck just applauds and shakes his head.

"Sooooooo," Russ says, leaning back a bit so he can look at me, "does that mean no Lenny?"

I laugh. "Nope," I reply, squeezing him tight. "No Lenny. Just you."

And after a week of false starts, miscommunications, and misdirected emotions, falling into a pool should be right up there in things that have gone wrong. But it's perfect.

CHAPTER 23

Since making out while all my friends look on is not what I had in mind, I let Russ lead me to the edge of the pool. Hillary and Huck lean down, each grabbing underneath an arm, and pull me onto the deck. I land with a squishy plop, water pouring out of my sneakers.

"That was super graceful, Liza," Huck says with a pat on the back.

"When we get home, we need to get you some swimming lessons," Hillary quips. "You went *straight* to the bottom."

"Thanks, guys, I'm fine," I say, but before I can congratulate them on their performance (and apologize for acting so crazy on this trip), First Mate Kevin steps toward us, thankfully breaking the spell a soaking-wet Russ has cast on me. He has his clipboard pinched under one arm, and his hands are cupped to his face in a makeshift megaphone. Everyone gathers closer to find out what we're doing up on deck.

"It appears that our little power outage had a residual effect on our electrical system that caused a bit of a false alarm. If we could all make our way back to the auditorium, I believe the judges were just about to announce the winners of the competition!"

Now I see the tension in my friends. Clarice grabs for Andrew's hand and squeezes so tightly he winces. The percussionists, who are usually tapping out a constant rhythm on anything that's standing still, are now motionless. Even Nicole, she of the newly found serenity, is biting one of her freshly french-manicured nails. Everywhere I look there are tense shoulders, nervous glances, and attempts at deep, cleansing breaths. Suddenly all the teasing and laughter is gone, and the band members turn quietly and make their way back toward the auditorium.

My brain won't let go of thoughts of Russ. I turn to find my rescuer rubbing his shaggy blond hair with a towel. It's a ridiculous gesture, since his clothes are still completely soaked through. His tuxedo shirt clings to his skin, the outline of his chest visible enough that my cheeks start to burn. I reach up and press my cold fingers to my face and look elsewhere, but my eyes just graze down to his black pants with the satin stripe down the leg, also clinging *super* inappropriately. And now the heat is migrating from my cheeks to other parts of my body.

I want another kiss. I want a thousand more kisses. I want to kiss until we get back to shore, and then I want to kiss some more.

But right now, I *need* to see my band collect their prize.

For the first time since I boarded the ship, I'm not nervous. Not about the competition or the band's future. They don't know what I know. They were up onstage, under the lights, in the middle of a tunnel of sound. They couldn't hear it, but I could. Tonight I stood in the wings and watched them give the best performance of their career, and I know they have a good shot at winning. And even though I'm supposed to be grounded to my cabin, I have to follow them. I want to see the looks on their faces. I want to watch Huck make his way to the stage and take the trophy *and* the check. And nothing, not even Mr. Curtis, is going to stop me.

Russ and I follow the band, fighting our way through cruisers with towels and drinks and plates of food until we arrive back at the auditorium. I shove through the doors just in time to see Huck leap up onto the stage to thunderous applause. First Mate Kevin hands him a trophy that's nearly as tall as he is, along with a large white envelope.

Huck hoists the trophy over his head and waves at the rest of the band to join him onstage. They clamber up after him until Kevin is practically mobbed.

"They won!" I say, turning to Russ and flinging myself into his arms. I plant another kiss on his lips, surprised at how normal it feels. Russ pulls back and points toward the stage.

"I think *we* won," he says. I turn and see Huck scanning the crowd. When he spots me wrapped up in Russ, he points at the trophy and waves us up to join everyone.

I take Russ by the hand and pull him down the aisle with me. We're almost to the stage when a sequined body steps out into the aisle. Demi is holding a slightly smaller trophy in her hands, but the tears from earlier are gone.

"Nice job, band geek," she says, but a friendly smile warms her face.

"It was them," I say, giving her a one-armed hug around her trophy. "I wasn't there."

"Take your glory, Liza," she says matter-of-factly. "You know you were there all along. You just needed to take a step back to prove it."

I feel the tears start to well in my eyes, but she swats at me. "No tears, geek! That's my job," she says with a hand on her hip. "Now get up there and claim your prize! I need to get back to my girls."

She nods at the Athenas, still in their sequins. They're passing around their smaller trophy, shrugging and looking sour. Coming in second must be a new experience for them, and for Demi too. I give her a quick squeeze, then head toward the stage.

I climb up, Russ close behind, and try to stay off to the side of the crowd. But my friends pull me into the middle until I'm face to face with Huck and the trophy.

"You know I can't take *all* the credit, right?" he says, his nose wrinkling in a smile.

"You guys have no idea what this means," I say, pointing to the check in Huck's hand. I can feel a lump forming in my throat, and my eyes start to fill. "I mean, this is huge. This is the reason that we can . . . that we can . . ." I break off as the words crack in my throat.

Hillary steps out of the group. "Liza, we know," she says. I glance up at her, and she crosses her arms over her chest, the edge of her tattoo peeking out from beneath the sleeve of her concert dress. "We *know*," she says again, one eyebrow raised.

I look around at the group and notice their smiles are wider than a regular win would suggest. Molly and Ryan have their arms around each other, and Andrew is behind Clarice, holding her tight. The percussionists are all bobbing their heads, and the flutes have their hands clasped in a long chain.

"You *knew*?" I ask, and they all nod, a few "duhs" rising from the crowd. "But how?"

Hillary swings around next to me and bumps my hip with hers. "Well, we knew *something* was up when you went all psycho over needing to win first place in the competition," she says.

"And then that Lenny guy told us at breakfast the other day," Ryan pipes up from the back. "By the way? That guy's an ass."

"So I've heard." I laugh, and Russ gives my hip a squeeze. "I thought if I kept it from you guys, you'd be more natural. You wouldn't freak out."

"And how did that work out for you, Liza?" Huck asks, tipping the trophy until the little gold band director on top bops me on the nose.

"Yeah, yeah, *you're* the boss now," I say, shoving it playfully back at him.

Huck glances around the crowd, shoving the envelope deep into his pocket. "Only thanks to your letter." He takes a pause and we look into each other's eyes and I know, even if I don't deserve it, that he has forgiven me. "So now that we've had our after-school-special moment," he says, hoisting the trophy, "how 'bout we go party?"

A cheer rises from the group, and the grins grow wider. As we file out of the auditorium, Sofia pokes her head out of the banquet room across the hall. A sculpted gray curl falls out of her elegant updo and lands in her face. She blows it away with her lower lip out, and then turns to us. "I hear there's cause for celebration?" she asks.

"There *is*," I reply, pointing at Huck and the trophy.

"Well, this is the place for celebrations!" she says. She pops the door open with her hip and gestures us in. Through the doorway, I can see that the room has been converted into a giant wedding venue.

As my bandmates gather around me, Sofia's eyes go to Russ, who's waiting, still dripping. His blue eyes are trained on me, a wide smile on his face.

"So I take it from the moony smile that strapping young man is giving you that everything worked out?"

I grin at her. If I weren't still soaked from the pool, I'd throw my arms around her and give her a hug. "You were right after all," I say. "Are you sure you want a bunch of high school kids to crash your wedding?"

First of all, in a sea of stiff black fabric, we're all more dressed for a funeral than a wedding. Plus, I've seen these guys at a buffet. They can *eat*. She may need to order a second wedding cake.

"Darling, the more the merrier!" she says with a wink. "That's life lesson number two."

With Russ on one side of me, my hand clasped in his, and Huck and the trophy on the other side, I know I have every reason to heed Sofia's advice. So I tug Russ through the door behind me, gesturing for everyone to follow.

CHAPTER 24

Sofia's party-planning skills apparently took a page right out of her own personal philosophy book, because there's more than enough food and cake to feed the marching band, the Athenas, and probably an entire football team. The room is filled with elegantly dressed partygoers in pastel silks and chiffons and crisp dark suits, the ladies with elegant floral arrangements on their wrists or pinned to the front of their dresses. Some are scattered about the various round banquet tables, munching on wedding cake and sipping from champagne flutes, but most of the guests are gathered on the parquet dance floor just to my left. They're paired off, swaying to the sounds of a gentle jazz band. A few of the more ambitious couples perform more elaborate box steps, spins, and dips, but all wear wide, sparkling grins, heads thrown back in laughter as they move about the floor. In the center of the crowd is a group of women who seem to be elbowing and jostling for position while trying to act nonchalant. Sofia stands on a raised platform in front of the jazz band, a circle of white and pale pink roses atop her head.

The band stops, and all the couples turn toward the front with a round of applause. The lights all dim save for the ones over the stage, casting Sofia in a swath of warm light. When the crowd quiets, she looks around, raising a bouquet of roses that match the ones on her head.

As soon as Sofia spots me standing just inside the door, she gives me a wink and a smile. Then she turns her back to the crowd and tosses her bouquet. Only it's a bit more than a toss. It's a full-body, two-handed heave, and the bouquet soars high over the crowd. It's coming straight at me, so I raise my hands to block it from beaning me in the face, and it lands right in my grasp.

Rose petals rain down onto my sneakers, and about forty well-coiffed heads whip around to see who stole the bride's bouquet.

I peer through the flowers at the looks that start as confusion and soon turn to frustration. You do *not* mess with a single woman's bouquet, apparently, but I was only trying to keep from getting smacked in the face with a floral arrangement. I make an *oops* face at the crowd and attempt a shrug.

"Ah, my dear young friend Liza here is the lucky catcher of the bouquet!" Sofia chirps into the microphone perched in front of a saxophone player. "And now it is time for a dance! Who will dance with our lovely Liza?"

I turn to Huck. "Ready to cut a rug?"

Huck is still in his concert tuxedo, so he fits right into the crowd of wedding reception guests. In my frayed cutoffs and T-shirt, still sticking to my body from the pool, we're an oddly matched pair, but I don't care. I fling my arms around his neck. The bouquet smacks him in the back of the head, and I hear him chuckle.

"No need to resort to violence, Liza," he says, pulling away just enough to settle me into a slow-dance pose. "I'll dance with you."

"Thanks, Huck," I say, my words drowned out by the jazz band moving into a version of "At Last" by Etta James. I lean in to whisper an apology. "I never should have talked to Curtis about cutting you. You're the heart and soul of the band, and even if you weren't, you're my best friend. And friends don't do that to friends. I'm so, so sorry."

"I get it," he says, his eyes downcast. "I suck at oboe. That's not news. I just never thought I'd hear it from you."

"But I didn't care," I tell him, giving him a light squeeze at the back of his neck. "The band without you isn't the band. And you proved that up there tonight. And that's what I was trying to tell Mr. Curtis when you overheard."

"So you snuck out! I wondered if there was a jail cell strong enough to hold you," he says, wagging a finger at me. "We were good, huh?"

"Better than good! More like incredible. *You* were incredible," I say. I tap him on the chest and feel it puff up in response.

"Yeah, I didn't suck," he says. "Thanks for the encouragement, by the way."

I shrug. "You didn't need it."

Huck stops shifting from foot to foot and drops his arm, reaching into his back pocket. He produces my baton and holds it out to me. "I believe this is yours?"

I shake my head and push his hand back. "No way. That's all yours now. You are a way better drum major than I was."

Huck cocks his head. "You know, if I'm drum major, I'm going to need a partner in crime," he says. He spins me out with his left arm, then jerks me back in until my back is to his chest, his arms wrapped around my waist. "You game?"

I wouldn't have it any other way.

We dance through the end of the song; then the band kicks into Sister Sledge's "We Are Family," and the crowd explodes. Anyone left at their table is up and on the dance floor, hands waving and booties shaking. An elderly man who looks like he hasn't had his own teeth since sometime in the last millennium waltzes by, fingers waving in the air, his head tossed back in a big guffaw. A woman who looks to be his wife, or maybe just an admirer, follows him, flashing a mischievous smile as she gooses him on the behind.

"Don't get frisky, Lydia!" he calls over his shoulder, but he turns and winks at her in a way that simultaneously warms my heart and turns my stomach.

I see Sofia through the crowd getting dipped by husband number four, and I don't think I've ever seen anyone look happier in my life.

Huck follows my sightline, and when he spots Sofia and her husband mid-dip, he grabs me, pulls me in tight, and dips me low, too. I let out a laugh that comes straight from the gut. Huck gives me a tug and I roll back up to standing. I have to stop for a moment and blink through the head rush, and when my vision clears, I find myself staring at a tall blond football player in a tux.

Huck steps away so Russ can cut in, right as the band moves

into a slow song I don't recognize. Russ grabs my hand and pulls me in with a spin and a dip that practically has our noses bumping. I throw my head back in a full-body laugh. I haven't felt this happy, this *relaxed*, in I don't know how long.

Russ, it turns out, is quite the dancer. He explains that his dad, in an effort to improve his coordination on the field, signed him up for a ballroom dance class. Russ threads the fingers of one hand through mine and sets the other firmly on my waist. While most everyone else under the age of sixty-five sways from one foot to the other like we're at a middle school dance, Russ leads me around the floor in some kind of smooth two-step that has me both grinning and swooning.

"Hey, where did you get a tux on such short notice?" I ask.

"It's Mr. Curtis's," he says. "Turns out we're the same size. He brought it in case he needed to conduct, I guess. Luckily he didn't."

I glance over at Huck, who is slow dancing with the enormous trophy. Lucky indeed.

The jazz band transitions easily into a bouncy Latin rhythm. Huck hoists the trophy in the air and starts dancing through the crowd with a fierce butt waggle. It takes only a few beats for Hillary to join him, her hands on his hips, her head tossed back as she mirrors his booty shake. More and more people join up, band members and Athenas mixed in with the wedding guests. They snake through the crowd, grabbing people. The line makes its way past us, and I see a familiar gray head shaking in time to the music.

"You moving forward, my dear?" Sofia calls out.

"Yes, ma'am!" I say, and reach for her waist, pulling Russ along behind me. We shimmy and shake and trot around the dance floor. During the drum solo, I feel Russ lean in and plant a soft kiss on the back of my neck, and I lean into him. But I'm careful that, even in his arms, I keep moving forward.

Because if there's one thing I've learned from *Destiny*, it's that you never know what's going to happen next . . . and it just might change your life.

ACKNOWLEDGMENTS

This book would not have been possible without the support of the Paper Lantern Lit team, especially Lexa Hillyer, Lauren Oliver, and the tireless effort of Angela Velez. Major thanks to Wendy Loggia at Delacorte Press and to the rest of the Random House Kids team, who make my books great and put them in front of readers. Thanks to my agent Stephen Barbara for always answering my "HELP!" emails, and to everyone at Foundry Lit + Media for their support.

My books would be nothing without their readers, young and old, near and far. You guys are an awesomely enthusiastic bunch, and I love hearing from you. You're the reason I do this! I also owe an incredible debt of gratitude to the booksellers, librarians, and teachers who share my books with young readers. Special shout-out to the Little Shop of Stories in Decatur, GA, my favorite indie in the whole wide world. Your store is magical, and I'm honored that you keep giving me a place in it.

And finally, thank you to my incredibly supportive family, who all own way too many copies of my books and who never hesitate to claim me as their own. But the biggest thank you of all goes to Adam. There aren't enough movies about swords or Dairy Queen Blizzards in the world to pay you back for all you do for me.

ABOUT THE AUTHOR

LAUREN MORRILL grew up in Maryville, Tennessee, where she was a short-term Girl Scout, a (not-so) proud member of the marching band, and a troublemaking editor for the school newspaper. She graduated from Indiana University with a major in history and a minor in rock and roll and lives in Macon, Georgia, with her family and their dog, Lucy. When she's not writing, she spends a lot of hours on the track getting knocked around playing roller derby.

Visit Lauren at
laurenmorrill.com

Follow Lauren on Twitter
@LaurenEMorrill

Read Lauren's other novels:
Meant to Be and **Being Sloane Jacobs**